THE NEVERSLEEP

S.E. Smyth

As always, even when never mentioned, my wife.

CHAPTER 1

The clumping of steps approaching the porch announced a visitor, and Jill cringed. People. Someone scraped their feet on the mat. Curfew started at 10:00 p.m., and no one visited this late. A rapping knock at the door caught Jill off-guard. She picked at the hairline crack in her hundred-dollar ceramic mug, the one with all sorts of clocks and gears on it. At first, she leaned back, not ready to find danger or peril, or someone upset with what she had once done.

The moonlit night pushed its energy into Jill. The glow radiated, a dull beam hummed in the night, now consistently darker than ever before. This stable light stayed strong despite the growing heat and sporadic torrential rains during the day. The rain did not insert itself into the night. Jill, wrapped in a blanket on the couch, understood she must answer the door. But she didn't go. Her forty-two-year-old body relished the care, the comfort of being able to stretch and contract at whim. She fiddled with her long wavy brown hair, twisting it with her fingers. It would never fully curl.

The rapping returned this time with an impatient immediacy. "Hello? Hello? I'll come in." The gruff man's voice hit a wood door and muffled the sound, but Jill still heard. Jill guessed it belonged to a man of a larger stature. She picked up her mace.

Jill rose to answer the door and meet the wayward stranger. He had something to say. An odd man in a white button-down shirt, top button unbuttoned, and navy dress pants stood on the other side of the door. He arched his back as if he had just gotten up to stretch. Maybe he'd had a long drive. His reserved face told it would be shocking news.

"What time is it? We aren't allowed out."

"It's 10:52 p.m. I am allowed. Let's just say that ma'am."

Jill patted her thigh for her wallet knowing he counted as an authority and might ask her, in a reverse set of circumstances, for her wallet. Her eyes burned from tiredness, but she didn't itch. Sudden moves in front of enemies and authorities might spiral a situation.

"I'm a doctor," the man said.

"Jesus. Right. Everyone's a doctor or a lawyer or a cop right now. It's February of fricking 2029, apocalyptic 2029 … and, right now, you can be whoever you want to be. What I want to know is what do you want?"

Dillan had died, the doctors at the institute said. Two months ago, the doctors had said Dillan disappeared. Now, a doctor leaned on the door frame of Jill's house, he himself weary, saying they had found Dillan's remains. She had killed herself.

"Dillan Maxson is confirmed dead. Suicide." The echoes would follow Jill, she knew. "We just wanted to give this to you. We have a severance for you." The man said.

He lifted his arm from the shoulder instead of bending it at the joint. His whole arm pulled stiff as if the movement of shaking hands in the business world had transferred to everyday life. "I'm very sorry for your loss."

Jill opened her eyes wide, and her bottom lip dropped ready for the news he would deliver. She needed to hear it. She had so many questions she couldn't bring herself to ask. She wanted this moment to be over.

"It's for her work with the lab trials. We are so grateful—" He held a piece of rectangular paper taut as he pinched it between his thumb and index finger. He waved it a few times. The heat mimicked mid-May maybe. He didn't need a fan.

Jill slumped and crossed her arms. She found herself out of harm's way but itching to pick a fight. She flicked at her cuticles imagining she was flicking away the check.

"Look. The check might not get delivered via mail, so I'm here."

"Where am I supposed to cash this?" Jill bowed her head looking at the extra-long, extra-tall check made out for two-thousand dollars. The trim held small washed out blue spots. After a quick glance she folded it twice in half and pushed the square into her pants pocket. A thin string trailed from the corner of her red on black t-shirt pocket. It only made her feel more underdressed in her own home.

"I'm so sorry. This is really it. This is the end of the world. You have to tie up your loose ends. That's what I agreed to do. Tie up some loose ends for lost souls," the doctor said.

"What is the pill? If you're such a doctor and you're so smart?" Jill said. She chewed a lump on her lip that was a scar from stitches, a reminder of an accident she had snowboarding.

"Sure. I guess I can try. The medicine is similar to midodrine and promethazine that astronauts are required to take to counteract loss of balance and dizziness. When the earth's provoked gravity shift happens, when the polar ice caps totally melt, well, you'll need that medicine. There's a threshold at least. You really should. If you're on the fence. You really should take it. It helps with anxiety, mania, there's some super antibiotics in there." He smiled.

"You know …" Jill moved to sit on the front stoop as the man leered in as if he wanted to come in and be served a cup of coffee. "I don't often tell strangers my life's story, but it is the end of the world, as you say. Last time someone came knocking at my door like this, they told me my parents were dead." She leaned her back onto the edge of the concrete step, hoping it would cut her. It wouldn't. The rough, solid surface was not sharp, just blunt. "We already knew. So, you see it's uncanny. We had already heard. And we had to sit there for his sake and listen. He might've been a cop. But you see it wasn't for me. I already knew. But me and my brother nodded and said thank you, our aunt is on the way. And, no he didn't need to say. Because, right, it would've been for him, so he might feel better."

Jill got up and went back through the door, turning to meet the man's gaze. He pulled back two steps away from the door, almost afraid to lean in. "So, you see. I'll be on my own now. Everyone is. I'd like some time. I'm sorry. I can't invite you in." She added pressure to the door to close it, one hand on the doorknob. The other she held closely to the latch. The door closed with the softest landing, locking, of the door. And then she let an awful howl, but tears wouldn't let.

The man's clumping steps sounded on the concrete and

then dragging and pushing gravel on the street's edge.

She returned to her spot, heaving in a breath. She re-wrapped herself in the blanket more tightly this time. She dropped the mace in a little dish covered in a glossy sheen that made it look handmade. Jill had bought the dish at a craft fair only to find it in some entirely different store, one that held a variety of trinkets, days later. This happened months ago. To Jill, it all seemed like it had been months ago. Everything was normal just a few weeks ago. It was the same, the same plane of being, as everything that happened in the last ten years.

Dillan had died and she cut her fingernail into the corner of her eye, itching it, wanting to cry. For some reason, as much as she wanted, mourning her friend, lover, who she had known for three months proved difficult. They spent three months holding hands at least once every time they were together, all as the world dissolved.

The TV, off, acted as a focal point, a waypoint for wandering eyes. Sometimes, she left it on and watched the nothingness. Most channels were just black screens. She watched the black screen most evenings, giving her room to think, falling back into her mind, her memories, and her future desires. The moonlight pulsed again.

The stress of societal downfall made its way into everyone's lives. Jill wanted to find a hole and crawl in, be an owl deep in a rut of a tree. The world would collapse in this climate change, and Jill saw through the fog. Societal collapse crept on doorsteps, dragged its way inside. Jill could be manic about it or sit in a rocker and watch the world go by from her front porch.

Jill breathed in one, two, three, and out four, five, six, seven. She wanted to wrap herself in a faint remembrance of her mother's womb. She tried to remember being cradled in her arms, how it soothed, but the image eluded her.

She recalled the time she scraped her knee and Mom came running, first aid kit in hand. She dwelled on a bee sting and Mom checking for allergic reactions and calling the doctor anyway. She remembered skiing in the Northeast in front of her mom on a tether and making snowmen out in front of her house. Her mom placed hot cocoa on the kitchen counter even when rain pooled on the windowsills, dripped a damp cancelation of winter fun. The sweetness lifted spirits. She waited for Jill to see, and she always did. She always smelled the gooey, sweet warmth of the cocoa from the other room, even while layered in wet wool.

She missed her treasure of a mom, missed the chance to bond with her and see her with her own family, one she had not yet built. Someone had come to the door just like they had just done for Dillan, right before Jill's eighth birthday.

Like most of the people on the planet, Jill shook herself to relax the tension every hour, every day. The only support in the world at this moment you found in yourself, your instinct, whether you had a family, a lover. She had never taken stress management courses or gone to therapy, but she tried telling herself to breathe, the key to calming yourself down. She had overheard it, or someone had said.

She didn't have a lover anymore. Hope still carried on. Killed or killed herself or went on her own way, Jill did not know. She was gone.

Jill grabbed her phone. A bit of liquid from her drink had slid under the case and screen protector. The planet paled beyond all hope, and she tried to recall where she last put the rice. She dried the screen with the corner of her shirt and dialed those frequently dialed numbers. She screamed for Dillan, but tears would not let. She tried to mourn. With all those that had died so far fighting the war in the arctic, would she cry ever again?

CHAPTER 2

Unlucky thirteen days later, Jill rose for the morning, the last morning's rise. She imagined she would never need a bed again. Or would it be like she needed to walk zombie-like day in and day out, the stress taking a psychic traumatic toll with no ability to recover? The pill would help with that, they said.

"Good morning," Jill sung to herself in a singsong rhythm. "Good last morning."

The planet is in chaos. Thousands of deniers are working to destroy polar ice caps in the arctic. Jill broadcast what she knew solely to herself mimicking the recordings that would play throughout the day.

Jill messed with the radio. She had indoctrinated the things she had learned already and was looking for more. Using bombs, missiles, oil and fire, exploding watercraft, whatever made sense to someone so determined to spoil the planet. It was hardly a morning to be loopy, but Jill rolled in sarcasm and irony.

She reached her arm from beneath the covers, the warm place she might never find again, and turned the volume up a bit. She heard static filter in and out and relaxed. She rolled over one more time in agony. Time stopped and she waited. Waited for something to happen.

Jill woke up for one of the last times. She shuffled over to her tile shower complete with angled floor, so the water wouldn't pool at her feet. Some hair and mildew had congealed at the edge of the glass door on the chrome hinges. She mumbled to herself how she never wanted to leave this place, this quickly rotting homeland. Thoughts bucked in her mind about if she would ever wash her comforter again, not when the Capitol would collapse. Jill thought about drinking tea in NeverSleep, not about the looting a few miles away. She thought about Dillan and Mary and how much love costs on this godforsaken planet. She must shower. She'd never use a comforter again.

Jill turned the lever one last time to hot.

From the window of the bathroom, she saw a child, eight, she guessed, with his mother. A rainbow formed in the steam. She rubbed a smiley face onto the window. The boy would never see it on the second floor.

"We were just playing being bad, Mom," he said.

Jill stared in adoration and confusion wondering what he was doing on her sidewalk and why he couldn't do the same thing at his own house.

She countered that no one should play that game. "We need to help the world, Jason,"

He refrained, why.

"Because we all need to work at being good. Now more than ever."

Wasn't it true? They all had to be good, and no one was. An inkling to be good would trick a person for a moment. One would think they should trudge on being their own good person hoping for a reciprocal relationship. But that was never true. Everyone found out that wasn't true.

"But there are no police officers, so Kyle said we can be bad," the young boy said. He adjusted his baseball hat with a thick embroidered A on it. He wore the expensive kind, the version it took time to make. The kind some leave the sticker on. He constantly fidgeted because he was a kid.

"More than ever, sweetie, we must be good. We must do good because there are no police officers," his mom said.

Jill's hot shower, glorious and trite, made her relax, pulled the fidget right out of her. She wanted nothing but to lie. And still, in the back of her head, she felt the mania of the moment mount. She would not let it out.

Jill lay down for hours waiting, wanting something more. Boredom wrapped up in pandemonium. They would take the pill that night.

When the sun cascaded, and the static became a little clearer on the radio, Jill pulled herself in a chair up to it like they had in the early 20th century. Listening. For news.

When the knock came to the door, Jill's pallor rose, and her elation and apprehensiveness magnified tenfold. She unlatched the lock, opening it with two hands. In bounded Mary.

Mary solidly claimed adulthood, settled in her maturity enough to act childish if she wanted something. But she often bounded in like a bronco in energy, action, demeanor, and character. Jill never knew what she'd get, never knew where she'd land.

Most days Mary came eager enough to charge. Today, she fully stopped in her tracks at the open door. Jill rose and sauntered down to meet her. At the door, she asked Jill if she was ready, asked her if she loved her, and then asked her if she could come in. The squawking of the radio filtered, faded in and out, from the kitchen to the front door. Both Mary and Jill skittered into the kitchen. There they froze and listened. The voice, gentle but firm, sounded almost like an android voice. Jill swore, almost positive the computer-generated voice came from the government, female to ensure less panic.

Beep … beep … beep. This is not a test. This is the American Collapse Broadcast. This goes out to the public at large. Those that are left. Those that can't be forgotten. As scheduled by the Antis, the Capitol fell. The staff and personnel left onsite have traveled to the Colony. Please take as assigned your Acclimation Pill, called by some the NeverSleep Pill, no later than 10:00 p.m. eastern time tonight. All children will receive the pill as directed at the proper time by the school authorities of locales still administering services. We repeat, if you do not take the Acclimation Pill, you will die.

"The NeverSleep would be a place of relaxation. Ha. Yeah right. Didn't the broadcast say if you didn't take the pill gravity would crush you; you would die right away. Never mind the struggle of ecosystems that are to come, issues will surface from the pressures of population should we all accordingly take the pill," Mary said.

"People are going to die," Jill said. Jill stuck her fingers into the corners of her eyes and then wiped them dry. She wasn't at the end of the world. She felt a little bit off like in the second grade Halloween parade, Alice in Wonderland. She didn't have the dress. The world was upside down and a pill would make it right? That couldn't be true.

Jill proved thin and agile, fit and limber. She could dodge a charging animal coming at her full speed like Mary often did.

"Did you get up today ... honey?" Mary said.

She hedged. "Yes. I did. My skin is like leather lately. It is getting worn. I'm getting old. The skin is from being out on the slopes. I don't know if I can go back next year. It will ruin my complexion." She laughed. "I'll be an old hag in no time. No one will want me."

"Aww. I want you just the way you are," Mary chided. Her words were singsong and delicate. Then she lingered in silence.

Jill used to pull Mary's thick locks in passion and in hatred, and in despair that day they broke up. It'd been seventeen years now that they had the right to get legally married. They had the opportunity at least. Jill loved Mary despite her always yelling through her teeth, cleaning up after Jill in a fury, shedding passive aggressive anger like loose clothing before she came on to Jill. For seven years now, they had worked on recoupling but never said that word.

Jill's ex, Mary, had resurfaced more frequently in recent weeks, partly to comfort Jill and her loss. Sure, they had loved each other for years. They visited each other and gave hugs before they left or after an evening walk. The embrace felt like security. They had shared so much and continued to be together, in a way, through it all. Through Dillan. Mary remained playing the role of the long-haul creature of persistence. As much as Jill's energy waned, she also wanted to jump headfirst into it—be together without added pause. Mary had the gumption, the fight, to break Jill away from Dillan. Mary tried.

"She's just not good enough for you," Mary had said coyly on the front porch one day as she left. She narrowed her eyes and leaned in, but not for a kiss. "There's so many of us out there Jill ... people who would love to marry you." She whispered the words, and then skipped down the stairs, kicking gravel in the distance.

"You mean you love me," Jill said. Her face lit bright, bold, and open. Her tightly pursed lips beckoned. She meant it.

"Of course, I love you," Mary said with a devilish grin on her face.

"Then you'll let me fly free. If I come back to you. I'm

yours forever." Jill said. Mary had heard the phrase. Early in the relationship ten years ago, she had said it to her. She thought it was a residue of her own former lover.

Jill had broken up with Mary because of the anger. Mary kept it bottled up, and like a carbonated drink, it fizzed with the slight turn of the cap. The sweet sticky mess of anger found itself difficult to clean up. She never raised a hand. Never created a controversy about lesbian relationships being brutal. But she didn't do it solely behind closed doors. The occasional outburst on a public street while they took a walk, or a fist inappropriately slammed into something Jill owned, was always apologized for, retracted. Half the people on the streets were acting out, so it wasn't so abnormal as it might otherwise be.

But in her other life, in her work world and the things she did after work, her friendships, their friendships, Mary created fissures. Jill saw it. Mary wasn't so nice all the time and it affected Jill and scared her. Scared her into hushed moments. Mary pried constantly.

Mary didn't want to hear about Dillan. Jill assumed Mary's jealousy came with the package. As much as Jill relished the words when she talked about Dillan, as much as she wanted to linger a bit more on the topic, let the words come back up with a certain speed and excitement, she knew she shouldn't go there with Mary. Mary had started to pull back in even before Dillan came into the picture. She came by more often, then unannounced. She called Jill simply to ask what color flowers to get, or if it mattered. But just when Jill thought she'd bring the flowers by, she didn't. Jill was scared a bit of renewed love, of old fights, and wicked tempers regardless, cried in private with no one around.

"Did you hear the new broadcast?" Jill asked.

"Yes. They are replaying the old broadcast now. Not the one with the robot lady. It was on when you came in. But that one this afternoon. It sounded kind of weird. It had live people. The voice gave some double talk. She contradicted herself and said the government won't be there now. There is no Colony. They said they were evaluating the NeverSleep pill." Mary said this swiftly. "I talked to my brother and a family member is doing research, had done research in D.C. Why would all this work be done and then simply pull the plug a few days before the due date, the last day on Earth? It sounds like a hoax to me."

"They're like zombies," Jill said. "They believe everything the broadcast says. Maybe if you listen to it over and over, it brainwashes you. You know."

"Well …"

"The kids already took it, I'm sure. That weird broadcast wasn't until about 1 p.m. The kids were supposed to take it in the morning. They're probably all conked out now."

A long eerie silence collapsed the place, and Jill transported to a new view, a position of calm and quiet where no destruction was happening, with Mary. Jill laid on her bed in her bedroom, a room with an ill-framed closet door and just enough room for a bed, bureau, and nightstand. Mary flopped into bed with her, petting her, calming her.

"Jill. I think we really should take it. The pills. I mean iodine for nuclear meltdowns? Does it really work? No. Probably not. Do they give people hope? Yes." Mary paused again. "I guess what I'm trying to say is that it can't do any harm. There's no arsenic in it, right? How bad could it be?"

"Well, one broadcast said that it would kill you. That eerie lady's voice said normal, typical, expected things this morning. These other broadcasts, though. They said the whole thing amounted to a sham, over. If you take it, you'll die. The government wants to control the population. That's how I'm interpreting it, but it's scary, you know," Jill said.

"Why would the pharmaceutical people say that about their own pill?" Jill said.

"It went south. Something is different," Mary said.

"What could they possibly add?" Jill said.

"Maybe it was a combination they found out after the fact," Mary said.

A long paused killed the sense of place. Jill traveled somewhere else, a rabid bystander in time and space swallowed up by manic thoughts and a tremor in her left hand. Her eyelid flipped a few times before she held her hand to it.

"Jill, you want kids." Mary said she clanked her teeth.

Jill took it as a sign she should perk up and pay attention.

Jill toyed with the idea one more time. They discussed it every night for months until she met Dillan. Then, one day, Jill thought the time for kids was over. Her periods were every other month. Jill wanted kids more than anything. At this moment, she wanted kids. She loosened her jaw. "Jill—it's me. I'm here for you. Be with me. Find me where I am. We can make it work."

Jill wanted to understand.

"I'll get you kids," Mary said. "We'll make or borrow or steal, I joke, but we'll be there as a family. You must take the pill with me. It's the right thing to do. We have to do it. The alternative is death. I'm sure of it. There haven't been any broadcasts about the polar ice caps. There haven't been any more earthly disaster stories. They are still planning to melt the caps, though. They still have the bombs, fire power they need to see it through. It will happen, and it's in code on the broadcast."

"I love you. Hesitantly, yes. Hesitantly, we'll go on this adventure. Give me time." Jill said. She asked Mary to call her in the evening. The worst thing possible would be to end up next to a dead Mary after the LongSleep.

"I'll give you a call tonight," Mary said.

Jill sensed the eagerness, the true devotion.

CHAPTER 3

"Jill. We're going to take it," Mary breathed in and stopped up her exhale. The static on the phone was more prominent than it had ever been. She waited and said, "We must take it. It's our only choice."

Mary worried about Jill. Jill fell off the rails a bit, their friendship a casualty when Dillan died. Jill couldn't handle the loss. Mary watched Jill hole herself up in the room all summer. Despite Mary's push, Jill avoided getting a second job as the ski resort season ended. The bike shop would've hired Jill, but she didn't pursue it in a prompt fashion. Mary sat by and watched Jill slump back into her old ways, sleeping until 1:00 p.m. Mary judged her and questioned her passion for an absent woman. They rarely ate together, and Mary guessed Jill didn't eat. She saw her once donate food not yet expired, not yet eaten, to the food pantry in town. Mary often witnessed the overflowing sadness when bringing food over and encouraging her to eat. Jill's depression manifested itself in many ways; she, in Mary's opinion, had reasons to be sad. She mourned something, always. No one, especially Mary, told her no. But the violent tears left marks on Jill. Mary could see it. The corners of Jill's eyes slivered. Paleness overcame her.

Mary worked for an architecture firm as an Architectural Designer. She had a regular job and schedule with a decent income with regular raises. She had health insurance. Her mantra to herself was that she had it together enough to help Jill and be with the woman she loved. The situation was ideal. She pled with Jill to meet her halfway on the emotional things, and they would make it through. She wanted her to snap out of the depression and work. Get back to a routine. Walk outside once a day, for Christ's sake.

But Dillan's death devastated her. They were only together for a short while. Jill must've thought Dillan was the one, and this unmeasurably hurt Mary. Mary could only imagine that stress abounded in an otherwise barebones world, and that the stress caused Dillan to kill herself. The politics that ran through the news months before the Antis declared they would melt the polar ice caps filtered through communication channels, provoking one gasp after another. This was real stress for everyone.

Dillan was great. They all got along, even though a suspicion in Mary's head reiterated that she and Jill should give it a go again. She had nothing against Dillan, a perfectly fine someone with whom she could settle down. But Mary secretly wished that Dillan was out of the picture, so it didn't appear that Mary was jealous. So, she didn't look too eager or imposing.

When Mary called Jill that night, she told herself she wouldn't bring up Dillan. Jill often became triggered and spiraled when the name came up. She wanted to do a tribute to Dillan, create art about her, a foundation, or do a speaking series about suicide. None of these things were doable in the world as it lay. No one frets about such things. She had no room right now.

All this meant that Jill wasn't over Dillan. She wouldn't be able to come to terms with Mary and what Mary wanted for them both. For them to be together.

Mary realized when they both spent too much time together, they were volatile. The communication became toxic and drove them apart each minute over a certain threshold. But if they both had jobs, hobbies, and preoccupations, why not? They had learned after all and regrouped, learned in smaller increments on Saturdays of every week.

But the world was collapsing, and they were here now. In this new but alternate reality and, well, seven years is a long time, but they were so much stronger for it. They could give it a go. Recoupling for this catastrophe presented an opportunity, necessitated a bond. If one ever found a normal again, they would survive that too. Thick as family that fought, they would get through it. The two of them would make it work. They had to pull together and live through it.

"Jill, you're on the fence. This isn't the best moment to do that."

"I like the broadcasts ..." Jill said in a fading voice. She started again, "It's just I have a sense some people aren't. They will not take it, Mary. Not everyone will conform to this madness. For what purpose?"

"To simply live, Jill. To live. That is the goal." Mary shook her head and sighed.

"I'm scared. It's so new, Mary," Jill said. "I mean the gravity thing. It would otherwise collapse lungs, give me cardiac problems. It seems a bit far out there. Can't we just see what the next day is like, then take the pill?"

"Absolutely not," Mary said. "You'll be dead. That's what they say."

"No one is going to do it. Am I the only one who speaks about it?"

"Ask anyone. They will. The government told them to. They will all comply if they value their lives," Mary said. "It can't be any other way. Take it with me," Mary said. "Have tea when you wake up. It'll smooth things over much more."

"Government issued tea. Great. So much more attractive than those blocks of government cheese," Jill muttered flippantly about running out of money and being hungry as a kid.

"Look. I'm going to go," Jill said.

"You have one thing to do, and I'll be over after the Long-Sleep," Mary said. Her eyes fluttered, but no one saw them. She hung up the phone and held it in a cradle as she thought about calling her back, seeing if she had done it. She might call in an hour to see if she was alive, at least, or awake.

This was a new journey. Environmental change created a new society, a new way of being. Would there still be government? No. Would all agricultural activity stop? Yes. Would the economy dissolve? Yes. Mary guessed it wouldn't be a society then. Religion might persist. She would pray, Mary thought. Before she would go to sleep, she would pray for basic things that made them human. Even though she wasn't religious, never had been. She would find a moment to reflect and hope.

Jill had said that the Antis probably lusted after the survival mentality, so much that they would want to destroy the planet to feel it. The Antis would rather ignore truth, an accepted truth, than agree that the world is dying and will die without an intervention.

Everyone must be Environmentalists. That was the government's marketing campaign to get people back to working on being "green." It was the trigger for the Antis. They balked, made up their own slogans, and, eventually, they tore the earth down to destroy it. Jill said it was to taste something they lusted after, the survival instinct that they said they had, that would weather them through it if need be.

But didn't the good-hearted "green" citizens of the United States also lust after the government, after rebuilding? Didn't they want to see a new, better democratic nation rise? If the constitution burned at the hands of Antis, surely, they would write a newer, fairer one. Mary, even, thought this might be sexy, inspiring. It pinched at her sense of adventure and growth.

Lesbians lusted after the apocalypse, Mary thought, a genuine test of survival for the butch. This world proved a morbid playground for them as well. Get out the tank tops, cargo pants, and bandannas; smear some grease on the forehead; peel out on a motorcycle. All these things resounded in Mary's vocabulary as a lesbian. Surely, she thought, she and Jill couldn't thrive in this type of life, but oh what a sexy life it seemed.

For everyone, life teetered on the thrill of the moment and the terror of a myriad of possibilities for doom. They awoke to a new and scary world, but the one thing everyone agreed on was the sheer lunacy of the ideas behind the coup, and the recognition that the last shred of sanity they had would disappear when the day turned over one more time, maybe the last time.

The world would be something Mary understood. It will be a new place tomorrow. She would have to cope with the inability to sleep, or the death of animals and plants, or the torrential climates. Or, if the Antis really found themselves right, she scoffed to herself, then a world without government and order. A mess of looting and disobedience, self-law, things that had already been happening. A torn apart society rearing its ugly face made for scary circumstances. The course of history climaxed, and no one bet on what the future would hold.

Beep … beep … beep. This is not a test. This is your last chance to take the Acclimation Pill. This is the last attempt to reach you. You have four hours left until the Anti's mission is complete.

"… Wait. What? What is—"

People with gruff voices interrupted the broadcast on air, but she was sure it was a hoax. It was a last-ditch effort to derail everything. The Antis had found the broadcast location before. Mary thought she could make out the President's voice.

The Acclimation Pill, aka NeverSleep Pill … It does not work. Repeat. You will die if you take it. It is not worth the gel it's capped with. Take your chances with the arsenic that is releasing in Siberia. You'll have a better chance there.

Someone coughed very loudly and cleared his throat twice, and silence set in. Mary wasn't sure if she then heard static or if the words had been formed in her head all along.

She hesitated by the phone. This wasn't enough to steer Jill away from what it was they both were about to do. She wouldn't call back.

Banking on fate, Mary popped the pill ceremoniously in her mouth and took a swig of the tea she had. She got some extra from a friend bound to die. To waste what someone left in her house weeks ago amounted to criminal behavior. The chaser now was only for good luck.

Rubbing her head into a pillow, she counted down, watching sheep jump fences to calm her nerves, her anxiety ridden fear. She made a little wish, a hope for the future with each jump. She thanked the world and society for something that had happened in the past to save them all when the sheep landed.

One of her last wishes before she tapped out came and blew away with the wind. She focused on remembering the want, focused on seeing it be true. She hoped goodness happened, that Jill would be with her every day, not just Saturdays. The trip would be their escape into what they used to have for good. The trip presented an opportunity to find themselves again, forever this time. She only hoped it would be true, but when she saw it as a dream came through, she sighed and rested. They were there, married at a waterfall.

Jill in her mother's dress. Jill in Mary's arms.

The pull of her desire, tragic and wanting, pulled her to sleep. The fear of the world and the hope of love were heavy at hand. She would find Jill either way. They would both find their way if they both did the same thing, took the pill. They might both die together or have their second chance at love. The lustful journey of new lovers in a devastated world, post-apocalypse.

CHAPTER 4

What seemed like days later, what likely was days later, when Jill woke up, out of her bedroom window, Jill saw large smoke plumes enter and escape the clouds, stitch up and at the same time drive the world apart; She watched tires on stone gravel kick up the dust on the ground; and she heard the bellowing rumble of engines sound all over the earth. Gear, shift, peel out. It caused her eyes to pull back from the night's sleep in the shimmering light of the last morning. Fear begot apathy. The coal rollers became more frequent in recent weeks. Coal rollers, trucks that were rigged to use diesel fuel and purposefully spewed substantial amounts of smoke, owned the landscape in the past few weeks. All along, their intent was to ruin the environment but there were much more efficient ways of doing that. They were in the Artic, doing what they could to blow up, melt, do away with, the polar ice caps. The coal rollers protested the NeverSleep. They were deniers. Those that didn't take the pills subsequently were to fall dead when the earth shifted. When a change in gravity spread eternal changes, headaches would ensue, the brain would swell, and insides would collapse.

They, the citizens of the United States, amidst a developing war, hesitated, unsure why the pill would work. The government told them it would; it's what they formed as tenet. The world would change. In or out. Quick decide. And that's why in recent days, the people of the unsettled country called the news propaganda. What they had agreed to two weeks before now appeared in contention, failed to make sense. To deny the government suddenly, at the end of the world, surfaced as the sentiment of the week.

Jill slumped deep into her mattress, her weight in place, sinking deep, wiggling her butt in. This LongSleep, the several days of sleep that preceded the new state of being called the NeverSleep, made Jill think about her own mortality. People in comas sometimes didn't wake up. She realized that much. She did not want to live in this day, because of the heaviness of the world and what the planet had become. The unknown she would have to rise to scared her more than any other day, tenfold the stress of a day at work. She fidgeted in her silly slump.

Her arms stretched wide, then flopped on the bed outstretched. She shook her head back and forth. She propped up, still awake. A light groan hummed within her throat. She imagined the flapping flags as they faded into the distance. Two minutes passed, too late to look. Five seconds elapsed. She rolled away from the simple light of a lamp. She reached for the curtains, rolling the fabric between her fingers. Her eye peeped through a sliver of a gap. The brightness of the light, mild as it might be, burned deep into her retinas for the first time. She internalized the heat, and her mind collapsed from knowing. Her glossy eyes captured images of herself in the window glass, a mirror. Then a scorched earth this world will be. This is what Life is like. This is what it is like to be doomed. Sleep ceased.

No one speed walked to start their day. No one hustled to work. No one would ever find another love. The bakery at the end of the road had shut off their lights. This was the closest to death she had ever been. How will we survive?

With simple pursed-lip sips, she tested her tea, a morning fixation. Earl grey, the flavor she learned to like early on. Now drinking the murky water would be for behavior, habit only. When the double-sized wheels of the coal roller rolled passed again at the other end of the block, the fumes puffed out a rooster in the morning before it crows. No other cars plagued the day. The streets were barren, and the mechanical clock showed 6:00 a.m. No one mowed their grass. The scent of fresh manure from an agricultural complex a few miles off was mysteriously absent. Only stale, acrid air, air like death, dust, and gasoline, lingered in the wind and on the tongue, potent in a giant pull into the lungs. She did this without an alternative. On exhale, she wondered about death, about the NeverSleep, guessed if she tried harder, the smell of the smoke might waft towards her. If a spark should fly from a metal exhaust pipe against the road, she would drop to the floor all at once, crawl, a marine in the trenches. Terrified of the rumble and apathetic about death all at the same time, she counted breaths in and out to calm her anxiety.

The bellow of a horn rang out for approximately twenty seconds when the heap of metal pulled up to a stop at the intersection. The icebergs had melted overnight; it seemed to say.

When she pushed the door open, she extended her arms pulling in sun, stretching, like when she drew her eyes away from lamp light and toward the sunlight in her bed moments ago. Nothing looked brighter. The world would not sleep, was the public consensus about the situation. So, she took the pill. And then she washed her hands. Because if people, those left living, caught some type of illness, even though they shouldn't, they might pummel each other. Instead, they would die trying to win a fight or stay alive.

Jill sipped her tea over the sink, looking out the window, waiting for the truck to come back around. The dark foggy pool of liquid tasted bitter, stronger than usual. She had steeped the bag in the water longer, not wanting its flavor right away because the ritual now manifested as a habit. She waited for the truck to circle back, sound the siren again, but the vehicle did not. The world had ended, or the world might rebuild. Or, Jill realized, people might finish it off, in their last sleep, by failing to rise, while the icebergs subsided at the same time. Bombs were bombing. Missiles were firing. Oil was burning in the Arctic.

Jill poked the key into the ornate interior lockset and turned, opening the aged, wooden front door that had seen just a century, a century of snow blocking its opening. The inswing door had never opened to invite the snow in to melt on the threshold. Jill had always stayed put when the snow piled so high access was limited. She guessed Colorado bears weren't as scary as the snow decades ago. This March, the sun glowed at the horizon, reddening the hue on the adobe-orange front door. Jill sauntered with a lilt of a swagger, as if she might be the first risen. She could be the only risen. She sighed empty and alone. The steps extended wide and hard. Cement stuck to the back of her legs as she tipped the mug toward her mouth, tasting the heat, then the black, black tea. NeverSleep would affect everyone. The wobble of gravity would affect everyone for a few hours, make them sick if they awoke, itch in their innards as the squish, tense and release, occurred. That they expected. The preventative, the anti-squish, was to be controlled by taking a pill, a new improvement, they said. The NeverSleep would ensue.

She looked down at her tea and tapped her fingernails, which had grown long and hazardous against the ceramic. They had grown out in LongSleep. They said distortion might happen, irregular growth, splotchiness, yellowing. The people of the United States, not anymore citizens, were vampires in coffins. The smart placed things in their rooms, houses, anything in their domain, in a particular way for a particular reason in case it was years until they woke up from the LongSleep or in case they never woke up. They had been given time to plan. While asleep, one would never find out if someone came in and checked their pulse. Watches and glasses on nightstands, she guessed, they all had taken the pill. They all had said. Sleep before NeverSleep would last days, but everyone's experience would prove to be slightly different. A short sleep before NeverSleep was thought to be an inconsequential anomaly. Sure, it was. She pinched the handle of the mug. The appendage looked, felt solid, real, a thing. The composition of the ceramic registered undeniably unalterable. She torqued the mug to examine it, and a drop of tepid liquid cascaded onto her thumb.

The empty mug clanked on the cement steps as she stood. Her digital watch glowed. She would be able to charge it, the electricity had not yet been turned off. Her cell lit up but not the bars. Her eyes didn't focus, and she imagined a cartoon, whose hands circled in all directions. She lifted her toes, and the dizziness subsided. No one could make a home now. No one owned any one place more than anyone else. No one should be born to this, not in this world. Not a place without humanity.

For the past few nights, she had slept in a LongSleep but were it any other day after she fell asleep, Mary would have come by the house. Mary always came over on Saturdays and Jill loved the time although didn't always show it. They enjoyed the exes date night. The company made them both a mite less alone. The aloneness had gotten to Jill, she knew it. It started with an apathy called depression. Misplaced tears would erupt for vague reasons of loneliness. Stubbed toes would cause a breakdown. She failed to cry, bawl her eyes out, for Dillan, for the true loss, despite being able to mourn, and that's when she knew she was depressed beyond reason. Perhaps that's why she conjured noble causes, ways to honor her name. Mary lived forty-five minutes away. Not necessarily someone she'd call in an emergency, but Mary still listed Jill as a beneficiary on her 401K.

The LongSleep wouldn't be without its issues, though no one was entirely speculating about the damage, the problems that would come about. The government said that there would be side effects, all of them. As everyone waited for the NeverSleep, after the LongSleep, people forgot common tasks, housekeeping. Bodily functions might change. You could lose weight in the LongSleep or develop headaches. Jill grabbed at her hair, which had lengthened, grown out. She tilted the dry and sharp split ends toward her face to examine them. They severed this way and that for a good inch.

Jill twisted her left wrist with her right hand. She never took her watch off, wore the timepiece, old and new at the same time, to bed. The impression of the dimpled underside pushed into the skin, slight but noticeable. It mapped to where she had slept and where the watch stuck to her wrist. She lifted her arm. She would have to shower.

Her fingers tapped on the phone that sat in her lap, dancing, until she picked it up. The phone wouldn't show internet service. The phone service was cut as well, but she dialed anyway. Dead. She would wait as she picked at her fingernails. Ripping them off as she once had when at fifteen. Mary would show. This would be their time to go. Get in the car. See the country. Like they had twenty years ago when they met. When they would never break up.

The pillowy black smoke came from two blocks down this time. The thick, dark cloud smoldered with heat as a beast of a vehicle kicked up its back wheel; it bucked like a black stallion of death. No other cars traversed the streets that morning, just after dawn. The smoke drifted a bit in her direction, coming for her ever so slightly, then dissipated. The wind blew south. And she laughed at the idea that gravity spun them in another direction.

It might have. They could've said it. Someone believed it. Jill was here now.

Minutes passed, and she glanced down the street, up at windows, mentally knocked on doors. No one ventured out into this world. If melted icebergs flooded the planet, surely, people would take to the mountains. They would come here. There would be only so much room. She might lose her home. The struggling looters would test their conscience at so many points.

With gaping eyes, she swallowed as a man in a camouflage ski mask walked his dog on the sidewalk. Jill wanted to bark at the man as his dog lifted a leg on a bush she owned outright. A piece of land owned jointly at one point by Jill and her partner.

Mary's partial payment was swallowed up in the breakup years ago. Jill lived on her own. The uncoupled pair did not quite identify as domestic partners and did not quite play well with lawyers. They shook hands, and Mary sold out her half of the house but took most of the rest of the savings they both held. Still, Jill struggled with money. Jill remembered the clasp, her sweaty palms against Mary's palms' dry heat years ago. She wasn't as nervous. For the past several years, after a several year break, Mary visited the house and Jill. And so, she was on her best behavior.

Today, Jill needed Mary. Mary would ease her down. Jill never, ever calmed herself down without a thorough discussion. She made an easy sigh just thinking about it. It wouldn't, didn't matter. Jill felt left behind by Mary and smothered at the same time. She was hopelessly hooked on the things Mary did for her, but couldn't let her back in. She understood the emotions and actions that would arise if she did. The relationship was over, and they both should move on. Mary never, ever let Jill go, and that was half of her own angst.

They had made a pact and put the words in writing. If the end of the world came next year, like the experts predicted, they would travel together to find their own bliss in mayhem. It wouldn't be safe to be alone, they wrote, signed. To them the document was as good as something legally bound, and as they wrote it, would beat all words to the contrary or take-backs from that day forward. A childish sentiment with hopes for a bright world's future. Lingering in the back of their minds resonated the warning, the gravity, the icebergs, the environment, the mayhem and looting, the last days with a loved one.

She wanted to bark at the man and dog to make a point, and her mouth gaped. Chin jutted. She would find a mechanism to say things were different. She strove to be unlike the rest. She wiggled her toes as they peeked out of the sandals, toenails longer than usual, longer than ever before.

Jill looked back at her phone, grabbed her hand, and then pulled at her flowing hair. In quick motions, she loosely braided the hair behind her as she had when she was at the youthful age of ten. It had always been soft in the braid and unfurled easily. She hated that about her hair, the softness, the inability to control it.

She rubbed her hands over her face, and the skin gathered. The water had flushed from her body, or the age had given a sag to the taught skin of her twenties. Wilted flowers bent over before her, or rather towards the street, the cascading sun. Just like her, she thought. The flowers dipped to touch toes, stretch in their age. Jill relished a good yoga session, despite the aches and pains afterward. She resorted to recorded videos now that the studios had closed. Summer had gotten on and the last bugs started dying off with the annuals.

"LongSleep, eh?" The man with the dog looked back, pulling at the leash as he did. He bowed to look into her eyes and stood back up. "Look it."

She didn't know whether he was talking about himself or not. The dirt around his eyes, the crevasses of his hands, nails were caked. The man looked like someone had put him inside the smokestack of his truck. Someone had powdered him in the smoggy dust.

She looked up and his big black truck had snuck into a spot caddy corner to Jill's house, two streets down. The truck had finished horizontal laps and then combed crosswise, working on the vertical. But he exited the cab to beg her a hello or to just look, peer into her eyes. The person who had been watching Jill finally spoke.

He turned to move back to his car. "I'm no doctor, but you look tired already."

The day's sun grew strong. The light hadn't fully risen. Mary hadn't come. Mary would be there soon if they were both lucky. If they both wanted to start a caravan of two to another coast. Drive all night, meld night if night existed, into day.

He read as an even-tempered man given all that happened in the last several days. His rugged demeanor came across like the others, those that drove similar trucks before and after NeverSleep. They were fighting a war of politics that wouldn't end, even without a leader, without citizens. His greased jeans mimicked those of a mechanic, or a person dedicated to a similar craft on weekends. It was an eternal weekend of sorts now. He carried a buck knife. His job now included protecting himself from this world he had looked forward to with the others. Had they won?

"I was always cold as a child," the man said. "My father would crank the A/C in the summer because we had it. 'Electricity bill be damned,' he said. He didn't care about me." He chewed on a wad in his mouth. "There's no reason not to think it might get hot or it might get cold or both. But we'll live with it. We'll find a way."

"What is your point?" Jill said.

"You're my point," he said. "There won't be an insurrection. The Capitol fell on its own, and we don't want to rebuild. There is no president. So, there's your news. Oh, you'll see me now and then, if only so that you know there's one of me for each and every one of you. We've got to watch out for who is left. They'll try to rebuild. But I don't think they can."

"I'm not running for president—"

"Oh, but you're forming opinions. Just … we're everywhere. Remember that."

The man turned and spat in the other direction and gave

a jerk to his dog's leash and then flopped the slack into the air like a whip. Offended, he moved on as if he never spoke to her. He carried on as if he hadn't ever stopped and as her focus blurred a bit for what may or may not have been the wobbling of the earth.

Looking back, he said, "Do you want a dog? I can't take this thing into a new world. I can't care for it. I've got to take care of myself."

"You're heartless. What's your name anyway? Who are you?"

"I'll take that as a 'No.'"

As she stepped back inside the house, the knob on the lockset stuck when she turned to close the door. The dust kicked up in the light of the window as she entered. Mary was not inside, wouldn't be home for some time, if at all. In this quiet, with only rumbling from the storm, she found boredom. She wasn't sure if people would issue from their houses tipping things over, standing on cars, screaming bloody murder because they were awake. They would enter the world to tip it over, likely at 3:20 a.m. when sleep ceased.

She flounced onto the couch, a big overflowing puffy thing they had bought together. It sucked her in, made her relax, if only for a moment. She must've been the first up, the first to want to go back to sleep, and it hurt. A wincing pain ruminated on her frontal lobe. The eye strain of the sun she took in on the porch, the bright light along with the Vitamin D, or agitation from the smoke, the idea of smoke made her hurt. It wasn't quite right. She avoided the pain. She moved to the desk chair.

Her pen in her hand, she only thought of the pain, not the writing. She wholeheartedly warmed at the thought that anything she wrote would be historic. Future archivists might look back upon it. Or it would be just for her selfish reminiscing, she thought. Her apathy came full circle when she doodled a shiny car, a cartoon with a plume of smoke that ascended the whole page. And then listlessness overcame her, and the firm desk chair poked into her bony butt.

So, she moved to the kitchen to make some cereal. Most people at breakfast at this hour, after all. But when she sat on the bar stool that wobbled, one leg slightly lower than the rest, she wavered more off balance than in the previous two spots. None was quite right. As she tried to eat the cereal and then just simply flipped her spoon in the milk, she relented. Her appetite was gone. Another side-effect perhaps? The day was now a trio of maladies. Was Vitamin D to be her only sustenance? Today it would be, positively.

Jill heard a knock at the door as the wind-up clock read 6:58 a.m. She gave it another crank. The damn thing usually came close to the correct hour. The day was early, and she rolled her head to the right, then to the left, begging for the sun to come around. This was a tomb of sorts, a room to move around but buried alive, locked in, never to venture past thick stone walls.

Mary approached, shuffling her feet toward the door. The boards under her creaked. She paused and ran her hand up the edge of the cracked door of the house they used to share and entered, almost sneaking through its sliver of an opening. She hesitated. That was the same caress she had given Jill so many times. Mary flipped her blond locks back as Jill turned her head.

Mary entered the foyer. "I mean, really, Jill, we had such a big house," Mary said.

"Truly is. Room enough for two. There's so much more of a need to pass the time." Her words lingered.

"You have the Jeep. Is it ready? Two days to California. Perhaps the best thing is not having to sleep. We'll be there in no time. How far can a car go without taking a rest? That's our maximum."

"No rest until we get there?" Jill said. She hardened her glance. She felt her age, stretching her arm over the opposite shoulder to ready herself, gather some energy. Jill knew this would be a long trip and hard on her body and mind. The state of the world itself was enough mental strife to make anyone want to stay put.

"Who knows what we'll find if we stop? Is it worth it? Should we test those icy waters?" Mary said. "This is the day we hoped for, the day we pinky swore on. Right?" Mary's eyes lingered.

Jill's persistent hesitation butted up against the last hours they had left to decide. Every child had made a promise to a friend to reconnect in adulthood. Jill's pledge to Mary rang no different and all in the same completely foreign.

"Here we are. If we don't rip each other apart, I'll call it a win," Mary said.

"I love you." Mary shoved hands in pockets and looked up. "But they'll be up soon. It'll be best to get on the road. Pandemonium, I'm sure. You don't feel earthquakes if you're in a vehicle," Mary said. She turned away as quickly.

The looting would come. New zombies, daylight zombies would enter, unable to catch a nap, recuperate, rest. Jill had tasted it already. She knew what would be coming. She knew the end of the world, saw it as she rolled around in her bed, trying to get back to sleep.

Jill packed a bag by 8:30 a.m., and she speculated that the world would soon end. At least that's how the tension in the room buzzed. Jill moved to the window after she zipped up the last bag. Brushing the curtains back, she thought about the world in a new way. She looked for people. A person. A clue. In this mystery of a world, she didn't know where to begin the investigation. Jill held a magnifying glass, but things didn't yet appear bigger.

A bewildered older man bent to his knee on the sidewalk, perhaps off balance from the unfulfilling last minutes of sleep, the inability to roll over and cascade back into sweet dreams. Someone is left alive, Jill thought. The lack of people, the blankness of space, told a different story. She didn't ask him if he knew of any others, even though her question persisted, and he eventually got to his feet, shuffled on with his walk.

How many people were dead in their beds? How many people had just failed to leave their houses yet? Usually, by 8:30 a.m. this place, this corner of life, amounted to a bustling corner, struck with mayhem. Peel outs that woke the dead by 12:30 a.m. Jerks in sports cars. Wanna-bes in mini-vans. And utility trucks making a point while on their way to work. It started three years ago. Jill rose early every morning, and for the millionth night, shaken awake by local hoodlums having fun.

Recently, the coal rollers inhabited the area. They became all that was left. The only thing that stated their presence. The plumes of smoke, the threats of mayhem. The reserve they showed with guns at their side might be called utterly amazing.

Not a peep, peel out, or honk sounded since Mary showed up. The LongSleep might've prevented the everyday restless sleep, but no pill lulled her mind from the impact of the everyday traffic of this corner. Jill confirmed the lack of cavorting to herself. "God, it's peaceful," she said. The noise loomed absent for hours. The world must be dead. Not her. She would never die.

Mary had parked the car out back, ready for them both to bolt, ready for them to career away from the gently rising sun, sing songs from the nineteen-seventies when trees mattered and people cared about nature, and they found themselves in it and proclaimed it to the world. Yet, no one quite listened because the coded warning sounded so sweet. Here they were, years after they shoved it down their throat that they were going to die. Months after it became real. And now they might die, and now Jill would finally find Mary amidst an impending doom.

A loud bang sounded off, louder than the siren when the asteroid hit. And the coal rollers swarmed again. The two ex-lovers sat on the front steps, looking out into the world. Car after car, as if they had all descended, those that supposedly wouldn't take the pill, they all appeared miraculously in that one spot. Because they were all there on that very block, not a single other person lived in the world.

Jill and Mary coughed in unison. They laughed at the act, in contrast to the seriousness of the smoke, the people behind the truck steering wheels. This world was on fire. Someone had lit icebergs on fire, blowing them out of the water with explosives. Turned the world upside down.

Here they still used trucks, with black matte paint jobs, trucks with dents, and dings, and scratches made from bumping into things to scare the last few left. Were they to kill them all, everyone, with fear?

Mary waved her hand to ward off any filtered smoke. She brushed her fingers through her hair, a last luxury she might lose on a trip for survival. She still packed the shampoo.

The Anti's trucks displayed their presence, and what was Life-after for the Antis. They showed the decisions of the nation, groups of citizens. Antis stood for belief in government. Loud and booming, they meant more to everyone that left, that must leave.

One of the trucks had a loudspeaker. Booming into the morning, it rang out in a garbled voice with a southern twang. They had come from the south even.

"Icebergs are gone. The inevitable will come. Sleep through it if you must. The interstate is down. You are officially stuck and so are we. Good to meet you neighbors." The words shouted from the loudspeaker atop a truck.

They traveled on, eventually rumbling out into the distance, a small horde of them.

"Well, we're stuck … if we sign on to the Anti's message," Jill said.

Mary tottered back and forth.

Mary rubbed Jill's shoulder as they watched a group of kids muddle and skip and dodge their way down the street. They were the first people up and at a time too early for kids who should otherwise watch Saturday morning cartoons.

The sun beat down on the hot spring day, but the heat had not yet rose quite to what they expected. March's heat mimicked July. The heat would collapse the world, the animals would die, Jill thought, but not before some of them got to a safe place, the Colony. They had heard about the Colony in California. The temperate climate, the bomb shelter like protection, the ultramodern technology. Of course, it had yet to be tested. They would get there if Jill ever agreed to leave. The only recourse included staying and getting swallowed up by the smoke of the coal-rollers, or bearing with headaches and intestinal cramps. One of these options would surface. They said so.

The kids bounded down, passed them into the distance. A shiny sliver of hedge trimmers popped into her sightline. Jill wasn't sure what they would need that for.

"What is it about you that makes you want kids?" Mary said.

"It's something I always wanted. What I can have now.

When I was young, a girl before I realized I was a lesbian with limited options, I used to name my children, thirteen of them," Jill said. She swung her hair back and pulled it together but did not braid it as she usually would. "Who would ever have thirteen children? This is the only thing I have wasted in life. My ability to have kids. As a teenager, I wrapped myself up in the lesbian game, I shook off the notion of having kids. I would be strong independent, save money and buy a vacation home instead of diapers. Then, it became where on earth should I live, and I forgot about ever having wanted children as a girl. The doll I had as a child literally got pushed to a corner of my room, then the back of a drawer, but I never got rid of it."

She shuddered and held her hand to her belly. Jill wanted children but felt pulled back by the world and by the apathy of her lovers about tiny Jill's growing up then wandering through the world. This was the stage in the cycle of her life that she wanted children again, just as she had as a child. It was also her last possible chance. "Mary, if I wasn't cursed and childless, would you have kids with me?" She pulled her hand back to her belly, knowing the blood only came six times a year now.

"Yes, of course." Mary looked intently at her fisted hand stuck on her chin as she leaned bent at the waist over the tall table in the front room. "I would have any child with you." They couldn't even check into a hospital if one of them broke a leg.

"That man, the one with the camouflage mask, I can sense him pulsing Anti. But why is he stalking me? He circled the block ten times this morning before he got out, let his dog shit on the yard two houses up and got back in his car and left. He relished the moment." Jill said.

"I'm not sure who this guy is you keep talking about. But those people are crazy, the Antis, they're crazy. Why are they even alive? Like the people who lived in vans and thought the world was going to end when the Mayan calendar reached a certain date. Twenty years ago, when people were wearing flannel and baggy jeans, yeah, it was weird. It doesn't, or it's starting not to, seem so ludicrous now, to live in a van and preach the end of the world. The end of the world is here. The thing that's weird, crazy even, is that they wanted it to come." Mary cracked her knuckles. The pop became a tell-tale sign that she didn't know what to say or couldn't articulate what she wanted to say. It gave the room a moment to pause before anyone spoke.

This altercation was the fight they would all have to have. The people who took the pill for NeverSleep were the last righteous people, who wanted to see democracy and goodness take over a world that had collapsed in ideology and turned, for the Antis, into a fight for doom instead of against. Spite. Pure spite.

That's what they had thought. They had hoped that the Antis wouldn't take the pill. And here was a herd of coal-rollers telling an awful tale. One last-ditch effort to convince the nation that the NeverSleep pill was a hoax, counteracting sentiments ongoing for months, years, since initial developments in the lab years ago.

A young boy popped his head in the window. He must've been nine. He held a pair of kitchen shears and laughed with a bold, hearty laugh, one that roared like someone three times his age.

Mary jumped back and landed squarely in the foyer chair. The chair's sole purpose in the world was to stop her fall. "What the fu——." Mary said.

The young boy grinned and looked Jill in the eyes. He snipped the scissors four times and vanished.

Jill darted to the window and looked out left and then right and left again. The pre-adolescent boy was gone. It tugged at her being, her will not to cry.

"We have to go to California. To the Colony. It's our last chance. There's goodness there. People will band together. We saw it in the commune we visited years ago. Remember when we loved … each other?" Mary said.

"I, I still love you," Jill said. "I really do."

"Then what is it to live or die? Why can't we?" Mary said.

"Because that's what's scary. Even if we live, we might die. That's the leap. I love you as much as I can now, but if we go now to develop that love more, it might all die. All of it will fizzle away. The last little bit we've had these past few years. Then, I wouldn't have you, whether or not I had the world," Jill said.

A loud pinging rose into the scent of the stale, still smokey air. It was like a pickax chipping away at a mined rock or a blacksmith forging a blade. Jill's eyes wavered, and she stepped back gasping, dizzy, from the front window. She coughed out and the dust of curtains not brushed or steamed in four years kicked up.

As they sat in the front room, a kerfuffle sounded out front. Both Jill and Mary moved to separate windows and, parallel, looked out into this new world.

The group, a mass really, of kids, about twenty to thirty, ran breakneck speed as kids sometimes do. Then ran away from a sole boy using an ax against the front doorknob. They all ran away from him as if, Jill thought at first, in fear. But they weren't afraid. They zoomed passed much faster than Jill ever imagined was possible. This time, all bared arms, sharp manual garden tools. One kid, about nine, took long strides that seemed somewhat slower and arching. He was in the air at a gallop. He looked right at the house and pointed. Jill leaned in to try to hear the mumbled words of what he said above the clamor of the crowd of children, but she shrunk back at the anger in his eyes. It was as deep anger only mustered in adulthood. The world had bitten him. It was different and now was their time to run and be free to change it all or have the time of their lives before they died. Let the kids play with sticks, sharp metal.

Jill moved to the front door. Jill counted five houses across the street and down to the next block, pointing at them with her finger. She saw kids storming the fifth house, implements in hand. A window broke with a crash. A small shed tumbled onto its side, with four kids rocking it over. They scurried underneath its open floor to steal more tools and weapons.

No one appeared from the house. When Jill realized this, she locked the front door. It was good or bad. No one or no one now left. The lock clicked, and the deadbolt snapped over. They would just have to break the window to grasp the deadbolt.

She saw someone push the end of a shovel into a small crack of a window in the next house.

Two children sat on it, bouncing until the lock broke.

Jill never noticed if either of the houses were ones that had children: if a parent or two lived there or the age of the little ones that lived with them. She hadn't been that observant. She was selfish, turned into herself. Sure, she saw kids day to day, but she never wondered which home they came from. She never spied on or tracked. That was for jealous beasts. They got off the school bus and dispersed. That was as it always had been. Despite that, she wanted one of her own. After witnessing this mayhem, this morning, she realized that the kids usually on their social media or creating creative video content had rebelled. An ultimate rebellion, one with more power than any kid had ever had before. They were free, and they were unpaired from their parents. They would change the earth.

"Jill, I've been pinning to go. But really now. Eight houses down? We both just saw that. We both can't dismiss it. Just wait here. We can't go down and tell them to go home to their parents. For Christ's sake, they might go home to their parents with pitchfork weapons. No one would have the gall to ground them right now for multiple reasons," Mary said.

Just then, the man in the mask crossed the window that Jill had stepped away from. The green camouflage of the mask stuck out, created dissonance against the deep red orange of the front room. His pale skin showed just below the mask. This is the closest she'd been to his face. He placed his truck just across the street. They must not have seen him come into the commotion, as Jill and Mary began to fret and raise their own voices.

He pointed at the truck, but Jill and Mary didn't hear him through the window. Muffled words emanated, and they tried to read lips. He darted for the truck as a lone child looked at him. The kid wielded a rake, a rake that might prove to do limited damage. He opened his fist, and the garden tool dropped to the ground.

"Jill," Mary said. "We have to go. The camouflage mask guy. The kids."

"What good will it do?" Jill said. Her apathy held down her emotion. She pulled in her energy despite the good rest she had awoken from just hours before. She was drained and without motivation: not marriage, not for the life of kids, and not for fear of a stale, gloomy man. She paused. She had no cause to act.

Jill mulled about trying to pace herself and her words. The tension of it all produced a single bead of sweat, and she reacted by trying to walk it off. In a swift movement, she pivoted on the balls of her feet and swung her body in the other direction.

"It's not like … I'm not there yet. This to me … we agree marriage is something else, something we'll never see again now that the world is NeverSleep. Something we never saw ten years ago. This would be like marriage. Going would be marriage. A decisive step," Mary said. "Post-marital sex, at least." She jerked her jaw back and forth and opened her eyes wide.

Jill responded, "Quit it with the jokes." Jill clapped her hands. "This is serious. This is our lives … what we didn't get to see. Going off with you would be like marriage. It would be the actual thing or as close as you can get without an officiant and a formal setting."

Mary cut in, "We have to get 'married,' as they say, or they won't let us into the Colony."

Jill jogged her memory for a light, a hope, or a whim that might change the course around. Some broadcasts relayed you had to be married to get into the Colony or the likelihood would be better. The government considered things like re-population and efficiency of numbers. The facility only held so many people and they had to decide.

People talked. Leading up to the day everyone was to take the NeverSleep pill, people chatted amongst each other. They tried to interpret what the government meant, what they wanted you to hear, and what would happen.

With no time to guess, everyone viewed their opinions as plausible. And soon, the pot of thought, the ideas of a nation muddled, not at all cohesive, and probably unbased and wrong.

"I know, but does it have to be real? Is it even real?" Jill said.

"We'll have the photos. It's the best we can do," Mary said. "And, yes, twenty-four hours a day, seven days a week together with few if any people left on the planet. That is, if anyone good is left, if it's not just people who drive coal-rollers. If the government we followed until the very end isn't dead, yes, it will be like marriage."

Mary ducked into the back closet and into a tiny corner of the tight space where they put the extras: snow pants, yellow running vests, odd clothing.

She reentered with Jill's mother's wedding dress. "This is for you. The one you didn't get to wear. This is for now. There will be no other time."

The dress was lacey and gorgeous. It had thin strings peeling from the detailing, but it added to its glory. This dress was an artifact, a tribute to a woman, a mold for a life as she always wanted to be. And the dress functioned as a means of forgiveness for Mary. Jill owed Mary this much to see her, to play dress up, to find a common ground in Jill's perplexing life. Jill owed Mary her whole self for always standing by. Yet still, Jill deserved Mary.

"God. It's so beautiful. That time … I never. I chose the new one with the slim profile for that night out. Do you remember? When we committed in 2012? Do you remember the crowd, all our friend's … Oh, God. God, I wish my mom was still alive."

"She would've wanted you to wear that dress …" Mary said.

"I doubt it. She would've wanted me to carry on the legacy. I would hope," Jill said. She honestly was unsure.

"I'm sure she would've wanted you to be happy, at least, more than anything. Are you happy?" Mary said, chucking her eyes up at Jill, pulling her lips in.

Jill held her voice back, hand over mouth. She all but bit her nails. It was a moment to think. The anxiety, the immediacy of it all, would not hit. "When I was young … she said I should've worn it. She said she wanted me to … But it might've all … she might've just said it …" She dipped back in time somewhere into her head. She heard her mother's voice drift through the void. If she found a thing called sleep in NeverSleep, this was it. She heard her mother in a lucid dream.

Mary jumped and smacked her feet on the ground. "I can't. I can't make you go, but it's time. We have to find our place. We have to at least start on our way." Mary grabbed a top hat and cane from the back of the closet. Her wool trousers were already packed in her bag.

"Will you ever leave me?" Jill's eyes implored Mary to be gentle but to take her swiftly, fulfill her promises of safety. So much was loaded in that question.

"Of course not, honey." Mary paused the longest minute she was able. "Everything will be fine. You will be safe with me. Nothing is going to happen, and I'll never, I promise you, leave you for one minute."

Jill shifted, adjusted, trying to find a sigh.

When the air released, the time was right. It was neither forceful nor coercing, but Mary grabbed Jill's hand and made for the garage.

Jill did not resist and flew swiftly behind Mary. Apathy let Jill go because her sentimental self understood they still had love to kindle. This knowledge let her move toward the door.

CHAPTER 5

"I just want to go home," Jill muttered as she opened the door to the garage. "I just want to go home." Her breathless remark sounded just out of earshot. "With you …" Her voice trailed off. Her eyes tried to stare through the door she was closing, maybe for the last time.

The broadcast several nights ago relayed that the government was getting situated and cell service might continue post-event. They said there were some qualifications to get into the Colony because they expected limited space. The broadcast indicated you had to prove marriage to get into the Colony. That the government, the last shreds of a pseudo-liberal government, was compromising in case Antis wanted to take the NeverSleep pill. The act might just be the last jab at forgiveness and compassion, neither of which Antis had.

The Antis would never gulp down a single pill. Everyone balked. They shot back their rules. If certain things happened, they would comply. The ultra conservative beliefs they put on the table included having a religion at the head of the table alongside a government president. It vowed allegiance for a hierarchical system with Anti associators in ultimate power. Asked for closed borders. They outwardly condemned respect for minority rights, the gay community, and common democratic ideals. They would not accept the legality of abortion. No, kids won't die in NeverSleep, they said. No one killed children. And promiscuity was strictly prohibited, especially the model of sexuality promoted by the gay community.

Jill was flushed by the attempts to call out her community specifically, her friends and lovers, past and current. The Antis were trying to tear down everything, the least of contentious things, as the root and build a society no one could live in. It would fail ten times over, and Jill saw this for a fact.

This place they were walking in now, this completely other place ridden with no rules but two hard last minute spoken rules. Abide or don't take the pill. Get along. This is a last-ditch effort.

It could bring about the demise of the gay community, people historically marginalized repeatedly. This world would not work, would not prosper without them in it, she assured herself with positivity.

Jill and Mary got into the beat-up Jeep, the one with the ragtop. The sturdy machine fit into this world like it had been run over by a coal roller. The royal blue shone strong in the morning light, even though a few rust spots on the edges above the tires poked through. Jill brushed a spot with her sleeve and saw a child skipping, crossing the block, in the mirror reflection of the back hatch.

Mary fiddled with the key to the ignition. It was loose, as it had been for several years. Jill was no mechanic. Mary was no mechanic. The Impreza might not handle the hilly roads of California. The Jeep was the best bet, except Jill hated driving. This was the same Jeep, brand new at the time, that they got married in and renewed their vows. They were one of the couples from the early marriage equality days, who wore rings, even though it didn't matter. Even though, in some ways more than others, to people who didn't understand, jewelry flashed and sparkled for no other purpose.

"He was so calm," Jill said. "It's how I thought I'd be in the NeverSleep." The pill was supposed to wipe out all possible mental strife: anxiety, depression, anger. Jill wasn't sure about the anger. It was a base emotion. Everyone needed to get angry now and then. Especially at the cable company. It was the only way they did business. The elimination of the cable companies weeks ago also did everyone good.

NeverSleep pills were developed to counteract the bends and the pressure from the environment. It would save lives. Right then, a headache formed from a swirling pain in Jill's frontal lobe. It was the mental strife being awake twenty-four hours a day. They said you should lie down when you are mentally exhausted, like a vampire in a coffin. They said to lie flat on your back to encourage the idea of relaxation and sleep, then close your eyes. The broadcast was very vague but said people would dream awake. They said the dreams were so vivid they would take people to other places. Everyone would realize in time. When the tumultuous dreams crept in while you were awake, when you saw the truth, you were to lie down and let them take over. The reason would be revealed. Those that were left would understand. Jill was not yet … tired … yet mentally exhausted.

They told those who lived that the pill would help you through this new world. It was the closest thing to a cure for everything. Everyone thought it was a farce, a scam, at first. But the test results showed positive aspects. Most conscientious doctors got on board. The ones who didn't scream blasphemy. That it was anti-human. Antis, of all people, made an argument for the humanity of it all. Jill had sat back and laughed, watched, waited. She had a fair amount of skepticism toward anything. But it came down to who she wanted to die with. The Colony would only take people who had taken the pill because of the proximity, because the pill cured all common colds and illnesses. Did she want to die with them or the Antis? The choice was straightforward. When the alarms sounded for them all to go to sleep, she took it, called Mary one last time to make sure she did too. The broadcasts said the world would be different when what was left of society woke up. People would see differently depending on if they had taken the pill, because it had some anti-psychotic medicine to keep emotions and panic of the public at bay. The last existing radio channel had hushed them all to sleep mumbling about the world and the pill and now and then a disaster: the water levels rose on New York, a nuclear facility registered on lock down, or the Anti's had taken the National Museum of Art. They brought spray paint with them.

Here they were ready to go on a long drive together, into the world like they had never seen it before. They wouldn't last through the summer if they stayed. It would get that hot. Lore had it that the sun would boil your skin if you didn't go.

The Anti were infuriated by the new accelerated drug meant to cure many ills, protect from so many others, combat emotional illness, and regrow healthy cells. They wouldn't admit that the world would eventually end, that we needed to plan. They didn't like the science above their religion. The second coming would be that of God, not of science. It wasn't to be explained like it was unraveling.

So, they made it happen before their plan of fruition, the coming of the end, could unravel. It was in their hands, the religious, the pious … the "humanity" of the world. They would usher in the world and the Supreme, the Anti they nominated to lead the quickened downfall, would be the messiah. They all fell in line.

"It's sort of like the same. You know," Mary said. "The pill we took. We resigned in a way to it. It was our last hope. We thought we got on the bandwagon just like everyone else."

"You took it, right?" Jill said. She looked sidelong at Mary as she kicked the car into drive and then stopped at a stop sign at the empty intersection. "Wait … you didn't take it right away."

"I took it right away, hanging on to those last words. If it was a bad pill—" Mary said.

"What nonsense is that?" Jill said.

"Didn't you hear? The last broadcast, the President came on and said it was all a hoax. We shouldn't take the pill," Mary said. "Jill. No one's left alive. Everyone is gone. It wasn't a hoax. They must've looped that broadcast. When I heard it, I was done. Did you hear it?" She looked up into her eyes.

"I … I did, but I popped it in. I went to sleep. I turned off the radio. We had made our decision." Jill's face turned to stone. "What if the result was the opposite? What would you have done? Why didn't you call back?" Jill took a wavering breath. "Did you not care?" Jill said.

"Jill, you're alive. I'm alive. That's all that matters." Mary looked down at her nails. "I couldn't make that decision with you. I couldn't bring it back up. So, I did what we said we were going to do, and I pushed myself to get to sleep. That's it. And now we're here. With not so many other people."

"I just wanted to know that if we had different results, different outcomes—If I died, would you regret …" Jill caught herself, unable to get the rest out.

"More than anything, Jill." Mary caressed her cheek with the back of her knuckles.

They sat in silence until Mary's anxiety surfaced once again.

"Where the fuck is everyone? I am like a fucking apoc-alyptic cowboy and the world has collapsed." Mary's face flushed red.

"It has, Mary. It has collapsed." Jill stroked Mary's arm and tried to calm her elevating stress.

Her shoulders shrugged and then fell limp, as if Jill's hand weren't even on her body. After Jilled sighed and smiled, Mary raised a hand to meet Jill's fingers still lingering on her shoulder. "We will be okay. I promise."

"There's no sense in this world. Just like the last one," Jill said. Her dark apathy grew as the hours ticked on. No one knew what would happen at night.

Mary fiddled with the two suitcases in the back. The Colony would only allow one per person. They needed as much space as they could keep. People needed to breathe, be able to move.

"Tell me you'll wear the dress. Please, please, please. At the Lost Falls. Let's do it there?" She pleaded.

"Fine. At Lost Falls, but I brought scissors. We still need the photo. If the camera on my phone still works, if it isn't shut off like everything else on this planet, I want to look good for the photo. I need to charge it is all."

"We need that photo," Mary said. "I have my camera."

The pair would register for the Colony as a married couple. Though technically separated, they passed. As Jill and Mary saw it, they weren't really married when they were partners but qualified for common law marriage at Jill's job. It caused some discussion amongst them. It was never important for them to get a document. They didn't need to tie the knot with a big cake and party before a judge because they'd been together so long. Jill thought Mary would back out at some point. That's what rang true in 2014 when Mary didn't want the marriage certificate like so many others did; so many others needed to have it. That's what started the downfall, a four-year descent, the fissure, the rift, in their relationship.

They would pit-stop at the falls before moving on to the Colony. No one would deny they were married if they had a cheesy photo in wedding outfits and accouterments. Somehow it made sense. If they had a photo, they'd let them both in under the marriage clause. The rent would be cheaper. The health care better. The chance at a job. There were already pecking orders for jobs. Men with kids' stuff.

"We have to get the cake," Mary said.

"That's where I'm going," Jill chided.

They sped along the narrow streets easily, the Jeep smoothly gliding along the road. An outline of a warehouse, with no people going into or out of it. Trucks parked, some willy-nilly along the docks, were abandoned. Stunned by the absence of anything, any people or motion, Jill guessed there would be vagrancy. People along the side of the road asking for a ride. People congregating in low voices planning the next step. The Anti's traversing the streets with baseball bats. Instead, they had only seen children this morning. Two adults. Kids in action, being kids in a way, but also more violent. Unbridled and let loose. Witnessing a child's catharsis, Jill had stepped back. She avoided the intervention, conflict, and the explosion of emotion.

Jill jerked the car off the road and into a gas station. "How long will we be able to get gas?" She popped the car into park.

Mary chided that she'd fuck up the transmission and then they'd really be screwed.

"Does it look like we don't have options … right now, that is? Look around, Mary." Jill's anxiety rose. She had turned from apathetic meandering through this new world into a woman bent on survival. She got out of the Jeep, leaving the door open, and pulled on the passenger door of a car parked in front of the station. "This one has keys. Let's take this one?"

"Not a Buick sedan." Mary crossed her arms. "It's just not something I'd pick. Even if it's for free."

"Where the fuck is everyone, Mary?"

"Just calm down, honey," Mary mumbled, uncrossing her arms, and loosening her clenched fists.

Mary calmed down Jill, every time. No one else had the ability. Jill flipped on a dime. When the dog died. When Jill lost her job. Explosive emotion for an hour. She eventually got tired, and Mary had hushed her, made her twelve again, listen, and she was the same person she had always been, always was if you didn't count outbursts. Jill functioned best with low stress, never a high-stress job or high stakes job. Pressure, a strong urgency to act, was overwhelming her.

"Look," Mary said. "We have to go. We have to use our heads. The danger is real, the absence of people. You do too. What are we going to do when, as they said, the mind gets tired, but you can't sleep? Will the stress, the tempers reappear?"

"It's why I wasn't sure we could go." Jill said. "If it was why we couldn't stay together years ago, how could this situation possibly be different? My stress stuck after all that you said you couldn't handle."

Jill folded her hands and spoke calmly and directly. "It's the time we've had together since then … It's been so great—You think I don't cry after you leave? You think I don't throw my keys when I've had a dreadful day?"

"Why didn't you ever tell me?" Mary said.

"Because it's why you left. It's the rift between us. Isn't it?"

"I'm here for you now. Aren't I?" Mary said.

"Yes. Yes. But it'll build up in you, and then you'll have enough again. Isn't it true?" Jill said.

"I will not say it doesn't wear on me. And you are selfish—"

"See," Jill said.

"It's true. It's always about your career. Look. We haven't had this fight in how many years? How can we be here five minutes in? Is it commitment? The mere fact? Is it the word marriage? Do we need the damn cake?" Mary said.

"Saturday night date night is boundaries. Deciding from there to spend the rest of what might be a brief life left together is commitment. One we tried to handle. One we weren't able to handle."

"We can try again—"

Jill stomped away into the empty station and got three gas cans. She pulled some chips and muffins, unexpectedly a plastic container of celery and carrots with peanut butter in the middle from the shelves and into her arms. She grabbed a few very unstylish camouflage t-shirts on display, barely glancing at the size. Some candy and snack foods also made it into her arms. She held it all, loose bits falling. She hobbled back to the car, as an untied shoelace became the object of her attention. With a shift, a swift heft, she threw the junk food into the back of the Jeep and re-collected the gas cans.

She ran her growing fingernails along the plastic of the pump handle. The video commercials were off. Food ordering keypad—off. The broadcaster had said they'd leave the pumps on. Jill had been nervous, but they were on. She took her fill of gas. And here at 11:30 a.m. on the first day of the new world, it appeared that no one was around. They took as much as they wanted. Jill wasn't sure if they'd end up along a long stretch of road with no gas stations in sight. Or if another Colony had popped up in a rural mountain area. Perhaps it was just this state that was not yet … awake?

Jill put the gas cans on a rack at the back of the Jeep.

"Road flares?" Mary said.

"They came with the roadside kits," Jill said, her face brightening at her own brilliance. "I got a first aid kit and some rope, ahh, a bunch of things from the miscellaneous tools and products section." Jill held up a flashlight and several packs of batteries. In between her left index finger and thumb, she held a camo shirt. "So, we fit in."

"Honey? We are going to be okay." Mary's voice was calm.

Jill exhaled, blowing air out between pursed lips. Still, her own tension rose and won the battle with calm. She gasped out the words, "We are," in an instant of tension, unable to contain herself. "We have to get the cake next." Mary acted nervous and anxious as if suddenly in survival mode. "I mean? We really need the cake." Jill said. To get into this, through this, she needed cake. After some quiet thought, she decided that neither of them needed the cake. It likely wouldn't be in the photos, but for Jill to put on the right face, she had to have something a little sweet and sentimental. "Otherwise, the marriage is off." Joking, Jill blushed as she heaved in a breath. "We're going to follow the plan," Jill said. Shift. Gas. Acceleration. "That's the only way to stay sane. Follow the plan they gave us." The peppy car cruised down the road.

Mary pulled a shirt out of the back of the car. The shirt, an extra-small, long sleeve with pink camouflage sufficed as a rag. Much too small for either of them, a child's shirt. The shirt bore the words Princess across the front. Mary held the unworn fabric out of the car window and let her wrist break and hands open.

"What if we needed a bandage or something?" Jill said. She grunted in disapproval.

"Jill … it's going to be okay. We're not going to get into a bloody fight." Just as she spoke, a loud siren rang from the fire station. It echoed in the air from several miles away. Jill looked out her driver's side window, and the car swerved a bit.

"See, there's someone out there. Stay positive," Mary whispered.

Mary was looking beyond her. Scared to the bone, Jill put on self-assurances to get her through it. Oh, what her therapist would say now.

CHAPTER 6

"They said we needed to recharge." Jill said.

"Yes. They said we'd need to relax. Rest. If we are to believe anything, it's that we'll eventually get mentally tired," Mary said.

"I'm there. I must be," Jill said. "I'm no longer wide eyed and bushy tailed. It's this fatigue like I've never experienced before, it's like an upset stomach or hunger, but it's in my head. My brain, not headaches. Like the circuits shot off one too many times and now it's just flickering until it dies."

"Honey. Lie down. Please. This is too much for you. For both of us," Mary said.

"I'm tired. Right. It's so soon, and I'm exhausted. More or less … Brain's exhausted."

Jill leaned back in her seat, tapping the back of her head lightly on a headrest that was pulled up too high. Her head hit the bottom edge of the feature, and Jill held it there and rubbed up against it to scratch an itch. Then, she popped her hand over her head and, holding down a lever on the other side of the headrest's base behind her, bopped the headrest of the seat down.

Fidgeting with the lever at her side to recline the car seat, anxious, Jill tried to go someplace she hadn't been by closing her eyes. She tried to find the sleep that they said she wouldn't ever have again. They wouldn't need it, they had said. Still, she wanted to rest. With a jerk on a lever, the seat was flat, and she stared at the smooth but slightly fuzzy fabric on the ceiling of the Jeep.

The bumpy ride to the grocery store was no more. It was just her and her dreams wakeful, but not restless, NeverSleep dreams, coasting along, almost flying. The static of a paused radio broadcast became the background of her sight. She saw, but she wasn't alive. She sighed, now calm, and she was out into a memory, into a trance, walking in her sleep.

Suddenly, Jill was in that memory she had started purposefully. In her dream, Jill saw Dillan edge into the room. Dillan hadn't had her dinner yet, and she was cranky. Her eyes darted left and right, and Jill thought Dillan wanted dinner. Something Jill barely ever bothered to make. Perhaps peanut butter on toast would do. Jill was only vaguely hungry, always, and she never quite figured out how to solve the problem. Jill never possessed enough reason to make a sandwich. Dillan still had not learned.

This was Dillan's fill in, in between work and her apartment, but it was also an opportunity for Jill to find home with Dillan. It was a momentous time for decompression and building.

Dillan had knowledge of the LongSleep. She was aware of things about NeverSleep too. She said it was those late nights at the hospital washing dishes that helped her find her place in the new world. It was a place where she would find herself, where she needed to find herself before she leaped into a relationship with Jill.

"I got a little sleep at the hospital today. It's wearing me thin," Dillan said.

Dillan's hands appeared firmly on either side of Jill's leather belt, pausing until they ran around her waist. The hands circled ten dishes a minute in hot soapy water, soft and pliable, butter. Dillan bent leaning her breasts into Jill's back and running her hands under her shirt at the waist. Her hands moved to the belly button and then pulled back until Jill felt Dillan's plush lips at her neck. Jill tensed and released. The stress of her own day followed in time. Dillan was devilishly young, and it showed in her actions. Dillan tempted Jill like a child grasping for an adult's cherry cordial. Their ages reversed every time. Dillan took control of every chance possible.

Her back had hung over the sink for hours, so Jill thought it must've been a relief when she bent backward. As she pushed an arm around to her spine, she smiled a painful grin. The narrow-eyed wince told Jill that Dillan's day was tough.

Jill gathered herself for the words she really wanted to hear from her partner when they first came in the door: "How was your day?" She was projecting, and she knew it.

"How long did you wash dishes for and how long did you

sleep?" Jill said. "NeverSleep? Is that what it's called?"

"They did more testing," Dillan said. "They said I have some special power. I'm a prodigy. They said that. A prodigy." Dillan sighed and slouched her shoulders. She cocked her head to the side and looked at Jill.

Jill absorbed the seductive energy Dillan was giving off and, as always, she welcomed the passion. Jill melted under the pressure of Dillan's eyes. "Lover of a prodigy sounds like a good title to me," Jill said.

When they made love minutes later. When Dillan called her lover repeatedly, they giggled. Jill never did this with a partner before. Laugh in bed. The words tickled, erotic, and she mumbled her requests, became a quiet child pining for her desires. When Dillan relaxed, Jill knew they would find a oneness with time and as a matter of course.

Dillan leaned on Jill a bit too much about work and the testing. Jill understood it as her responsibility to pull Dillan out of the madness before she got too deep into the experiments, the testing, the studies. And it must've been Jill's fault when Dillan died. Jill decided it, so it must be true.

Dillan didn't come home one night. It must've been three months ago. Her work shift at the hospital was over and she didn't say that she was going to be involved in any overtime NeverSleep studies that night. They called it "the studies" from the beginning. Only about three months ago, everyone guessed the qualities of the NeverSleep, the side effects. Most people across the country, across the globe, started figuring out the riddles. The broadcasts started using the word.

When Dillan didn't come knocking on the door, it was all different. It was like someone pounded on Jill's back and the wind gushed out. Her face looked run over by a car from hand to face, rubbing. She added pressure upon pressure to make the headaches go away; Guillotined without a single soul watching. Except Mary in the wings. Mary was the failsafe, a rock unable to now never, ever, leave her.

Jill drove to the hospital, and they showed her around the facilities. They promised her that Dillan fulfilled her obligations in the studies to the utmost degree. She did everything she was told to and was safe, respectful, and honest in everything she did. Jill had muttered to herself. Of course, she did, because she also worked in the hospital kitchen and valued her job.

They didn't know where she had gone but agreed that Jill's lover, Dillan, had not shown up the next day. They agreed, they said. Jill confirmed the action peculiar.

Jill reported the missing person, but the police never followed up. A great panic had started and soon everyone except the police, hospitals, and government, fended for themselves. Temptation called to every person in uniform to end the day.

That nurse had given her a shot when she entered the hospital for a tour of the testing and study rooms. The shot functioned to keep her immune to the contagion they studied. Trace amounts presented issues, a chance. All the doctors and nurses had gotten the shot. They must've gotten it too. They must have.

Jill remembered pushing to see all the rooms. She did not push for the shot. They gave it to her quickly and swiftly in a weak moment and she wondered, just for a second, if she would go missing too.

Jill rubbed her arm, head still back on the headrest, remembering.

Jill shook herself too. She was on the way to the grocery store. It was five minutes of remembering. But then it was different. It was somewhere dark. At first, the dream welled as dark as possible, as dark as it could get in the middle of Mammoth Cave. It was a hollow emptiness that swam in her belly and mind. She absorbed everything that was nothing into her body and soul, and still more of it released. It. The void. Jill thought, "green."

Then a thing grew and behind it must've been light because she could see. There were eyes on her face. A tiny sprout of grass wobbled loosely in what became unpacked soil. The sliver of green waved in the ground. And that must've been wind.

The green thing, a dimly lit being in the world, appeared first before Jill looked down at herself and saw that she was also there, in the silky-smooth darkness that wrapped around her body, kissing her neck. She pulled a hand to it looking, in a way, for Dillan. Her absence sent a shiver down Jill's spine.

A sole star spotlighted the green. And the star, a distant spot, a light fed off the green, powered the unworldly mass.

When Jill looked back there were more, tens of thousands, that were always there and had not yet appeared. And they shone down possibilities for the dreamer, for those who might travel more freely in the void. They were there. She was sure of it. She sensed the human heat and the mortal souls that might come, if she shed a bit more light, a bit more green. More developed. A tree, a bush, awkwardly placed and unassuming. It was a building block of a grove. A minute gesture of the mind on an otherwise blank canvas. And then Jill was tired, exhausted in her NeverSleep. Jill didn't pretend to be a painter anymore.

"Oh, mother earth. So perplexing," Jill said. Sucked into an upside-down world, she knocked without a fist at a door that did not come to be. Only to have it appear moments later. There for her to understand. She was in a virtual world, a video game, a holodeck in her mind.

She knocked again.

This image of herself terrified her. The projection of her being in a world that had yet come to be was startling and foreign. She sucked in a deep breath as if there wasn't any air to take in, but she made it and then it was there to use. Leaving behind the empty canvas covered in gesso, a new world, she somehow gathered that she was to be there. She was about to help. To create.

CHAPTER 7

"Oh honey. Did you choke on something?" Mary said. "You look almost blue … scared blue."

Mary let her hands slide to the bottom of the wheel for a second to relax. Tense, she had been waiting for something to appear on the road: a person, a car, anything. The highway was vacant. For a second, she swore she saw a zombie, a wayward man with a gun. Was it at all possible? Everyone left alive must be experiencing fear and chaos, but nothing threatening appeared. It was eerily calm. She scanned left to right trying to anticipate danger as she drove. Not a soul entered the view. Not a soul confirmed they were not alone.

"I thought I saw a man with a gun. Isn't that ridiculous? I must be hallucinating. When I looked back, he was gone," Mary said.

"Not so outlandish," Jill said. "I thought I saw Dillan. I thought it was her, but it wasn't."

"Honey. Dillan is dead," Mary said. Her knuckles brushed, as was becoming typical, at her cheek. The smooth skin caressed her face. "It's been months. If she didn't contact you, it's not because she doesn't want to be with you. It's because something happened."

"Oh. Don't be cruel, Mary," Jill said. "Dillan was special. We hadn't known each other for too long, but she had a magical twinkle. Something that lit worlds on fire."

"The glow probably surfaced as a result of the nuclear testing they did on her." Mary chuckled. "Okay. I'll stop." Mary continued to scan far off, looking, and quietly the words mumbled out, "You love me. Don't you?"

"Mary. We had something. And we, the two of us. You and I are just starting," she paused, "again." Jill bowed her head as if she had a loose tear. "But you and me, it's like starting over. It really is. We had a lot of rocky moments. For a long while, I thought it was too many. Even though devastation hit this world, we are starting over from point zero. This is a new beginning."

"But we're getting married in a few days," Mary said. She snickered to herself again.

"Jokes aside, Mary. I love you. Always have. Always will. But we could kill each other sometimes on Saturday night friend date night. There is so much … managing … we have to do with our relationship. And it's on. Oh my, it's on. The world is exploding, and we must find out now, at this very moment, if we can live side by side for the rest of our lives. We really are the last two people on earth. We must try." Jill clasped her hands, now fully awake.

"I love you, Jill," Mary said. "I joke. I'm jealous. But we will get through this. Our lives really depend on it. Who knows what this world is now or who we are in it." Mary, with both hands on the wheel, stiffened and relaxed her arms.

Mary had leaned in on Jill relaxing. She donned a kiss on her forehead, even, but Mary didn't even turn to look at her. While in some sort of trance, she didn't look like she was sleeping, but she didn't look awake. Her lips quivered, and it was like she was at once in REM sleep. When Mary shook her shoulder, she didn't come too. She was rigid, unrelentingly clenching her muscles. So, it was a trance, but it was a deep trance. Not a limp coma, not a placid sleep. A deep, dark trance.

Mary had loved Jill for the longest time. It was true. She pined after Jill, but she did it with a smile, so she didn't get hurt. They jabbed back and forth with jokes about their past relationships, the several year fight. It was possible two people just weren't supposed to be together twenty-four hours a day. They agreed on this.

But when the world started shaking things up, when the idea of NeverSleep came and stayed, Mary saw it as almost romantic. While scary for Jill, Mary looked at it like an opportunity. Mary wanted more than anything to escape away with the girl of her dreams, be it whether the world was falling or not. She held onto this in recent weeks. They would have a life together. She was sure of it.

Dillan was great, and everybody liked Dillan. Mary was

particularly intrigued by her, albeit from afar. But to have her live with Jill would've been a lot. It would've been a trying time for all of them. Mary's jealousy bit down and ground teeth. A deep pit appeared in the corner of her heart.

The issue was that in the past year, Mary had just seen Jill as so special. At the end of the year, even, they decided if the world would end … before all this nonsense, before it became clear that the end of the world was coming, they would take off together.

The memory of them discussing it last year remained vivid. Laced hands almost kissing. Mary and Jill had said, "Nah …" in unison and shuffled to each other's corner of the couch. But they went back to it, repeatedly. An attempt to get close. It became a code word for the sex they wanted to have but would not broach, the uncrossable drawn line. The line they both drew to keep them together, which was only keeping them apart. Months later they had signed a contract, like the one they needed to have made to break up. After they signed, they didn't have sex.

"What if the world ends, Jill?" Mary had said months ago when she visited for a dinner date, playing with Jill's hair as they both sat next to each other watching the TV. Mary was admiring her hair and gave it a little twirl. She wrapped just one curl around the finger and then she pulled away, letting the curl drop. Mary put Jill's chin in her hands, and said, "I want to be together." She ran knuckles against cheek, opened her hand, and then searched for the smooth skin beneath her fingertips.

"But we're bosom buddies, right?" Jill said.

They both let out an apprehensive laugh. Mary brushed down Jill's hair where she might've messed it up. She would've done anything to kiss her. These emotions had subsided for years, but recently rose again. In hindsight, Jill started dating Dillan for this reason. She wished intently for a mutual relationship, for a shared friendship at the very least.

"Of course, we will go away together," Jill said. She looked down at Mary's eyes. "Should we try a vacation first? To prepare for the apocalypse we'll have to live through to be together for the rest of our lives." Jill laughed, holding her hand to her stomach until the noise trailed off.

Jill really did plan a vacation to Rocky Mountain National Park almost a year out, but she and Mary never went. When the broadcasts started coming, everyone lost their plans, their money, so many things.

It was a romantic notion Mary thought she shared with Jill until the world unraveled. When Mary heard the first broadcast, on all the millions of channels there were for a few more weeks, Jill backed away. It was as if she remembered that moment when they agreed to flee together if the world would end. Jill backed down and wanted to find Dillan, bring her with them, leave now, kill herself, anything but flee with Mary. And, yes, it hurt.

When they took the pill, the act was at Mary's insistence. She would hate to find that Jill feared the pill because of what it might mean for them both together, but then again, the hesitation was normal. For so many people, apparently now in this blank world, the hesitation turned into a rejection of ideology or the government trying to impress a rule. The world bucked, and it wasn't pretty. This aftermath. This blank landscape with children running wild, rampant, a literal Lord of the Flies, Children of the Corn in some places.

No one stole Jill away from her now. She would do her best to step up and defend her soon to be wife, be it a sham marriage or not, and fight anything that came in their paths. Right now, it seemed to be children with sharp yard tools probably playing clean up the yard. That's what she'd tell herself. They were playing clean up the yard.

CHAPTER 8

They pulled up to the grocery store five minutes later. No more words were said.

"We're buying a damn cake," Jill said. She smiled as if all they had said and not said melted away. And it some ways it did. And Mary smiled back.

As they entered, they took to opposite sides of the grocery store. The bakery was in the back, that much Jill garnered. They each took a cart. Mary would stock up on fruits and vegetables while they still had options. Jill would get dry goods. The back of the Jeep had a generous amount of space. The groceries might be allowed in the Colony when they got there. Apparently, waste not want not did not apply. There were few people around, and Jill reasoned there would be an array of groceries to pick from. If the nuclear facility some forty miles away melted down, they would all die for sure. They didn't need to pay for the food. Vacancy riddled the great state of Colorado, and Jill was nervous, still in shock. She sensed the emptiness, and the void wasn't hunger. Yet, she continued to push perishables and nonperishables into the cart.

Jill held a box of Cheerios in one hand and a box of Wheaties in another. She squeezed the box. The cheerios were stronger, stouter than the other. They were heavier. Jill thought back to her childhood and her mother, who had mouthed for her to loosen her jaw and popped them in one by one. They both would bob their heads and giggle. Jill wiggled her feet and legs feverously. It was one of her first memories of being young. And the hazy days, her father's cigarette smoke, came back as she closed her eyes to rest them.

She must've been six. Every day after the cereal pop-ins, she put on her shoes for the day, with her mom. One loop over the other. They had made it a rhyme. They had practiced every day. And soon when the Velcro shoes showed up, they never sang the song again. Jill's temper tantrums had been bad as a child. Emotional episodes didn't prepare her for life after her parent's death. Although the moments of fussing escaped her, she remembered the Velcro shoes and mumbling to herself every morning when she put them on, without her mom. All this, all the emotion, before her mom died. After her death, Jill quickly became an adult. The excess emotion from childhood dissipated when a bit of real life hit her.

"Wheaties just ruin your sex drive, right?" Jill mumbled to herself. She tossed the Wheaties over her shoulder, and they fell to the floor. Grabbing two, then three boxes of Cheerios, she stacked them neatly in the cart. The store was vacant. No one was there to run the register and scan food item by item. No inane beeps. She was able to go straight to the car.

She looked up at a surveillance camera as she chewed at a nail and then over at the big broad windows, just past which was her Jeep. A matte black paint job stood out in her vision, and she pushed her shoulder into the shelves and craned her neck to see. The same enormous cylinder of an outlet for smoke protruded from the front of the truck. The same huge Anti flag trailed from the back.

"Oh, shit," Jill said in a murmur. She didn't know where to find Mary or if she was in danger or if she had moved to safety. She threw the rest of the Cheerios into the cart; in case they would have to run. She didn't have time to find the peanut butter. She didn't have the sense to look for the milk. All that was on her mind was Mary. She must go to her.

As she dug her hands into the handle of the cart, committing to her next move to go deeper into the danger instead of outside to potential freedom, to run, her shoes squeaked on the still slick waxed floor. As she launched forward, she simultaneously retracted her body, the cart, her will, her sense. The man with the camo mask took one giant step into the aisle. Like Jason in the woods or a stiff zombie from hell. Like a man with a vendetta. That's how it appeared.

"Stop," the man said.

Jill recoiled. "I just want to talk."

Jill pushed her cart in front of her like she would attack him with it if he came any closer. It was so futile, yet the action was comforting to her somehow. She widened her stance.

"You're wondering where they all went ..." The man's voice lingered in the air, and he held his mouth open, jutted his chin to the air.

Intrigued as she was, she didn't ever meet this man. She didn't have any reason to sign onto anything he said; it might not be true. She bit down and gnashed her teeth. "Get out of the way. Where is she? What did you do to her?" Jill said.

"Didn't touch a hair," he spoke. "I promise." He now held his hand up in the air, patting down the region of air between his hand and the cart.

An urge to plow him down came over her.

"It's just ... One minute, please Jill," the man said.

"How do you know my name? You're so creepy. Who the hell are you?" Jill chomped her teeth down one more time and gave an angry look. "You'll be sorry."

"Look, I'm here too. But most people are gone. Most people didn't take the pill. They chanced it and poof. They listened to the president. Said they'd take it the next day. So many things. They're gone." He held his hand upright as if swearing on a bible. "I have no reason to lie. I took it, that's it. In an unexpected turn of events, a few didn't believe the radio, the president, gun to his head, and a few daring soldiers live still too. They found their way out in a pill."

"Who the hell are you and why are you stalking me?" Jill said.

"I'm just concerned," the man said.

"You're here to kill us in the afterlife? After all of that? After melting the icecaps in bitterness, you have taken the fucking pill ... which worked, by the way ... And you are going to knock us off in our own world ... our own heaven's eve ... one by one?" Jill was flustered and tense. Her brain was about to explode, and she needed her calm self to take over before the eruption got her into trouble.

"It's not. Look, it's survival now. You shouldn't be paranoid, but some were scared. The parents were. The kids took it at school. If the district gave the pill at all, they made the kids take it, even if they were screaming and kicking. They lay down and went into the LongSleep, a side effect of the NeverSleep pill. They would sleep for several days in a Long-

Sleep before they entered the NeverSleep. Parents thought their kids were dead because they took the NeverSleep pill. They didn't wake up. They didn't take the pill. They left their kids for dead. When the president said not to take the pill, it made sense to the vast majority of adults." The man relaxed back on his heels and chuckled. "The funny thing was it was an Anti with a gun at the President's head." The man's smile turned flat in an instant with Jill's blank reaction, her inability to smile along with the man or even sneer.

"Look, I'm not sure who you are, but I don't trust you. I'll get out. I'm going to find a way out." Jill tensed her body, and anger grew with the force of her stiffening. She focused on her ill-will and contempt, and her blood grew hot. Thought was the only weapon she had.

She jerked the cart back and in front of her. Yelling Mary's name, she bolted down the aisle, only to find Mary milling around the candy bars at the checkout. "Jesus. We don't have to check out. Right now. We need to get out. I'm serious." Jill's voice was elevated and commanding.

Together, they leaped for the door. Mary somehow understood. The underestimated tension in her own voice, loudly overpowering rang out. "Get to it. We've got to go." Jill motioned with her hand as she pushed her cart toward the door.

The man had the ability to catch up to her. He wasn't trying to kill her, just watching. His intent, his presence, his purpose perplexed her. No one overturned the cart and made things harder. But his words confused Jill. What he said made her question it all, who was out there, and what would become of those left over.

Jill chucked food into the back of the Jeep with vigor. She moved some of the first aid kits and road flares into a backseat pocket. She tensed with each throw, each placement of the things she had gathered, what she thought she would need to survive.

The man meant that things were different. This information was valuable, and she wanted, in a way, to ask more questions: To see into their future, what would happen on their trip. But this prized information was elusive and hidden behind a man with a mask, one meant to intimidate and confuse. Jill tried to guess his purpose. What they would do was so valuable to him. Why hadn't, in this world of chaos, looting, and vacancy, the man in the camo mask shot both Jill and Mary. One thing that still worked like magic, which didn't need electricity or the internet, was a gun. A steadfast gun able to kill.

"We should've gotten bags, at least. Why so much rush? What is wrong? What is wrong?" Mary looked agitated.

"The camo guy. He's in there. Look." Jill pointed toward where she had seen the coal roller. He could not have left before they got outside. They had run. With the truck gone, some of the man's menace left as well.

On the beautiful spring day, Jill lost her head a bit more than Mary. Birds still chirped. It might've been a little hotter than normal, but not a cloud came into sight, not a dead leaf.

"You're just tired," Mary said, serious.

Mary intentionally slowed Jill down by taking the groceries from her and placed them in an organized manner into the back of the Jeep. She moved some bread to the side and pushed the rest into the trunk. The cake rested away from other groceries in a corner. The cake and icing looked rock solid.

"I talked to him."

"What did he say?" Mary said, hands on hips, annoyed she didn't get a chance to meet him.

"He said all the adults in the world didn't take the pill. People followed the President. An Anti pointed a gun at him while he talked. Somehow, they must've ransacked the Capitol, kidnapped the President. Can you believe it? What if the Antis were behind it all from the beginning? I mean the broadcast, playing with people's last wills."

"Then why didn't we hear about it?" Mary said.

"Not sure," Jill said.

"Then why is he still here?"

"Your guess is as good as mine," Jill said.

Jill slowed her movement toward Mary. She was almost in slow motion. She almost said aloud that what had happened had not. She almost swallowed her sanity, her mental health.

"Let's just take it easy today." Mary extended her arm onto Jill's shoulder. "Drive for four or five hours and then rest.

Close our eyes and rest. Try out that NeverSleep again," Mary said.

"The mind will do crazy things now that we've taken this pill. That is the most of my knowledge. If it's real, the dreams, or if it's keeping us alive, I'm not sure. I know a few things from living this many years. Too much sleep or too little sleep can kill your being, the way you are, suck life and soul from you. I got it down pat when I slept until noon every day after I spent hours awake, hoping Dillan would walk through my door, wondering where Dillan had gone. Worried sick." Jill clasped her hands even though she didn't believe in God, didn't pray.

"But in this now," Jill said, "an hour with your eyes closed will turn you. The things I saw were tantalizing but dangerous. I smelled the danger. It sapped my strength to live in that world. Much as my mental collapse in this Life is imminent if I don't sleep. It's not safe being awake or asleep. Someone could kill you in your sleep, or you could kill yourself, your mind, staying awake. This world for some reason they call it out as Life. This world we're in when we're not dreaming, will crumble." She let her clasped hands relax hoping they weren't all doomed. Hoping her NeverSleep dream was a way out.

CHAPTER 9

Jill and Mary took to the road for a three- or four-hour drive. The beautiful trees and deep gulleys that captured Jill before had lost some luster. The low green vegetation, weak weeds and flowers, were not coming back this year. Since the environmental collapse began everyone had said the green growth was lush and strong. They talked about how it had always been there but might not always be. The pines would last for a bit. They were resilient. In time, the weather would erode the cliff sides and topple the rocks to the road. Water from heavy storms would flush out the pavement, preventing access to this place again. Nature's gouges still created awe, and the greens gleamed for Jill at that moment but not for long.

Despite all the beauty sinking in, something other than the gloriousness captured Jill at that moment. Jill had something else on her mind that was much more fleeting, elusive, and temporal. NeverSleep had overturned her intentions of finding calm in rest. It boggled and perplexed her and would keep her up at night if night ever appeared again.

She tried to describe it to Mary without saying she had the strange power, the ability to control things and events. She talked about vegetation blossoming and the beautiful stars. Mary said it sounded like a pleasant dream. Jill thought privately that it was much more than that.

Eventually, they stopped for a rest. Because Mary fidgeted her back as she drove, and some pain surfaced. She asked to take a break, and they agreed they were in no rush. They had no deadline. No place to be. For now, it didn't seem like they were running from any danger. They had it all under control.

They adjusted themselves in a small grassy spot just outside the Jeep, bedded down, with a single pillow for each of them and some wool blankets they had hidden where the spare tire was years ago. In the rush to leave, they remembered the pillows but not much more. In the grassy spot, slightly harder and slightly more comfortable than the car seats they had been sitting in consistently for several days, Jill turned to look at Mary. Mary looked back into her eyes. She seemed a bit scared, a bit wary.

When Jill looked up at the sky, she saw the madness she had gone into. The mass of openness both tantalized and terrified. She wanted to meet the sky, this Life of madness, halfway. It would have been less frightening if she flew out and met the birds, birds that might die with her in the climate changes, than to go back to NeverSleep, that beast of a state of being.

Silence persisted. Noise from airplanes usually filled a thick swath of mid-air. Voices, screaming, playing, chatter, often filtered up to the sky, and the recent frequent gunning of engines and plumes of diesel smoke was absent. It made the dream of traveling so much more enticing. The pathway rolled out like a red carpet; they were all alone.

Still, no one got there. No one found the easiest solution to be in the sky. Work, fixes, survival, must be picked at for everyone's sake. Those few astronauts sent on a voyage in recent months would linger until their death, Jill imagined. With no stopping point, the astronauts hurtled into deep space, returning only a long, hollow scream for help. These would be the last people left, caught mid-drift in a space not meant for human occupation. Now, so much like this place here.

When Jill closed her eyes, in a moment her very real body was vulnerable to the elements, she tried to imagine a peaceful place. For the first time, the dreams did not take over. She took them over. She imagined the swirls and sparkles of the sky and the temptations of light to be close. They were as close as they had ever been. She removed her hand from the sleeping bag and grabbed at the air in front of her, eyes closed, to see if she could feel.

The NeverSleep promised problems. Jill read about the potential issues in the papers until the news ultimately disappeared. And then listened intently to the radio programs, then the program. Your body would still be tired until you gained enough strength. A person would have to rest the body, not necessarily the mind, but maybe the mind if psychotic features arose or if anxiety overpowered a person. It was best to rest the same way a person always had. "See you on the other side."

The unknown of NeverSleep fooled everyone. So many people could not guess at it all. They only watched a few case studies. They only took a bit of video proof. Oh, but wasn't everyone on board? The NeverSleep pill would counteract the wobbling of the earth, nausea, and the ability for the body to cool. The drug, a new combination of cures for every common cold, illness, STD, encouraged people for a while. The pill might cause cancer, they said. But the cell regrowth feature proved promising. The pill of all pills, developed in a bunker away from the Antis, was built on science, they said, experimental science. The world might end.

Mary clasped Jill's hand. "I'm so happy to be here with you. There might be no one else," Jill said. Her introspective nature came out full force. "What if we're alone in this world? What if the man in the camo mask is the only other person?" Jill shivered.

"You mean besides the kids?" Mary said.

Jill banked on the idea that there would be more people than just kids. They were, after all, in the rural mountains of Colorado. They would be in rural areas, on rural roads for some time.

"Yes. A world full of children is overwhelming to say the least. Can you imagine the crying, the screams? You've read the books. One bad kid starts everything. Can you even imagine?" She gripped the inside of the fabric cuffs of her shirt, digging in the ends of her nails, scarring the fibers.

"We're lucky the high schoolers weren't required to take the pill," Mary said.

"Or are we? Don't older children have some sense?"

"Hormones for sure. So glad we don't have one of those, a teenager. Those problems. God knows what I did to my mom," Mary said.

She shut her eyes then blinked off the bright light that had formed on the backs of her eyelids. "We'll find them, the commune, the survivors. We'll find them. Find this world."

Off in the distance, Jill thought she heard hands clapping, sounding off. Mary shuddered.

"I want to help them, Mary," Jill said. "I really do. But they are a horde. This planet will overpopulate with certain species of wild animals, wild beasts immune to the perils of a new world, in ten years."

"The kids, younger kids, were all given the pill in school. It was a last-ditch effort of the government. Feed them the pill. Whichever kids went to school yesterday got the pill. They got NeverSleep," Mary said.

"Surely some parents didn't let their kids go to school that day. Positive. Some parents would not take the pill even before the President said they shouldn't. It's unrealistic to conclude there are even too many left on this earth. We might be close to it, given the circumstances," Jill said. "Except, right, the kids I saw." Jill questioned herself and wrestled with the emotions behind it all.

"Hush, children," Mary whispered to herself. "You scare us."

Mary rolled to her side and gave soft kisses on Jill's neck and cheek. Jill guessed she wanted to start something. With a tight schedule, they might only stay a little while longer. Jill wanted this but had never let herself have it. She was torn. Close. This is what her mouth wanted. Lips on soft skin. Lips for her, for them both. She must have it to be satisfied. Mary dragged her knuckles across Jill's cheek bones. Still, Jill did not reciprocate. She enjoyed every moment of Mary on her and moaned softly at the pleasure. Let Mary know it was okay with a simple, "Yes."

As Mary pulled away, Jill asked for more. "Don't stop. You know I don't want you to," Jill said.

"You're conflicted. It freezes you," Mary said. "We get married tomorrow, and we haven't even had sex. Not in ten years, at least. Is it possible? You're wearing that wedding dress, and I will come for you. Oh, I will. I will find you in your place. We will find us together. I will do whatever you want or nothing at all. But you must tell me, we must find it together. Marriage can be so many things, but most of all to me, it is being by your side. Being with you when no one else is—," Mary said.

"But no one else is," Jill said.

"So much more reason for us to be together," Mary said.

Jill hushed Mary back with sweet kisses on her lips, one to the forehead. A return of what she had gotten. Then she collapsed flat on her back, eyes still where the moon might be. She had shut them for the entirety of ten minutes, looking for clarity about the relationship. She would find something.

Jill nuzzled her nose into Mary's shoulder. "This is how I always wanted it to be," Jill said.

It was how it had been a few nights ago. They lay together and talked about those pleasant moments. Each had stopped just before they spoke about an awful moment. They laid without sex, and knew, together, that was all they needed, to lie. Sex was such a crux. They found passion without being together, located that moment of ecstasy. They would lie together and meld minds, find compromise, and calmness together, everything they couldn't when they were together before. When they were ready, they would have sex.

A precocious howl came through the night, and Jill thought about jumping up, running, but she didn't.

"If there was a stray, alone, then we would rescue them. Save them from the horde of beasts."

"Jill, you really want a child," Mary said.

"If we saved the child, it would be humanity, you know? They would grow apart from the savage beast the pill has made them."

"Jill, their parents are dead. They won't be anything else."

"I wish. I wish I knew what the other side was. What if we hadn't taken the pill? What if these children weren't so messed up?"

Jill pulled her hand out of the bag to flick at some ants congregating close to the end of the zipper. She rolled slightly to her left and held the position, even though she neither held it all night, nor saved her from the ants' impending doom, a swarm into the warmth she had created. The warmth her body had made was one of the few possessions she still had.

While staring at Jill's body, Mary unstably shifted in her direction. Her lust glinted in the corner of her eye.

For the first time in an extraordinarily long time, Jill thought she might've been too close. She might've been right about the two of them.

"Jill, you'd be dead. The world would be dead. We must hope for a single other person. There's only that man. I mean, really, who is he, Jill? I've barely caught a glimpse of him."

"You saw him?" Jill said.

"I heard the wheels when I was in the grocery store. Those were yours. And I heard the footsteps on the other side of the aisle. I might've seen his shoes. His … dark … green or brown … jacket?" Mary said.

"Thank God I'm not delusional. What is this fucking world?" Jill said.

And she was, again, experiencing a delusion. She had seen the stars up close. She had gone there in her mind. Not yet searching for someone, but some place. Soon, she was on the verge of finding someone out there. Screaming with her mouth shut into the ether.

Jill's eyes were as open as Mary's, and they both discussed leaving. It wouldn't be the bears or the spiders or mosquitos that killed them. It would be the children with hedge clippers. At least that's how Jill and Mary imagined them. The scene from the house, from a distinct quality of rambunctious, was burned into their minds.

"We've got to go," Jill said. Jill shuffled her sleeping bag down her body as she stood in an upright position. She wasn't sure how she'd risen. Once out of the bag, she stomped on the ants. At the very least, the ants were still alive. The doom of the world would begin at any minute.

And without engaging in NeverSleep or sex, Jill and Mary gathered their things to take off in the Jeep, into the night, into some sense of safety. Pushing the start button on the console like it wasn't ten years old, the car roared to life. A bunch of lights flashed in the distance. Jill saw it in a haze of a memory or a hallucination. Had they known they were there, alive, awake? Had these kids been some two hundred miles away? Had they wanted to kill? Was that true nature?

Jill steered, hands tight, pretending other cars on the road careened like she did. Like it was a long stretch of road to the end of the planet. She hunkered down over the wheel, staring out into the night to focus and forget what had just happened, pretending that the world had not collapsed that all of it amounted to a game.

CHAPTER 10

The arduous drive sucked the life from their bones. The next morning their blood curdled as they attempted to relax, for all that it was, in the car. Each of the three times they stopped in the night, they laid their heads back on the reclined seats of the Jeep. The seats went as far back as possible with all the junk in the back, too much to move, too much trouble for a lost sense of initiative. The NeverSleep wreaked its toll.

They stared up at the roof of the Jeep. Jill blinked. That precious state of being, the NeverSleep was sad and exciting all at the same time, scary and bold.

"I want to find that place," Mary said. "Where you saw the new world or whatever it was. The 'blank canvas' is that what you said?"

"I just had a dream in a memory. Really, nothing," Jill said.

At early dawn, they started their day, but the day had never ended. It meshed with the night and the weariness glowed through. As the sun rose on the horizon, their vehicle tucked into an enclave at a state park. Jill couldn't see its beauty.

"Do your guts hurt?" Mary said.

Jill looked out at the horizon, eyes fuzzy, trying to find something in the distance.

"Well, there's that," Jill sighed and looked at a pack of Reese's peanut butter cups that she essentially stole from the grocery store. Stole was the opportune word. To think the world had collapsed was one thing, but to actually know was another. "No. No bends like they said would happen … But my eyes." Jill rubbed at the itchy dry sockets and left her fingers pinched in the tear ducts, head down.

The couple shivered at the idea of wild animals, but not as much as at the notion of the children who had swarmed in the night. They feared the pill they took. Jill's thoughts fluttered back to the moment she took the pill, confident in double-speak. She had convinced herself, and here she said out loud, she knew the whole time it was a lie.

"Mary, you knew it wouldn't work, didn't you? All of it, call it propaganda?" Jill said.

"Yes. In a way. Isn't it all propaganda? Someone trying to get you to believe what they say is true. Isn't it always someone who really, really hopes they're right, even if they know they're wrong?"

"Should we not have taken it?" Jill said. She tapped her on the toes of her feet, almost like a child. Wasn't she, though, in disguise? Dressed up for Halloween as a zombie, someone who never sleeps.

"We still don't know if they're alive," Mary said.

"Who's they?" Jill said.

"Everyone ... everyone but the children." Mary choked out. "Are you okay?"

"It's all so much. I'm dizzy. Yes, of course, the children are still alive. Thank God we have children," Jill commented in a dreary haze.

"Jill, wake up." Mary turned in the driver's seat and patted Jill's cheeks with her hands. "This is real. This is us now."

Mary mumbled something that Jill could not hear. "It might have been loud," Jill imagined. "It might've been something I could hear." Jill might've spoken. She drifted as she hung on to Jill's words. Garbled as they were, they came in and out of Jill's consciousness, mingling with what might've been her own.

Black.

When she came to, Jill had so much to relay. Her memories were vivid, as if they had just happened.

"Where did you go? It's been two hours," Mary said asking question after question. "I slapped you silly. You might still ... Yup. There are red marks on your cheeks. Your eyes were open. You were here. You mumbled, had full conversations with me, but I wasn't me. You blinked your eyes, turned your head. There, but not. You would've been speaking in tongues, but you weren't. You were lucid with no concept of me. Tell me what happened."

Dizziness overcame Jill, and, confused, she grasped for words. "There are people with ice and once it's in place, the world will be good all right … for all who's left. How come you don't feel the NeverSleep? Why are you so awake? So here for life, for living?" Jill said.

"I don't know. It hit me differently. That's all I can say. I don't need that place … wherever you traveled to alleviate the NeverSleep symptoms. You were terrible before you went full zombie, speaking not in tongues but about the end of the world and shit. Scary stuff," Mary said.

"I'm so 'repaired' now. Is that what we call it? 'Repaired.' I am awake and alert. True, I got sucked into that place, but somehow, I'm back. I'm me again. It was disturbing, but reparative … somehow. Wasn't it just sleep," Jill said.

Her words lingered on, "Wasn't it just sleep?" It wasn't. The NeverSleep manifested itself as a magical place, and she floated there. She witnessed the hope … looked down on the world in a way that must be true. In no way could she have conjured it. No way, the NeverSleep wasn't a lie. She convinced herself this place she went was the earth … will be the earth … Life will be all okay.

The rocky cliff in front of them had been a toy for climbers, a beginner climb. When Jill got out of the car for a moment, a definitive moment of pause that Mary should not join her for, she got a closer glimpse.

Gear lay strewn across the area. Almost as if they had been having a day of it, a picnic in the woods when the earth exploded. But the world didn't explode. In her dream, it didn't.

A pair of climbers snuggled up in their sleeping bags told so many tales. Jill might've thought it cute and dear, but the smell caused her to not move closer. The odor that filled the air was death, was a last attempt at sleep.

As she gazed over, taking one last look before she turned, she examined their faces close together, as if they drifted off to sleep mid-kiss. They had done what they loved during the day and ended it with their love. Their staged death curated as a send-off to the world and also what they would do on any day, any weekend day, for fun. Their love wrapped up in normalcy, a plea to the gods to keep the most stable thing they had, a rocky climb they defined as fun, defined as what was between them.

Jill turned and got back into the passenger side. "Please, you drive?" she said.

"Of course, with where you went. Yes. I will drive," Mary said.

"God. Can you believe it?" Jill said. "They died kissing."

"We count as witnesses now of the end of people's lives. Can it be any more touching? And tragic. I'm sure we'll see more," Mary said. She rubbed at her eyes, squinting in the blistering sun. "We better get going. We have a waterfall to see," Mary said. "And I just might marry a prophet."

"I really don't—" Jill started.

"You witnessed the truth, Jill. You verified the happily ever after and that's all I need to hold on. Hold on to something. I'll hold on to you," Mary said.

They careered through the gulfs of mountains between Denver and Utah. The couple took the major route. Water fell from the rocky cliffs still. Jill's lucid dream feverishly pitched her thoughts this way and that about a world without ice then a world without water.

"It's glistening. The water on the red cliffs. The yellows … I've never noticed how bold it is," Mary said.

"I see it too. Like I have prisms in my eyes now." Jill said, only half understanding Mary. Understanding her passion should be both of their passions. The beauty she took in, Jill hungered see, to share.

"I will marry you under this waterfall if you let me." Mary pointed out the window at a cascade that ended up a trickle at the base.

Jill wasn't sure where the water went. The stream flowed so powerfully at the top and drifted down, dispersing, taking shots of rock elsewhere, finding its way back into the crevasses. It dripped a narrow but steady flow into the gully just off the roadside.

"This will be the place. This will be our place," Mary said.

"Oh, Mary. The earth really is so beautiful. This vision is so much for us both. We'll live here. It'll be our one spot."

When they bumbled out of the Jeep, their legs barely able to walk, they moved toward the cliff. Jill flipped a butterfly knife, pulling it from pocket, making toward the rock, and carved their names. A childish heart surrounded it.

"Oh, honey." Mary's face filled with a red glow.

"You gave me this knife," Jill said and snickered into her fist. She didn't want to show her how she really felt. "Everything I do with this knife is your fault." Her childish grin took over her face until she grabbed for Mary, now fingering the grooves in the rock, and deepened the carving of their initials in a heart. "We'll go to MOMA in New York City, the MET even. We'll get whatever painting you want and hang it here. Who will ever care? There is no one here to stop us. Will that be a better marker?"

"I love you," Mary gazed hard into Jill's eyes, creeping her body toward her slowly. When they embraced, Mary wouldn't let Jill go. Mary wouldn't let Jill veer away from the intensity they were forming. Jill tensed, fell loose, and snapped back into Mary.

Jill leaned in and reclaimed the love they once abandoned. She pulled the passion from her and mingled it with her own. This was the moment they cultivated all those years. The weekend date nights, the day trips to hike. The planned kayak outings. They would never have to plan again; they were stuck with each other for what seemed like the foreseeable future.

This act, their attempt to recreate a marriage that they lost, would be their last bet. Their last gawk at the horse track. They would either come out of it alive or doomed to separate, but for right now, for this moment, they had each other and beautiful scenery. What is not to love?

Jill changed into the wedding dress, awkward as it might be in so many respects. No one to help her zip up the back. No one to carry her train. The lacey trim gathered in the mud. No screen to keep her body hidden from the road, not that traffic would ever traverse it again in the same way. And, of course, her propensity to overact femininity in the face of her burgeoning masculinity. The latter she eased into easily and with comfort. The former she tried to hold on to, but it was slipping away at a growing rate. Looking at her graying hair triggered thoughts about what might've been, what came easily, and what society put upon us all.

She pushed up a grin and shuffled still in sneakers toward

Mary, holding the dress up in the crooks of her arm. She turned swiftly without words, and Mary zipped the dress easily. Jill's subsistence lately consisted of no more than nuts for nutrition and tea for good measure.

Jill's gaze dropped to her feet.

"It'll be full-length photos, but don't worry one bit." Mary held pins in her lips, pulled moments ago from her the pockets of her tailored suit jacket. The jacket was the one she wore with Jill over a decade ago. "It's the closeups we'll frame." Mary smiled and talked at a breakneck speed. "You've been preparing for this. I know you have. Fits like a glove and you haven't been starving yourself since January. I did that, right? I got you to eat again?"

"Isn't this performativity to the tenth degree?" Jill said. "This is just a white lie, really, in an eye-popping world where nothing is ever as it seemed before."

"It is honey. It's so someone will let us in. The Colony doesn't take singles. At least you have a better chance if you're not." Mary's shoulders collapsed.

Jill flattened her dress on the lap and knees. The flowing fabric gathered in bundles, fistfuls, but she still loved it. It felt like her mother. Even if it was on her mother for only one day. It's a day she held in her memories, as Jill, at that moment, looked for her own memories of that same woman in the elusive prospect of a certain death before the photos were even put to use.

It wouldn't work.

"We are selling our love." Jill bit her teeth down and then a light smirk appeared. "Only we know the truth. Whether it is or isn't love?" She picked up her hair and pulled it over the front of her shoulder.

"That is the problem," Mary said. "We don't know if we really do." She gushed a breath out. "We really put the cart before the horse. We really aren't getting hitched at night in Vegas. It's worse. Isn't it?"

Jill used reverse psychology.

"We are getting hitched, not knowing if we get along and with the odds stacked against us," Mary said.

Mary teetered around in her sneakers, pulling at her pants,

raising them an inch away from the soil, the mud and muck, the pooling leaves damp with water that might become precious. Mary's favorite wing-tip shoes hadn't made it to the bag, so Jill handed her back her sneakers. Dress shoes proved to be impractical regardless.

"Worse than mail-order bride style?" Jill shifted the waistline in small increments, as if it all mattered.

"Yeah. I guess. It's before we even meet and late in life marriage all at once," Mary said. "We are the inventors. We are the start of the future. To find someone you once knew and pair up for the sake of humanity is powerful. Isn't it noble?"

Mary donned a top hat and cane to compliment the posed photos they would take to act as evidence of their marriage instead of a marriage certificate.

Her hat was the velvety kind, one Burlington Bertie might have worn.

Jill plucked a thin piece of evergreen twig sprouting spikey green needles from a base of sappy wood. She stitched it into the thick band of the hat. "You looked too English." She snickered. Jill, hands on hips, sat back in her posture, resting her weight on her lower back.

"Do I look good?" Mary took a soft breath.

"Baby. You look grand. I'm going to die right after these photos." Jill bit down proud and adoring. She warmed at the thought of others seeing her with her beautiful bride.

They held hands and looked into each other's eyes. They would be acting out a scene with forever and ever implications. They might never actually get the piece of paper. And to Jill, the whole staged event didn't really matter, but Mary said it did. So, then, to Jill, it mattered more than ever.

"This world will be better, Mary. This world will be full of order and regulation again. We will get the paper. We will make it official," Jill said.

"I know you say it, and it's all that matters at this moment. We don't need the paper. We don't need the issue of the government in our business, not with how the world has turned. The world is us. That's all I see, Jill." Mary sniffed in. "That's all I need to see." Mary brushed at her Italian wool trousers that might've had a hole or two from being in storage over a decade. She adjusted a belt Jill had gotten her for Christmas a few years ago. She fidgeted with it in the belt loops. "Something borrowed, something black." She changed the tone.

"I guess that works," Jill said, still staring out into space. "Something new—this world."

They gathered closer to the waterfall, taking tiny steps, holding hands. Jill looked up at Mary and she came back to Jill. When a piece of loose rock rolled under Jill's foot, Mary dove to hold Jill. From beneath her, still holding tight to her waist, she looked up at Jill. "I have always loved you."

Jill couldn't quite get over how sincere her words were while they drifted into the farce the photos were.

It might've been the mood of the moment, the lace and fine wool. Her bare feet and the light spray of cool water. The grocery store cake, extravagant as possible, awaited their appetites. The tension of the larger world and their flirting made Jill weaken and a warm heart beat. She loved and shared her energy with Mary. They would have the happily ever after, a sham wedding or not.

We are now falling in love. Farce or not, we are falling into this play of marriage. It's taking us away. Jill let herself be vulnerable.

"I'm afraid to let you in, always have been. But you're in. You have been to every Saturday date night, every Friends Thanksgiving, every moment I let you saunter in through what was our front door. I love you. But I'm telling you this now, because it's our last, it's everyone's last, really, only hope," Jill said.

A few gazes and a kiss later, they paused holding hands, leaning back, gazing again. Jill stumbled on a rock. Click.

The camera clicked from over by the trees. The timer had blinked five times, and they hadn't even seen it. They both agreed that one photo was the sincerest strategy. The one where Jill looked down and picked her dress out of a rock puddle, almost laughing about hope. And Mary bowed to take up her train for lack of someone to assist her. Her strong cheekbones and stiff gait, her masculine poise pushed through.

CHAPTER 11

The couple, fake married, dried off from the splatter of water and changed into their normal attire. This often-coveted event, the wedding, was held for show.

Jill cherished being close to her mother one last time in a dress she never thought she'd wear. She belonged to something now, a unit of people, a family, a bit more than just being one. Part of someone else, now bonded, unabashedly linked, Mary and Jill committed for better or worse till NeverSleep they part.

At 7:00 p.m., they ate their plums and peanut butter sandwiches on wheat bread under a tall pine tree, saved the cake for later. It would likely be forgotten. Jill stole a pack of smoked salmon jerky from the grocery store and tore into it. The shade spread a coolness that was more glorious than any she'd ever felt. When the needles were all shook off and the tree then fell, the blazing sun would singe anybody left on this earth. Leave them adrift in heat and dust. The tree was huge, old. It could topple just like them in a matter of moments, months, or a year. Who was really to say?

Out of the corner of Jill's eye, a man in a thick green pullover jacket and bright yellow pants sauntered over to the pair. His multi-colored scarf wrapped around his neck and extended almost to his knees. Jill made out snowflakes interwoven into the pattern.

"Hello. It's the yellow pants, isn't it?" He dusted his hands on his knees and tapped them three times before he rose back up. "I use them not as a warning of doom but of friendliness. Some people have hidden in the woods, these woods, at least they've started to. You'll notice it's cool. It's cooler higher up. Also, far from food. Unless you know how to get your own. Hunting and whatnot. They'll eventually filter up there. He pointed."

"You'll have to excuse me. We haven't seen people yet,"

Jill said. "Well at least not in a bit." She leaned away from Mary and their intimacy.

"Except for the man with the camo mask," Mary cut in.

"Oh, camo mask man. Very suspicious. Does he need help?" The man leered in.

"No. We didn't ask," Mary said.

"We ask everyone to come with us. We'll ask you in a bit, after you get to know us." The man gesticulated with his arms more than most, almost an ambassador of sorts, welcoming them to his lands.

A group of small children followed behind him. They sat and pulled out a deck of cards. Giggles emanated from the forest, as if in all directions. They ran down from up a hill. A small boy frowned, as one often does in the mix of others having fun. He didn't get what he wanted. They didn't choose his game. He shrugged and pouted.

"They're so good now. Not as wily. They were wild when we found them. Of course, you know … the schools fed the children the pill. Unexpectedly. Rouge. Elementary only. Maybe some middle schools, but mostly at the elementary level only. Based on recent lab results." The man looked at his dirtied nails. "For some parents, though, rural middle American and the south mostly, red states, it was convenient to follow a certain trend. They didn't let their kids go to school. They had some separate broadcasts. Didn't come up here. They waited." He sighed and cocked his head. "Aren't we all still waiting? Waiting for it not to work."

"I'm sorry. Where did you come from?" Mary said.

"We're from Idaho traveling to Kansas. It'll be a place we try to regrow. We have time, you know. A few years. Things might be better without all the people. Things might turn around is what they say. We're going to plant. This place. This earth has literally almost zero carbon emissions. No cars. Electric right? No smokestack factories. It's all our earth again."

"But the weather …" Jill from the beginning didn't want to get into these arguments. She didn't want to tell the man the climate wouldn't allow it. The world was changed. Nothing was impossible, she assumed he would say. Wasn't it what all the Antis said? Optimism never died. She never wanted to get into the arguments that led Antis to melt icebergs, ruin the planet, what the earth was now. She shut her trap.

"So. These are your kids?" She knew they weren't.

"Two of them are mine, yes. Two of them have the same blood. But shouldn't we all look at children like our own in this day and age?" The man in the scarf winced, skeptical.

Jill interpreted his actions, the verbal quality of his face, as asking for concurrence. He was right. This was the world now, overpopulated with children. No one liked to see a child struggle.

"They were so helpless. We had to help them. They were crying and screaming, really, out loud. They wouldn't stop until someone gave them some attention, a moment. What would you do without parents?" The man stomped his foot, trying to get across meaning.

"My parents have been dead for decades," Jill said. She flipped her hair and scrunched her nose, offended, and looked him in the eye.

"So that makes you what …" the man said.

He folded his arms, closed to her responses.

"Independent," Jill said.

"You should get yourself some kids," he said to her. "With proper training, they can help. Live fruitful lives. You'll need discipline. These kids have real trauma. They're everywhere. And be careful."

Jill hadn't ever been a mom, and that's why it stung so hard because he knew too, and he was using it to pick at her vulnerability, questioning her ineptness and viability. Gathering up children and carting them around wasn't noble.

"I don't really want any kids … to take with us …" Jill whispered quietly, but her anger roared. She absolutely did not want to tell this man she wanted kids.

"So, I'll ask you to come with us … but we have kids …" the man said. His long scarf dipped almost to the ground. He spread his arm out and motioned behind him like an ambassador. And a leader he was. More children, dozens, and several adults came from behind a cliff and out from nests of trees. They all waved in half-hearted attempts. Hand raised and sagged, washed invisible windows as a motion, and a few children even bowed. The man handed each that bowed a cookie, gesturing his hand to have them come closer to him. With his arm around the children, he said simply, "Welcome."

"We're on our way west … I'm sorry." Mary gestured in the general direction.

He dropped his head in dismission.

"Oh, the Colony?" the man said. The man guessed it straight away. "Good luck with that. They didn't want to let us in. There were like three people. They blew the whole place up."

Mary mumbled. "He's lying."

"You're group. Is it growing a lot?" Jill said, staring at the man from a seated position. She identified as the vulnerable one, and he went on abusing his position.

"It is," he said arrogantly. "We've put up flyers for people to meet us in Kansas. Painted on billboards." He puffed his chest. "Why not start in the center of the world, the country? Will you, won't you come? His eagerness pervaded.

"My wife and I are going west, as she said," Jill said. "We are looking for a place to rest for a long time. One place to call home."

"Oh right, the Colony. 'When the world dies … call this place home' jingle jangle. Lie I might, but about this … no. It really is in shambles. You think the Antis didn't know, that they didn't go out there first? Good luck is what I say. They'd let you in if there was a door. I'm sure." He grinned a broad, patronizing smile and nodded.

The children appeared now as if they were fresh out of school, some in T-shirts, some in jeans, a few in shorts. The cool air coming off the waterfall gave Jill a bit of a shiver. It likely still got cool at night on top of that hill.

One child in plaid pants and a crisp white button-down shirt moved toward the group. He wore his Easter best. He kicked dirt a bit and lifted his head, chin pulled into his neck. His arms outstretched in a plea; he spoke. "Please misses. Please come with us. We need people like you to help take care of us." He dropped his head again and moved toward the man in the loud, streaming scarf.

"Here you go." He passed a rather large cookie to the boy

and spoke up again, this time in a booming voice, "He is right. We need women to come with us, raise the children."

"Oh, we're not qualified," Mary said. "We've never had children." She raised her voice at him as he badgered them.

"Aww. Tut. Tut," the man said. "You would do."

"Look. We're not interested. You'll have to move along," Jill said, defending Mary's honor to the end.

The man gathered up the group and hushed the children, who were rambling about cookies, what they did for a cookie, or could do what. They walked back around the corner of the cliff, almost as if it was a play that had ended. They clapped in the distance, and it was done.

"Well, suit yourself. Talk it out a bit." He winked. "We'll be in earshot. Just back up this way, over the hill, is a beautiful grove, and an even better waterfall to get married under. I hate to tell you. We'll be just up there and then down over the next hill to our caravan." He looked back over his shoulder. "We really need people to drive. We've got an eight-year-old who says he can, but I don't know." He laughed as he walked away.

When they were so far, they wouldn't be able to hear Jill's and Mary's whispers. The two huddled up, pushing the food aside. They would never get to the cake. Honestly, even in real weddings, the brides bought a cake simply for show and luck. They needed some of that luck, and that was a pity.

"But they were our connection with people," Jill said. "They were some semblances of a person. Not what a person was a year ago, but they were a connection so something that breathed, moved, talked if you were lucky."

"I thought you agreed. Headed for doom. The center of the country. The heat and dirt." Mary said. "That is Plan B. We need to know if Plan A is viable first, rather than gallivant across the country with some crazy traveling folk."

"But they were people," Jill said.

"They were. And for two days, we've barely seen any. Now we know they exist, but just as when there were many people, we can't make dumb moves. We can't fall for baseless propaganda."

Mary sliced a piece of cake to take with them. She brushed off crumbs.

Jill went to get the dress but thought the better. She draped it across the tree they sat under, as high on a branch as possible. "No room," Jill said. "Eventually there will be no room." Jill didn't even shed a tear because this was the place their love would stay and something so much more valuable than a thing, a dress that was worn once, and would get dirty. It would only count as baggage. The location they called their own, a place they went back to whether the pine needles had fallen, or the rock had eroded, or water filled in. They found this place, this spot in the woods, and made it their own.

CHAPTER 12

Jill and Mary had traveled through the night, with brief stops, sometimes stopping into, but usually staying outside of the NeverSleep in Life. They were trying to find what Life amounted to with the inability to sleep. The mood became grating and eerie. The deep night sky at 3:00 a.m. was foreign and beautiful at the same time. The pill prevented their eyes from drying out. It must've.

As they sat there at a break, stopped alongside the road, they held hands. The car had driven non-stop for two hours, so had their thoughts. Jill said she could not stare at the road any longer, or the overwhelming nature of the world. The stress beat back the anti-anxiety medicine in the pill.

Mary pointed to the stars and leaned over for a kiss. Jill felt the safety of the action and moment. She understood these things quite frequently from Mary now. Her love enveloped Jill and made her warm, protected.

"Will we ever get to sleep?" Jill said.

"That's what I thought as a teenager," Mary said. "I thought if I could just stay up extremely late at night, I would get so much done. It would be so much fun. I would never be at a stretch for time, unable to get my laps in at the pool or my homework done. I was romantic." Mary said. "Now, as an adult, I would be ten times more productive, but it's just this anxious sensation that I am not me. If I produce, do, or speak, the words or actions come from somewhere else. They are not the words that would come from me when I'm rested."

"I want sleep." The lull of the engine egged Jill's words on. Jill did not say anything more, and her silence was enough pause for her to rest.

Mary gathered her thoughts. Mary said, "Will we ever sleep? Does it matter other than science? Does this special power we have now make us superheroes? If so, I just want to be mortal. When the world is at rest, when they get the earth's rotation right, decades later, then they'll let us rest, let us have anxiety and anger. They'll let us lash out at each other as most people do … did. We'll be human again. Are we aliens now?"

Jill didn't answer but from it, together, holding hands, they broadened their emotional bond.

The Jeep chugged along on the highway. They had stopped for gas a while back. When Jill flipped the handle to get gas, it gushed just as she had hoped. She looked left and right, almost as if hoping to see someone. She didn't know what she would do if she had an encounter with someone left living.

An enormous billboard read, "Go to Kansas." And they both laughed a bit.

"The NeverSleep pill got to them," Jill said.

"Right. We're all really there and we just can't tell," Mary said, her voice drifted off.

Everyone would go to California. Jill was sure. Everyone should. Everyone left would get in their cars, drive four hundred miles until they needed to gas up, and then do it again. She thought up and down the east coast, it might be different. That a mass horde might come for the route they were casually meandering along through. They would stop for waterfalls; they decided to visit Canyonlands.

Everyone would go to the Colony. They weren't sure they'd get in, if space allowed for it, if a judging would take place. It was unclear what the politics would be. No one knew what would happen in this life or the next.

The pair were on barren highways, not a car in sight. But they expected that. The road was traversed less often than east coast roads and major thoroughfares near Denver. Still, nothing came into view until something in the very distant rearview mirror appeared.

"We've got to find a photo place. Like a pharmacy. The one with the red and white icon." Mary said.

"Logo?" Jill responded as a question.

"Yeah. It's a logo. Why are you picking on me?" Mary said.

"It's just your word choice. Icons are images of saints. They are considered a way to speak to the holy. You let the image speak through God to you. It's a soul window. That's what they call it," Jill said.

Jill watched as Mary fingered the locket she kept on her neck with several other loose chains. A memento of an old girlfriend. A rock she particularly liked. The locket held a photo of her uncle. Jill knew that much. She was tempting her past, too.

"Right now, there is no one to talk to. This world is all messed up with death and vacancy. We don't, no one must, know if anyone is alive even," Jill said.

"Who do you talk to at night?" Jill said.

"My god, before I go to bed. Well, I guess the people I knew. If you want to get religious … If at all … The people I knew that passed," Mary said. "How about you?"

"I think about you, Mary," Jill said. "About all the good times we have. Last night, with my eyes shut, let you come to me. I made us alive and not doomed, last night too, and dwell on all the good things we could be. We are so far here, together." Jill grabbed Mary's thigh as she drove the Jeep, swerving a bit when Jill first touched her.

"Honey … I feel these things too," Mary said. "What are we going to do when we fight?"

"We haven't fought yet. And that's a good thing. Show me waterfalls and remind me of my mother, and bam, you've got a month of no fighting … automatic." Jill said.

Out of the corner of her eye, Jill saw a big plume of smoke making its way towards their car. A shroud of smoke covered the front, sides, and trailed behind the truck, a smokescreen that would confuse anyone who followed them.

"That can't be the same truck?" Mary said.

"Oh. I bet it is …" Jill replied. "Why is he tailing us? What the hell. Of all the people in all the world …"

Jill trailed off, her mind racing to her parents who died when she was twelve in a plane crash. The smoke … she conjured up images of what the smoke looked like, drew for days in notebooks.

Jill just wanted to go home. The trip they were on, a vacation no less, was incredibly stressful for Jill, new place after new place. They were traveling all over Europe. Staying in foreign places, with foreign people and breakfasts. She cried to her parents. "I just want to go home," she had said. And they put her on a plane.

She was old enough to fly by herself, just thirteen. A family friend met her at the airport. Her brother called her every night. She ate ice cream for dinner for about a week, cranked the heat, and skipped school for a day.

Later that week, her parents flew back. They didn't return. Her brother, who had almost finished college, did. He explained in the gentlest terms what had happened. They were always moving, always finding a new place, a new home. Her brother was an academic, so Jill grew up around books: science, literature, and engineering. She preferred literature. Things with meaning, not a product. But, in time, Jill learned science had meaning too. It was basically all built on theory, finding definitive meaning before you do something.

Jill grew up here and there, the same as she did in size and mind. One place would teach her how to act like an adult. Another, when her brother took a job as an adjunct at a community college, gave her insight into adulthood. She grew up fast, learned to cope with people older than her. She learned to stand up for herself when they were quickly critical. With gusto, she applied her newfound knowledge and found herself cool, among others her age. When they moved to Massachusetts, it was her body that grew up, physically, through snowboarding. She matured and experimented with her sexuality.

She had always craved the mountains, which is why she eventually moved to Colorado. They were a home so big getting lost was easy, warranted, desired. But she always found a spot or a run of her own. She went to it whenever she was depressed or ill in spirit. That mountain, that spot, would never move.

Jill was a snowboard instructor, and it was just after peak season, the worst around the planet, of all time, she thought. An early mud season at best. She would have hibernated in their house, picked up an odd job around the town, a mountain bike shop or restaurant, and worked it. Then, NeverSleep came, and they were out of luck fast. And here's where they were.

Her brother off in Europe studied, took classes, as much

as she was aware, until the phones cut off. He was either dead or alive. Since the broadcasts started at the earliest, the world, Colorado at the very least, the United States likely, was left out of the news of the world. No one knew anything that was going on, only what would go on once the Antis struck the polar ice caps.

"Snap out of it, Jill …" Mary said. She was looking, chin struck forward, staring straight out of the window, one hand on the wheel, one hand held loosely in lap.

Jill was only trying to see her mother. Through a loose fog off on the side of the road, Jill thought she saw her and wondered briefly if they might stop. The haze dissipated and she could not, did not, go into the NeverSleep. She tried, she mused, to create her mom in NeverSleep but she would not be the same, only what Jill thought of her, only a creation of Jill with years missing, the years she didn't bond with her and the years that were gone.

"Take the next exit? We have to find that photo place regardless," Mary said.

A single sign for a fast-food restaurant hung at the exit. Mary hung a hard right several seconds later. Within a few minutes, houses began to spot the road. A single yellow line down the middle told them there wouldn't be any major throughways from there on out. They didn't see a single car on the road, and the homes appeared empty. Doors left open swung in the slight breeze, trash had built up on the curbs along with tree limbs and debris. A few cars pointed the wrong way on a one-way street. It might be that all the windows left ajar would attract wildlife. Uneaten food might go uneaten. The barren town couldn't have more than a thousand inhabitants.

Mary turned left and then right, avoiding a peculiar truck, and another hard right, going nowhere near the restaurant and potential pharmacy. Mary shrugged. "I mean, we have them on the digital camera."

"Yeah, but we took them today." They'll notice the date. It's in the metadata. Jill held her head down to her still loosely cupped hands. She knew it was too untrue, unbelievable.

Jill gazed into her past and saw all what they had built together become. She saw them as a couple for what they really were. Mary did this for them. For the bond, the renewal, and she, yes, it was needed, and yes, Jill would marry her. Jill only wished she had guessed Mary's motives sooner, so when she kissed in front of the camera, mumbled "I do" when no one asked a question, she would've known, would've confidently directed her kiss as not for show, not an outgrowth of the madness of the moment, but see it in the light of truth, as true of a love as she could give, as she was giving in her glowing beam of love now. It was all foreplay, anyway, and Jill was okay with it.

"But who gets 5x7 prints of their wedding in 2023?" Mary said.

"Right," Jill said.

"Just breathe, baby. Maybe they will just accept us, that we got fake married, because of all the chaos the gay community has been through," Mary chided.

"Doubtful," Jill said.

"Who are these people even?" Mary said, coaxing Jill to speak.

"I'm just so used to it. To the news. It leaves me remembering the last downswing. The last time gay was out of political fashion, they attacked other liberal rights associated with our issue. That's what turned the liberals, wasn't it?" Jill said.

"Not all of them. I'm telling you. It's your pessimism shining through. We'll be okay." Mary said.

"The Colony will reject us. Then we'll have to go back to Denver with those kids on our street. They'll eat us alive. I still say we should've never left—"

They pulled off onto a side alley and parked the car against a curb just off the main drag. The town, a humble but stately place, included a mix of older buildings with businesses from the early 1900s and a few influx businesses, mostly newer retail, fast food, and the like.

The side street was dusty, and the dry heat seemed to infiltrate the car as they clung to their seats, afraid to go out. Several empty cars lined the side street they were on. A door led to a bank, another a tax and insurance company.

A ringing bell came from several blocks away. Jill and Mary

both pulled up in their seat to see if they could get a glimpse of what was making the sound. The sound clanked with the quality of a cowbell, but rang unevenly: one ring, three second pauses, ring, ring, ten second pause, ring …

A youthful face popped out from the edge of a building, a federal brick storefront, at the end of the next block along the main street.

The face popped back in.

"Hello," Mary called out, window down. She unhooked her seatbelt and scrambled out of the car. "Hello?"

The vision, the face of someone small, was gone. Without the sense of warmth, the body, the emotion that the person brought, Jill only saw a barren town, ready to start a slow process toward crumbling to the ground. If only everyone were gone. But they weren't. At least one remained. Mary knew it was true. It wasn't a hallucination.

"Please—"

They both turned abruptly and stared hard at a little girl, about eight. Her cheeks were rosy red, and she brushed the knuckles of her tiny hands along the side of her pants at the belt loop. She stood on knobby knees on the precipice of a turning world. This land, the streets already littered with trash no one would pick up, didn't deserve her. She deserved much better.

"Good or bad?" the girl said.

"Oh, this is too much cuteness." Mary turned to Jill, filled with glee about the child's tiny bow holding her hair back and the skinned knee that needed a bandage.

Jill noticed the glint in the girl's eyes. She was untethered, a newly lost soul. She might be dangerous.

"They will come for you," the little girl said in a deep growl of a yell that only a child made up. She flipped up her middle finger. She arched her back as if no one told her for weeks to stand up straight. As if no one had grounded her for the way she spoke to adults or asked her to explain her role in the events, at least in the past two days.

They heard the cow bell again, and the girl was gone. She turned the corner, and Jill barely heard her shuffle for a few seconds before the noise disappeared entirely.

Out of the car, things looked different. A dusty haze permeated throughout the streets, abandoned cars, doors left open. Pillows and blankets poked out of several of them. Whoever was here, whoever rang the bell, might've been sleeping there. The people with them might've been sleeping as well.

Mary grabbed Jill's hand as they walked away from the car toward the corner where the young girl had stood. Her other hand held the camera they used at the waterfall hours ago. "Honey, this doesn't seem quite right," Mary said.

When they got to the corner, they peeked around the edge of the bank and popped their heads back quickly, one, then the other. "There's nothing there? Did you see anything?" Mary said.

"Look, I'm as freaked out as you, but that girl said they'd come for us," Jill said. She tapped her hand on her lower thigh in anxiety. "We'll get through this, right?"

"What? A bunch of kids? Yes. Yes, of course." Mary's head darted left and right and then left, and she peeked around the corner again. "We … we just have to find a photo machine."

"In here." Jill pointed to a department store on a corner across the street. Its door was open. It looked like it had seen some weathering, like management had avoided maintenance. The red brick was painted over, and the paint peeled off the brick in fist sized chunks. With the metal of the gutters rusted, and the connections showing wear, the building was less than inviting. The thin metal shoots hung off the roof, making their ability to carry water questionable.

"Okay. Fine. But this store is too small. It won't have the photo station," Mary said. "This is a wild goose chase, Jill. Do you even know how to use one?"

"I don't … Mary," Jill said, pulling her with her limp fingers toward the door. "What did you expect us to do? Why didn't we use that instant print out snapshot camera? A digital camera makes no sense. Were you even thinking?"

"Jill. I … I want us to be together. I'm sure they won't take the camera. They just look at them. Could we put them on a USB at least?" Mary said.

"Metadata. Look, Jill, we will get in. I just want to be as

prepared as possible. This is the only store in town. Folks have to make prints somewhere," Jill said.

Once inside, they scoped the aisle for goods they might want. "We have clothes, we have food …" Jill paused.

"We might need fresh fruit," Mary said.

"True," Jill replied. "I guess we can barter best with fresh produce for sure. When—if we ever get there."

Mary ducked down a dirty aisle to grab the fruit still in the chiller, though the power to keep it cool was off. "I'll be back."

"Wait, Mary, there's no photo stand here. This is a bust. Wouldn't it be right at the register?"

"Try upstairs," Mary said. "I've seen this layout before. This is a chain, albeit a poorly kept version of the same one we have in Denver."

"I've never been to it," Jill said.

"Probably never will," Mary chided.

Jill squinted her eyes as she tried to recall a memory. When she met Mary, they had settled down quickly. Jill led most relationships in the early phases, work and personal. Mary wasn't more vocal until her confidence in the relationship bolstered, which wasn't far afterward. It wasn't even a year, and they had moved in together. Jill had bought a house. The market was right. The interest rates were right.

She really wasn't trying to trap Mary, but, in a way, she admitted she did. As her therapist guessed, Jill was just looking for some sense of stability … a home, Jill thought. She needed a place to rest her head. Hadn't she always been looking for just one place?

The sociologists her brother hung around talked about three places. The first place is your home. It's your main place, the center of your life. Your second place is your work. You spend almost as much time there. But your third place, the one often defined as fun, is where you go after work: a bar, library, barber shop, café, anywhere you go to regularly.

Jill had a third place. It was the mountains. It was also her second place, and she didn't mind. She had messed up the sociologist's theory already. But her first place. The home. There were so many places to Jill and never just one.

She thought back on the sociologist's comments. That

everyone strives for third place. To have community, a sense of family beyond your family is crucial. Everyone should have a place to bitch.

All Jill ever wanted out of life was a first place, the given in the scenario. A place to grow roots, to learn family because something took it from her so young. Yeah, she had a brother, but not the history, not the history of a family house, or that of a grandmother or grandmother's grandmother. She did not have the quirks of her mother to build on, internalize, find meaning, recreate for her own children.

She had always wanted a place. That was it, one place. She finally had that with her partner and when they split, she wouldn't let the house go. She never wanted to leave unless the mountain called.

From the tip-top window of the attic of the small grocery section of the franchise department store, she saw them scurrying. Children at the playground. It was almost as if they hadn't a care in the world. Like they didn't give two shits about the absence of their parents. They still laughed and played. Three spun one around on a merry-go-round. One swung as high as he could for the trees. Another scooted his way down a slide he was too big for.

The last child Jill saw from the attic space, which didn't have a photo print station, was the same girl who had stuck her middle finger up at them both. She was crying, sitting cross-legged on the ground.

The young girl's eyes. Young. Her limbs. Adept. Both might be slightly supernatural. Her gaze swung up to the window in the attic, and Jill sensed the bead of her eyes on her. The child got up, dusted herself off, shouted something at the playing boys and girls and trudged laborious, heavy, sad steps toward the store. They weren't coming for her. She was leaving. In whatever capacity she could, as she was.

Jill surveyed the top floor, which was mostly left unused. Various products were strewn about. The glint of shiny metal racks with rough edges caught her eye. Kids liked shiny things. Jill guessed the disarray was from looting or forts. She moved to the stairs, where she could already hear the girl and Mary conversing. She descended the steps to see Mary on one knee, holding the girl's hand as she whimpered about something or other, probably the other children. Children are so horrible to other children.

"We have to go," Mary said.

The girl was at her feet, sitting, knees tucked into chest. "I want to go."

"What? Why? What's wrong?" Jill said. She also kneeled by the girl. "My name's Jill." She stuck out her hand.

"We have to go and we're taking this girl with us," Mary said.

"Okay. Can't I ask—"

"No. There's no time," Mary said.

Jill grabbed the camera she had momentarily set aside and, in a deep breath, sighed. It would be tragic if they forgot it, wouldn't it? They would let them in as a couple. They would be responsible. But this girl. This was a new story.

"If we take her, we can't leave her anywhere. She must be with us until we get to the Colony," Jill said. "She could have siblings here."

"I will tell you, but we must go." Mary's face was pale white. Despondent, her lips turned down heavy with recent news this child had delivered. Whatever the girl said did permanent damage.

They moved as a chain. Jill, who knew something must be wrong based solely on Mary's countenance, pulled Mary by the hand who had the child by the arm. The bells on the doors clanged, and Mary gripped them to make them stop. But when she let go, out of the door, they continued sounding out their warning.

The children were in Jill's direct line of vision when she appeared. They were attacking the Jeep with bats and small kitchen knives. Jill heard a tire hiss and turned away, taking one large stride, then another in the opposite direction. Mary hoisted the child on her back, and they were off.

"Look! A gas station. Cars … keys. Fingers crossed." Jill ran ahead. Even though Mary was in better shape, Jill wasn't carrying a not so small child on her back. They hustled to the station just as scurrying kids rounded the corner. They all paused, holding knives in the air and acting tough. The older ones had cut slashes in their shirts and rolled up the ends of their T-shirt sleeves. Collared shirts popped. They were acting out, performing for someone. For themselves.

Jill opened a door on an extended cab Toyota Tacoma as the kids charged closer. Although poised to attack, they lagged back.

Jill turned the key, and the car jostled to a start. The cab was shaking slightly as it idled. It was outside of the garage where mechanics worked on cars, so Jill assumed they fixed this one. Only time would tell.

Mary hoisted the child into the middle front seat and shimmied her own self into the passenger seat. "Belts," she said instinctively.

"Okay. okay."

"Millie, are you okay?"

"Yes. I just hate belts," she mumbled. "At least it's not a car seat."

From down the street, she heard the crowd of children coming closer. "Don't take her." "She's with us." They bounded down the street. "She's the sacrifice."

"Did he say she's the sacrifice?" Jill said.

Mary nodded, and they pulled out of the gas station. Mary turned a hard left avoiding running over the group of five children clamoring after them.

Jill accelerated and didn't look back. They were someone else's kids. For all Jill gathered, Millie was now theirs. They saved one. From death, at least.

CHAPTER 13

As they hit the open road in the gassed-up Tacoma extended-cab, Millie revealed bits about what had happened in the past two days. What happened in their small rural Colorado town might've happened in many towns, if parents weren't around. If they fell asleep and didn't wake up.

"We can do anything we want. We can eat chocolate. Steal from the grocery store. Bang shit up. That's what the boys like to do. 'Bang shit' is what they say." Millie was excited and breathless.

"Millie. What did you say to me at the store?" Jill said.

"My time is up," Millie spit out. The half-smile on her face turned into a frown. "The boys. My brother's friends put me in time out and then said my time was up because I escaped from time out."

"What does it mean if your time's up, Millie?" Jill said.

Millie made a long cut across the throat.

"Can't be true," Jill muttered off hand to Mary, who was for once in the passenger seat.

"They killed Nathan because he wouldn't kill Michael's dog. Hank hated Michael and his dog, but Nathan didn't. That's what they did. Killed Nathan. Pushed him off a building. We cried. Some of us cried … And now, my time is up."

The car fell silent, and they drove for a bit. "Can't be true," Jill muttered again, this time to herself.

They drove for another thirty minutes, quietly. Millie had pitched her head in the air. NeverSleep took over. When Mary rubbed her shoulder a bright flare of light cascaded inside and outside of the car simultaneously, and Jill swerved.

"What was that?" Jill shrieked.

Mary looked back at the small passenger in the back seat. "Honey, look."

Jill jerked her head toward the back seat, then toward the road, stretching a mite more each time until she got a glimpse of Millie's hand. A little firefly of a light glowed, and they felt it warm the car and their skin.

"Millie, what do you have?" Mary said above a whisper. The flickering light jumped and relaxed.

"It's a Life. I collect them. This one is my mom. They're not for squashing like the boys say. Never mind that they can never find them, anyway. Here, I'll give it to you." She lifted her palm and pushed it toward Jill, who swerved again. She sensed its feather weight on her supple skin.

"Millie. What is that?" Jill said.

"It's a power. You'll take it back to NeverSleep when you go. It'll answer problems."

"How do you know these things, Millie?" Mary said.

"School mostly," Millie said. She returned to playing with her book. She was bending the pages into patterns, a basic origami of sorts.

"I need to switch," Jill said. Jill didn't like to drive. She didn't have the right sense of things. Vertigo set in and nausea crept up her throat. She wasn't quite sure which, but she knew she didn't have enough gusto to drive.

The car halted, and the driver and passenger switched. "This is true love," Jill said.

"Jill," Mary said. "This is why you love me."

"It's not the only reason, but a strong one." Jill smiled and winked, pushing her cheek toward Mary almost as a kiss.

In the back, Millie clapped madly. She loved it. "You two are fun," she said. "Where are we going now?"

"School, Mary. Of all the places, wouldn't you guess kids learned more about NeverSleep than us because of school?" Jill leaned in deep and slumped her arms across her chest. One deep breath in, one deep breath out.

The conversation moved back to the front of the car. Jill, in concert with Mary had to decide what would happen. They couldn't simply leave a child in distress. Then again, in another day and age, they would be in trouble for kidnapping a minor. Did Amber Alert even work? This had to be the right action, in this day of this new age. They still had rational thought. Maybe not days from now, but now. They were reasoning through the world itself.

"We need to take her. She's magic, to say the least. If anything, we can save one. Whether she was supposed to die. Someone must repopulate the earth. Someone needs to be tame enough, tamed, grow up as a decent person, to repopulate the earth. Isn't saving one better than none? Right now, there must be one adult for two thousand children, if that. We must do our part," Mary said.

"No one is testing us," Jill said. She dug deep for a memory of her mother or how she might've been when she knew her parents were gone.

"We test ourselves every hour in this mayhem," Mary said. Her eyes got stern and bleak, as if there was no other answer. She barked with those cold eyes. "This is our child."

The sky was deepening into a dark blue and the horizon begged for a time that people would normally tuck themselves under covers, finding sleep one way or another. Be it after good sex, or crashing from a long day, whether it was sleeping pill induced or if one would just lie awake just long enough, counting sheep, to drift off for enough time to get them through the next day.

"Look, I should be tired. I'm on edge about that. How do you feel," Jill said.

"Exhausted from the world in chaos, but alert like I just drank a coffee," Mary said.

"I'm wondering when we'll crack when the sense of 'just had a cup of fresh coffee' will break us. When will things stop making sense? When will the psychological toll begin? They said they put an antipsychotic in the pill so that it would take the edge off. That's not it. There must be other repercussions, dimensions to thought."

"You're going there now. We should take a stop … a nap, so to speak," Mary said, looking into the backseat.

Jill wrapped her long, flowing hair around her body. They didn't look prepared for the apocalypse. She didn't have a leather vest, or a madman biker helmet, or even a survival pack. Her department store backpack bought five odd years ago and shoved in a closet did simply fine for a go-bag.

Mary combed Jill's hair with her fingers gently and tenderly as she looked out the passenger window, gazing into what some might call oblivion—an empty town. To Jill, it just looked like an everyday mountain town cleared out early after the snow finally melted. It matched resort towns miles back. Resorts she had worked at in season.

Out here, everything was barren anyway. National Park season was coming up, and that's when this place would see the influx of visitors, bent on a stamp and a bit of a sweat with some mosquitos.

"Honey, we don't have children," Mary said. She petted Jill's hair. Jill did not look in the back seat.

"I forgot she was there." Jill's voice was only a murmur. She saw something distant, an animal loose from a fence. It would soon find its way down to the road. "Someone's going to hit that cow," Mary said. "Actually, the population of the world has been cut in half. It might stand a chance. Someone might come along. Someone might shoot it. I hope they shoot it."

"For the love of God. I hope those people traveling to Kansas have the knowledge to skin and cook a live cow," Jill said.

They both muttered back and forth a little, thinking out loud about how ridiculous their lives were and speculating on all the things they didn't know were happening since the apocalypse.

Millie sat in the back seat, looking at the pictures of a gossip magazine that Mary snagged from the front racks of the grocery store they were at yesterday morning—the morning they woke up.

"Millie. Are you happy to be with us?" Mary said.

"I guess so. Mom and dad are dead. That's what my brother said," Millie said.

"Oh god, Jill," Mary said. "This poor girl. She's going to have temper tantrums and cry. She's going to miss her parents and needs to eat at particular moments of the day. Can we handle it?"

"So will we, Mary. So will we. When NeverSleep hits us, we'll freak out just like children. We'll be the helpless ones. I'll be glad if Millie keeps me in order." Jill smirked and jerked her head over her shoulder to see Millie, smiling, still paging through the magazine. Loving every minute of the ride with these strangers.

"Let's shave our heads," Millie said. "So, so. We're a real apocalypse gang. Just like the movies."

It was almost as if she read Jill's mind. She combed her fingers through her hair's twisted locks, as if playing with it one last time. She let it fall in front of her, passing her shoulders. If she tied the bunches together, she'd have pig tails. When Jill asked her if she did want pigtails, she said she didn't. She didn't even make an effort to pull her hair into pigtails just to see.

"This is barely an apocalypse yet," Jill said. The two in the front laughed and soon squeaks sounded from the back seat of the Tacoma. She was joining in, mimicking, or musing on her own. Jill would never truly understand.

They stopped at a gas station just off the highway with their guard up. Jill piled in water and candy bars, soft pretzels, as Mary held tight to the wheel. They got some gas and then took their time with the facilities, Mary taking Millie with her.

It was, God, crazy. No one was in sight. No one. The universe had disappeared, or had it? They were still on that remote stretch of land to Utah. They missed the ghost town that Jill had wanted to go to all her life. After the incident with the kids, they were on their way to find something, to find the end. They would need a break in a bit, they all agreed. It would help them clear their heads.

They were so close to Canyonlands that they made the detour.

"Can we get four-wheelers?" Little Millie squeaked.

"I suppose eventually. We have to find people first. If there are people there, friendly people. Then we can play as much as you want," Mary said.

They traveled along the dusty canyon road lined with ancient pine tree by ancient pine tree. "If any one person lived that long," Jill said. She cozied up to Mary, happy to soak in the warmth of nature until it became overpowering, unbearable.

The road seemed like it would never end. So many secrets in the age-old trees, but not one of them alluded to whether other people existed. Kids, of course, existed, but who else took the pill? Should they have taken the pill? What would become?

"We're here … Canyonlands …" Mary said.

Jill had been resting her eyes.

"And that doesn't count for pseudo-sleep," Mary said. "Plus, Millie needs to rest the brain."

"Is that what they call it? Pseudo-sleep?" Jill said.

"Might as well. Out here all alone. That is what we have. The ability to make a new world. Make new language. I'll abuse it. 'Lovely traveler.'"

"That's what I am now." Jill sat back and let out a howl. "I am a traveler. A term dug up from dystopian novels of the twentieth century and beyond. Personally, I'll let it unravel before me. I'm not God."

"I hear you. None of us are God," Mary said. "Millie lie back. Jill lie back. We need to rest our brains. We need rest. Let's just call it that."

And Jill knew she had quelled emotions that gather speedily inside her when she faced tension and immediacy. Things like the world collapsing, the end evolving via a band of Antis who purposefully melted the polar icecaps.

Vertigo had set in, and she only rested, shut her eyes, pulling for sleep to come.

"I'm going to lie over there on the flat cement." Jill lifted her hand and pointed her finger limply gesturing it.

"You always did like a firm mattress," Mary said.

"Is that why we were ultimately incompatible?" Jill said.

"No, no. You were spreading your wings, made space for you, you time," Mary said.

"It's true. I needed space. Like I need space now," Jill said. She carried herself flowing like water toward the Canyonlands National Park Service office, the covered shelter of a place. While there and not there at the same time, flowing into a warped world that moved as fluidly as she felt, she rested a hand down on the ground. When she thought she was there, she crawled down into place. "There. This is it. Just need a little shuteye."

They had said on the broadcasts you needed shut eye. Not necessarily sleep, but eyes closed. If you abused NeverSleep, took to the night like a raver, like someone who partied until dawn, you might just keel over. But they didn't know for sure. They said they didn't want to lie, so they wouldn't say for sure, but they guessed. If you took the NeverSleep pill … well no one even really guessed.

Her eyes glazed open, dry, and then shut dry. She pulled some drops from her pocket and dripped them one by one into her eyes as she lay on her back.

At an early age, she saw an eye doctor. Her first visit she kept as a horrible memory. She visited the eye doctor and squirmed and twisted to avoid the drops in her eyes. She wanted anything but dense water pushed into her eyes. The pressure might have popped her eyeballs right out. She writhed and screamed and when her mom came running; it was okay. She relaxed. Her mom pet at her head and cooed a nursery rhyme from an even earlier childhood.

The doctor said she didn't need glasses, and they left together hand in hand, mother and child, both knowing they would never go back to that evil man. All at once, the doctor, a vampire, a swamp monster, an evil character they would never need to encounter again disappeared from consciousness. To this day, when Jill saw a villain in a comic book movie, she always felt the glint of the eye, the sense of evil the character dished out into the world was still a bit like that doctor. A smidge of what he had.

And she was out into another world once again. Building in the doctor's office, over the office. With a swift crane and ball, she demolished it. She was an overlord willing the crane which way with her mind, hands on head, concentrating. And holding the construction vehicle between her fingers, shifting it back and forth to gain momentum. Wheeling the vehicle just over to the building. It crashed down.

Then she was with the children, on the ground building a new spot, a new place to live. This was an extravagant home.

"Only meant for one person," one child said.

"They're going to love it," another cheered.

They had the most remarkable acuity with tools, never slicing a finger or hammering a thumb. And their pace was breakneck. It all dissolved and appeared before Jill's eyes. Those eyes she felt now with her fingers, nails trimmed properly. They shut; she was sure. But she wasn't sure where she was. She was either in the rebuilding world or in the realm of the last few living. What she knew for now was to be in the only authentic place. She would wake up to it now, wake up from the NeverSleep, if she weren't drifting so far into the imagery.

The house was a barnish, steep gabled roof set on the top of a slope. What they called a bank barn out east. The windows were glass, reminiscent of a famous mid-century modern in Connecticut. Jill had seen it with her brother, the intellectual family he inherited by living in Massachusetts. Jill had tagged along, like always, slowly to find her own friend. Stiffly holding on to her brother's security, her last shred of a sense of family.

Inside, she saw a one person. Millie, the girl they took with them from the small town now miles back, appeared. Older and stretched out on the couch, she grinned and waved at friends coming to the door. It might've been Christmas if the warmth didn't swell so much. Jill felt the warmth.

A fireplace popped up a low flame, and smoke rose from the top of a clear chimney. Jill and Mary knocked at the door, too. They were visiting. Jill rubbed her hands together and held them in the flame. Jill, with her eyes shut on the cement floor outside of Canyonlands, missed the heat.

Jill rolled to her side. Her pain told her she still ached, and that she lived in a lucid place. She fought to open her eyes, and they didn't beg to stay shut, but they were stitched, unable to lift lashes from lashes. In a gag like reflex, they tried but snapped back like a bug setting off a Venus flytrap, clamping shut after the bug struck the jowls.

Jill didn't see the marble, at least the light that glowed in a flash before her. Millie's marble with a prism in it that stopped the world before them. Jill didn't see Millie's mom or the world she might've created. She saw a single small ball when she thought about it. It was one Jill had in her own childhood. The concept of a sphere, something to play with, brought fear, unknown powers. Try as she might, Millie's marble didn't appear. Millie's mom eluded.

The marble, the Life, must've been from the school, a way to tap into children to make them happy about their parents.

They would find their parents in the NeverSleep that everyone was talking about. And if they lost their parents, if the last day they didn't take the pill, lived without their children, watched them die because of what the school had to make them take, because of what had changed in the hours between that and the announcement, they could find their parents. The light of the glitter was upon them. And that's all the children needed to believe.

Millie evaded Jill in NeverSleep as well. On her own journey, she might be with her mother. Had found her, holding the marble in her hand. But Jill wouldn't know until she could break through this place, this wall of a prison where she defiantly created. Didn't she need people to survive? Was this to be done all on her own? Didn't she need to interact?

This child that Mary and Jill had brought into the fold was everything. Jill got what she wanted. She wanted to care for her and be close to her, shelter her, and comfort her. But she was not Jill's child and, more than anything, she wanted her to be with her mother. If her mother lived in the NeverSleep, more than anything, Jill wanted them to be together.

CHAPTER 14

Jill never thought she'd have a kid out in the world this way. How could you ever imagine? They had run across few adults. It seemed to be that all civilization was lost. In pockets of the country, apparently, whole elementary schools existed alive and well. Albeit the administrators and teachers may not have taken their pills. Except for masses of children spotted in the few towns they had stopped in, people didn't persist. Still, they had mostly stayed on the highways.

One child is something. One child in the NeverSleep Life is another. In no way were Jill or Mary equipped or experienced enough to handle either the entire school left behind or this one child, here and now. Jill guessed most mothers started this way, knowing nothing.

She would try. Jill would try to create a world for this child. It was not her temporary responsibility. Her goal for the rest of her life, she found thrown down without delay. She promised to provide for this child, learning to be a mother because she had to be a mother. This was not a temporary situation. They would have to be together. Jill let her assume the trauma of finding a third mother. Jill would be the second. Jill would be the last.

Jill batted around the idea of having a child for a long time. Since she was young, really. When her mom came running into the room early in the morning, Jill would toil away caring for a baby doll as if it were her job. Her infatuation continued in middle school when she collected miniature baby knick knacks, mostly porcelain pieces. She saw to it in high school that her egg baby, home economics project never dropped. She scared her partner off with a scowl and maniacal laughs. It worked and her egg lasted the duration of the experiment.

She was ready to have a child by herself in a year. She had talked to Mary about this. Mary had never been too keen on the idea. She used it as bait, as far as Jill knew. A playing card, they realized. Jill had waited to see a doctor about starting the process alone, if it was still possible.

Mary would wave her prowess in front of Jill in a certain way. "I am a wonderful mother," she said. "I can take care of things." She would go on about how she treated her nieces and the meaning of her intentions. Jill knew it was only for show. At least that's what she had thought.

She looked at Mary now, constantly looking in the rearview mirror, tapping her hands on the steering wheel anxiously. She hoped they would all make it out of Life alive, get to the Colony, find safety, and Jill thought sincerely, they would all be a family.

Mary put her hand on Jill's thigh just as she was thinking all these magical things about settling down in a post-apocalyptic world. Almost as if she knew what Jill was thinking, she said, "We'll figure it out. We'll find a way. This child," Mary said.

"Millie," Jill said.

"Yes, Millie. She is precious and unique and came to us just how any other child would be, one of a kind and assigned to us. She will be with us, and we will be here for her as long as she needs us," Mary said.

"Unexpectedly," Jill said. "It was so much more unexpected than any other child would come to someone."

"Yes, honey." Mary said. "It's different, but we are together. This is our life. Buck up because this is going to be a ride. You can't leave a child on the side of the road or put one out of their misery. God would kill you, strike down force. I don't believe in God, but it must be true."

Jill topped Mary's hand with her own. "This place we're in, this jungle of an apocalypse as you said it, is so much less scary with you. The idea of having this child alone and not knowing how to handle it all. It would be mortifying."

"We'll get through it," Mary said. "This place isn't so bad. Look at the landscape. We have a sense of safety. There is still some green left. At least, we'll have safety when we find the Colony."

"We'll find a mess of trouble with a child and if there are guns and looting involved, it's sure to be trouble. And if they even let us into the Colony, there's no guarantee we can also bring a child. We'll be lucky if we get a room with enough beds," Jill said.

"There are no people. You forgot. Literally no people. How hard could it be? There will be tons of space. We shouldn't be scared. We should go into this with a positive attitude. We are freer than we have ever been before," Mary said.

"Rabid children can kill. We've seen that," Jill said.

"So skeptical. Let's just get Millie to safety, ensure our own, all our safety, and get the rest under control then. It will be so much easier when we are at the Colony."

CHAPTER 15

Mary found herself apathetic about children for the longest time. She neither wanted them, nor didn't want them. She always thought she might be too young to tell.

What she knew she wanted was a woman to be her wife, someone she might live with for the rest of their lives, an eternity if it might be now. Jill. She desired Jill. If that's the way this turn of the world was going, yes, she wanted to take a pill to NeverSleep, NeverDie and live forever with the woman. Her woman, the woman of her dreams.

Jill had everything she ever wanted. But she wallowed, at times, in depression. Mary filled a void, didn't she?

Her hair flowed a luscious brown, much too precious. Her eyelids, a deep-set glory, raised during most conversations. Her qualities of character included a keen perception about people and unending care. She'd know your past trauma and deepest ecstasy in a gaze. If she told you, you were considered a friend, or a lover.

Jill had seen lost desire, the loss of childhood. Mary understood that much. Though she rarely talked about it, when her parents died it devastated her. Mary saw the scars that would not go away. Jill has been knee deep in fog lately. Mary knew it. Likely obsessing over the past trauma. She saw her mom she said one day almost a month ago. In a dream-like dream, a wakeful state she couldn't describe. And she reached out to her, but she was gone.

"It wasn't the NeverSleep," Jill had said. "It was a place I couldn't get to. A place no one can get to. And she was alone. Her vacancy pulsated with my want to speak to her, but I couldn't see her because she seemed to say, 'I see no one.'"

Mary thought it might be her desire to put her trauma back on her mother. The years of loneliness that resulted from her parents' death, she only drove harder back into this image of a mom, what could be her mom, but she was sure in several worlds it was not.

This is all Mary ever saw about anyone, because she was in love with just this one person.

Jill was peculiarly special. She had magic in her eyes when she looked at this child. And it wasn't just the magic of the NeverSleep. It wasn't her want and desire for a child fulfilled. For her, it was real, confusing but real. Mary, too, had opened herself to the possibility of nurturing someone else. She hoped that she might cradle, then grow another life. Her goal to care for and make better another's life, a delicate body not her own, was a bold first start.

Still, Mary doubted Jill's ability. Her want was greater than her ability. Her call to action was stronger than how things could play out. Mary second guessed Jill's capacity, her nurturing powers. If it was damage from her childhood, which it frankly could be, Mary's want to help Jill was ten times stronger. Wasn't a partner supposed to fulfill the weakest misgivings of your other half? And Mary might still be just a companion, even though they were sham married, but in her eyes, the bond was great. It was before as it was now, a way to get to the core, Jill's love, the companionship they both needed, that almost worked at one time. It would work this time. Mary was confident this time around.

She saw them raising a family now. In an instant, from across the room, so to speak, she saw that child in the rearview mirror of the back seat of her wife's car. This child would be their savior. It would not be the one that saved the world. She didn't seem to have any special powers, but the child would save Jill and Mary. She would save their relationship, cement it if you will, and bind them together. It was selfish, but Mary knew Jill would never let a family get away from her again.

"Millie?" Mary spoke up.

"Do you like Jill and I?" Mary said. "Would you like us to be with you for a while? Maybe a long time?"

"Yes." Millie hopped up and down on the seat, adjusting her hands beneath her butt. She still didn't realize what it all meant. What the world had come to. The child might be in shock. Not a peep was made about Mommy. Had Millie even seen her mother dead? Had she known that she was gone and cried for a day or more, since that morning, however long the LongSleep was for her?

Millie was a dear, dear soul, but even if she was kicking and screaming, calling for Mom, the two, Mary and Jill, would have to bundle her up, hush her down, and continue to escape to safety. It was their responsibility, as adults in this world, to look after just one child. At least one. That was what they could handle right now.

"Millie," Mary pipped up again, hoping to elicit some response from the silent child. One that had been hushed by something, everything, the world come down. "We love you. Jill and I love you. And we're going to take care of you. It will be alright. I promise. We swear to take the absolute best care of you. You would like that, wouldn't you?"

"Yes," Millie said, still quiet and now thumbing through a magazine for the fifth time. Amusing herself as much as possible. Quiet. Behaving. She was the best child in the world at those moments. But it might not always be so. A traumatized kid might prove difficult in the future. Right now, in this moment of stress, she was good. And that's all they ever needed to solidify the bond.

"I miss my Mommy," Millie said.

"Do you want to talk about it?" Jill said.

Mary was anxiously waiting for words, something to go on. Something to live the rest of her life with.

"No. I don't want to talk as much," Millie said.

"We love you," Jill said. "You don't have to talk. It's okay. We'll just drive for a bit. If that's okay."

"Okay. I like the drive. I like you both," Millie said.

They needed some kind of validation.

CHAPTER 16

The group of three drove into the canyons, passing rocky landscapes on the way to Utah. It was the next part of an unplanned journey with unplanned steps. The first part was over. Jill and Mary were married and had a child. Ironic as it was, they were a sort of family. It was at least the second leg. Jill was unclear how many more stops would be needed. Being alone in the wilderness made things very unclear. It was a NeverSleep Life wilderness where most people were dead and gone, locked up in homes, rotting as flesh will. That's all they could really guess.

Jill turned on the radio and checked the channels. A signal came in for a brief second, and Jill adjusted it with the tiniest increments possible by turning the knob and then turning it back again. A loud snap and an "Alert," spoken in a state of panic resounded and then silence again came over the place.

"What was that?" Jill said.

"Not sure. Somebody's out there. No NeverSleep broadcast though. Boy, do I miss falling asleep to that monotone voice," Mary said.

"Really?"

No one told them to listen or not to listen. Jill and Mary checked on each other regularly, and that was their self-check. They were children in the apocalypse's newness. Curled up in bed, they had pillow talk about what each new broadcast meant. They weren't lovers but entranced children, thinking about the current moment, mulling it over, coffee in hand, fretting as if it would never happen. "Not the future." They thought about the movies. "This will never happen." They would coast to their graves in warmer temperatures and bigger hurricanes. Everyone was safe. But, here now, in a car running from a wild trucker, they had to be adults in the aftermath. They were taking control of another person, responsibly reporting to their check-in location. And they were fending for their lives. It was not the act of a passive watcher, but of one catapulted into the battlefield.

This place was a time bomb waiting to happen and Jill and Mary were dumbstruck in the here and now. As much as they tried to be both here and anywhere else in the world. What was happening with coastal flooding in New York? How did the plains dust kick-up? Were the animals really dead? Did they even see them around them? Hills reserved for buffalo grazing, Jill knew, were populated year-round. These same hills were now vacant.

Right now, she saw only pines, tall, lush trees never meant for Santa Claus and chimneys. They trickled needles to the ground. Jill guessed twice about diseased groves and the effects of the shock of the climate switch. It was all relative to where you were. They were in the wilderness careening, mostly unaware, grasping glimpses of what might've happened with no viable news. This place, this wilderness, was still the closest to pristine, the best place to hide, the safest place on earth. Until it wasn't.

Kids played fort apparently. Leader of crisis. They, their group of three, also struggled with leadership. As much as Mary appeared to understand what she was doing, no one really led in a world overflowing with emptiness, a world on the edge of a shelf ready to fall off? Often meek, Jill herself didn't tell her otherwise.

The smoke gushed into and up against the windshield as if a cloud turned black, as if they were driving through clouds.

A screeching wheel turned and a truck skidded: skis on sheets of ice, a skater in the 1980s powersliding, a mud boggers dream. The vehicle leaped forward in a pulse and then paused and let Mary, the driver, cascade forward, passed the truck, gripping the wheel for life.

The car punched at the back end of Jill's vehicle. As she braked, the black truck gave a little distance in a jerk and then zapped back on the bumper. Millie cried out in a squeal. For the first time, she was vulnerable, and Jill could not help. Mary tried unable to return to a normal, safe speed.

Jill leaned her arm on the driver's seat and peered back behind Mary to see the travesty, the purveyor of smoke. Mary stared into the driver's side rear-view mirror. She leaned in, only to jerk back and keep the car on the road.

"Who is that?" Jill said.

"One against three. Do we have what it takes?" Mary said. As her car drifted toward the center of the road, she panicked.

"I would hope not," Jill said, intimidated and barely knowing how to fight. "Mary—"

"What can we do, Jill," Mary said. "This is stress if I've seen it." She wiped her brow, now soaked in soggy soot.

"Keep driving. He'll pull off," Jill said.

This masked man, from what Jill gathered, was not the same one that she had met at all. Jill understood from the very first moment she woke up from the LongSleep, these people who tricked the world, would want to kill. The Antis were serial killers at least, ushers of genocide more appropriately. Jill justified the Antis might live with several thousand or more adults, kids as well, who might not have the same beliefs. They might try to brainwash them as they built the new civilization. Or, as was becoming very plain, they might try to plow down everyone left in Life.

"We're after you …" a voice on the radio cooed.

"It's the radio," Jill shouted. Then, with a twist, she turned it off.

The car vaulted back, bucked, and sped to meet up one more time. The intimidation worked. And it provoked more fury from the driver. Mary continued on, steady, playing the solid soul.

A rabid man pulled most of his body out of the window, bared chest, tongue wagging. He hollered, "Yee haw." The car ventured up again, this time with fewer precision bumps. A shot to the back left tire made Jill moan.

"Fuck off," Jill said in a relaxed monotone. "Millie," Jill said calmly. "Hand me some things … big clunky things."

Millie casually, in between sharp screams, handed Mary things from the back seat. Mary chucked them out the window, aiming as best as she could at the car. A shirt at the windshield. A road flare at the tires. A flashlight at the windshield. Only the flashlight struck, and it hit the bumper.

If this wasn't debilitating anxiety and fear, Jill wasn't sure what was. But it was here in this moment that Jill was glad and ultimately terrified that she didn't feel what she should. Millie should've passed out from her emotion, from her sheer terror. Jill should've lost her head from the worry, placed herself under the tires to death. Mary should have rammed the car for lack of concentration. But they didn't. They survived with a man at their heels, the way they trained soldiers to do, to keep their head. It was a pill, a godsend, and a damnation. To sense this, to feel any deep emotion, empowered. Their brains relaxed. How would they deal if they were so dull, unable to hold love, unable to retain empathy? A curse and a blessing.

Out of the blue horizon, the one they were all reaching for, the masked stranger they had become accustomed to, pulled from the berm about five hundred feet in front of Mary. He let the black matte truck catch up. In the rearview, Jill clearly saw the mask, that same man. His truck a molting matte black beast with chips and dings the same as the one she had seen outside her house. The truck was the same as the one trying to ram them now, only a different make. Weren't they all essentially the same? She clearly saw his motions.

"He wants us to get in the left lane," Jill said. He motioned, looking back with a crisp chopping motion toward the lane they were almost in, but occasionally bumped or pushed to the limits. Jill had an inkling. "Trust him."

"Are you kidding?" Mary yelled.

"It's okay. Somehow, I know," Jill said.

When Mary adjusted her hands on the wheel, gripped it more tightly. In an instant, it was over.

The masked man's truck stopped full stop in front of the black matte truck. Mary kicked the accelerator to the max as he stopped. The black matte truck swerved sideways skidding, and the man vaulted out of the window. He yowled in terror. The truck skidding into the metal beam extending from the masked man's bumper. His car jumped and twisted, but it didn't roll. It could've turned on its side. The accident might've crushed a person, snapped their life out of them. But it didn't. And the three, Millie, Mary, and Jill, moved on.

"What was that?" Mary said.

"The man in the camo mask," Jill said. "He saved us."

"Should we go back?" Mary said.

"I don't think we can," Jill said. "It's too treacherous. What if the other truck … What if that guy lived? He'd kill us. I saw a hunger for death in his eyes."

They entered Canyonlands a little over a half hour later. Surely, no one would be there during a national crisis or perhaps they would want to claim the beautiful land. Hopefully, the bandit trucker had not followed them. Beauty might still be a commodity, something they'd have to guard with guns and numbers. Money is not so much. No one needed money right now. A penny might be flicked into the world and bet on luck.

Canyonlands was empty. Beauty wasn't too precious to seize.

The canyons were deep, and the air was hot, but the beauty cooled their souls. The group of three took the car through the park for some ohs and ahs. They saw the famous deep dips and outcroppings. They saw the beginnings of trails. No one would save them if they got lost. They touched the rocky soil and chatted about growth.

As they disembarked from the car, the three veered toward a cliff that appeared ready to drop from the sky. Millie skipped as Mary and Jill watched nervously. Jill wondered at what step, at which distance, a mother would intervene. She couldn't guess. At the edge of a peninsula of a cliff, Millie looked off the edge. It was almost too late. If Jill shouted, she might turn and miss a step and fall backward. But she didn't. She turned as Jill held her breath, and Millie skipped right back to them.

Jill, then Mary went past Millie to look over the edge. A one-lane road led to the base. A bike trip would be heart pounding. A walking stick would be necessary. The trail cascaded around the corners of the cliff. At first sight, anyone would call it dangerous. No one would want to walk back up. A wobble on your ankle, and you would plummet. A wheel hitting the rock the wrong way, and you'd fly for an instant before you hit your end. Right now, no one traveled the dusty gravel path. Not in the heat. Not in the world's dilemma.

It was almost dusk again, and night hovered above the

horizon. They were ready for a rest to take a dip in Never-Sleep. None of them needed it. None of them felt weary as they relaxed. NeverSleep was intriguing, but one must be awake, cognizant, and aware for it. It was the curiosity of it all that led them to delay their trip and know more about this world that they were in. They found the covered patio of the visitor's center and splayed their bodies in whatever shape was comfortable.

CHAPTER 17

A man rustled her shoulder. The stale scent of wet wool on his breath from the well-worn mask made Jill choke a bit. The breaths and wheezes sounded stunted, short, and a bit muffled.

"Was it you turning me to my side all along?" Her groggy words came out low, and she cleared her throat. Her eyes gently peeked toward the sky.

"Ha. Ha. You've had enough NeverSleep. You've had enough shut eye. Don't hog it all," the man said.

Now Jill saw parts of his face and polite demeanor behind the redneck mask he might've snatched from a truck stop gas station. They were like this all over, Jill thought. Jill wasn't sure. The men who drove the deep bellowing coal rollers started out east, they had said, but they invaded everywhere before the Antis melted the polar ice caps. She was sure every one of them fell asleep, didn't take the pill.

But here was this man again. Proving her wrong.

"Who the hell are you?" Jill said, leaning now on her elbows, arms propped upright, as much as the joints would allow.

"Who the hell sleeps on concrete? Ha." His laughs boomed, and he cleared his throat.

"I wasn't sleeping," Jill said. "I was—"

"I bet you weren't," the man said with a slight twisted twang.

The vocal quality said he knew where she had gone. Jill thought at least he would be bitter that the broadcasters were right.

"I have all the cigarettes in the world to smoke now. There are millions on shelves here to Maine. Here to Florida. Here to Mexico. There are millions. And I'm still trying to quit. Hell, nine dollars a pack didn't dissuade me then, and now here I am, taking a few puffs and throwing them out the window. Hell, I'll create a forest fire for sure." He laughed again. "Anyway, I'm trying to quit, not from the nine dollars now, but from the medicine. There is none you see. I can't find a fucking doctor, a sane doctor. Let alone get the chemo I need. That's why we're rebuilding. That's why we need—"

"What'll you do, ruin the whole place again? Why live to kill everyone twice?"

"Look. I'm here to make sure you're safe because we don't have many left. Most people didn't take it. That's what it said. The kids, the elementary kids, yes. The administrators at certain schools snuck it in when the parents weren't expecting it. That's a problem, all the children, yes. But we survived, the four of us and there are other people too. And you just married my baby niece yesterday, and why wasn't I invited?"

"What?" Jill sat up and crossed her legs. She had changed her shirt that morning, but the fresh T-shirt now stunk. A weird taste of metal lingered in her mouth. She figured it was from clamping her jaw. Her tongue on the roof of her mouth tasted bitter every time it touched.

"Look, Mary's over there in NeverSleep. Her … and your daughter … my God your daughter. I suppose theft counts in this day and age." He yawned and lit a butt. "If I wanted to kill you, I would've. But I don't. I want to make sure you're safe. Make sure you make it to the Colony. That's what you want, right?"

"Why did you—"

"You realize I'm an Anti. I was … followed the beliefs, until I learned this remarkable thing called NeverSleep, a rebuilding." He lifted his mask from his face.

Jill swore that she'd seen the face before or sensed the same presence, but she couldn't place it. Had there been Christmas or some other holiday?

"Nope. She never loved me after age fifteen because I was an Anti, what we were before we were Antis." He gave a deep cough, holding his fist in front of his mouth. "I loved her, though. She's the last of our family and we need to stick together. Don't you think?" He took a long drag on his cigarette and exhaled.

"You make it sound so cruel." Jill said.

"I wasn't the angry one, but she sure was angry at me." He spit. "I just want to see you all to safety. It's necessary for my rebuild." Uncle Mark.

"What the hell are you talking about, rebuild?" Jill said.

"We have to rebuild in the NeverSleep. That's where you probably went. I went right away. I really tried to get back to sleep, get to my wife and kids. That's, that's death though and I could. I just got to the vision place. And I built. I built the place I hope will be my own."

"Did we visit?"

"What do you mean?" Uncle Mark said.

"Did we come into the vision?" Jill said.

"I guess not yet. It'll get built though. I'll build it with my eyes closed in NeverSleep to see Mary. To see her on good terms."

"I have to tell Mary," Jill said.

"Not. Just not yet. She's still building."

"How are you sure?" Jill said.

"Because I was there with her before you were done with your daughter's house. See how fast she became your daughter and became part of you. She made you care." He still sucked on the white cancer stick. "It's the same for me. She won't love me. But … when you have no one to care for … Don't snatch her up out of the NeverSleep just yet. I still have to convince you."

Jill scrambled up. "I don't even know you."

He grabbed Jill by the hand and held it stiff. He could've been pleading with her not to go.

She only broke away the hand and stomped toward the Jeep. She kicked the dirt and adjusted her shirt in her pants.

"I mean good. That's all. I want to help," he said.

Jill shook Mary by the shoulder just as the man had shaken her. She opened the car door, and she didn't wake up. Jill had to pull her from deep nowhere, an indescribable black hole of a place. Somewhere you'd never want to leave but never want to go to again for fear you'd find the truth about being or the future. Jill, for Christ's sake, didn't want to go back. She wasn't God.

"Kids can NeverSleep too," he called out.

"Wha—What is it?" Mary was groggy, to say the least. Drool spit out of the corner of her mouth as her head jerked up.

"Oh my. You're a mess," Jill said.

"I thought I heard Uncle Mark? It was so ... And I built a medical center in my dream. I knew about these things I never conceived of hospital machinery, medical techniques. I didn't have to learn it. It was there. All of it. So weird," Mary said.

"Me too ... I mean, I built something, I guess. It was for a good purpose too," Jill said. "Your ... Your Uncle Mark is over there."

"By God. If I wasn't so excited to see anyone, any one person or living thing, I wouldn't give him the time of day ..." She gulped in air. "Is he coming ... That's not really ... Is he coming over ... Don't come over here!"

"Dear. Mary. It's just. You'll know when you're an adult. When your child grows up. When your family intertwines itself so deeply, it hurts. You banished me to the Antis. If you had given me a chance."

"Uncle Mark ... I can't believe ... And she's not my—"

"She's your child now. The kids can NeverSleep too. But they must be monitored, taught. The travelers were right. Hey, cookies work."

"You've been following us?" Mary said.

"You were at our wedding," Jill said.

"Bit of a lie," Uncle Mark said. "Bit by bit. I've just been trying to keep you safe. It was a close call with the children in Andersonville. Closer call with the black truck on the highway. I've done my job."

Millie muddled around in the back of the Tacoma. She was up. Until that point, Millie had been quiet, reserved even. Unaware of what was going on or unable to break through and realize this was really what life was like now. The change might not have sunk in.

But at that moment, the loud shrieks of a child came ringing through.

"They can go there too," Uncle Mark said. "Go to the same place, build. But the Antis warned us about this. They can't understand being builders. They might not understand the purpose or implications. Children just don't understand the weight of it all."

Mary patted the girl's head, rubbed her arms to quell the disturbance that was developing because of the anger in all their voices.

"The Antis knew? All this. They had … intelligence?" Jill said.

"Fucking propaganda. Their intelligence is a crock of shit. And there's no way. I'm not any more than anyone else," Mark said.

"Yes. They knew. And yes, you'll know. We're building 2045," Mark said.

"If they understood the choice," Jill quizzed. "Why did they fail to take the NeverSleep pill?"

"Because of you … Because you were taking it … Because it'd be populated. The world would be populated by people with liberal beliefs. If they couldn't kill you all, they'd kill themselves." Uncle Mark walked back, turned, and kicked dirt. Then, he pulled a full stride and kicked dirt again. He danced along over the hill and neither Jill nor Mary stopped him with a yell or a motion. They both looked to a slightly calmed Millie, whose had her cries quelled when adults spoke over her noise, which was the very loudest she could make. It was still not loud enough to squash the voices of the adults.

"Hang a left at Albuquerque …" Uncle Mark bit into the air. "You rascally rabbits."

"Bugs bunny reruns. We used to watch them …" she said. "It is everything to breathe in and pull a genuine memory from childhood. But I will never ever forgive that man."

"Even if he was one of the last men on the planet?" Jill said.

Mary slid deep in her seat and shrunk her shoulder over her body, leaning in on the steering wheel. "You'll never guess what I dreamed," Mary said.

"Oh. I remember. And it wasn't a dream. You were a builder, right? Did you hear some of what your uncle said? Did what he said resonate? The NeverSleep," Jill paused. "Is just meant for the last few living. To build. To be something. To make the next world. I guess. I guess that's what it is now.

We're making the next world."

"Something I did as an Architectural Designer, but something I never thought I had the ability to do in my sleep."

"Millie, do you want to go for a walk?" Jill said. "Maybe to the potty in the enormous building?"

"No, I don't have to go," Millie said calmly. "I just want to be with you two. But no yelling. It makes my ears hurt when adults yell." She smiled and adjusted herself in her seat. "Is everything gone?" she said.

"Well. Things are different," Jill said. "But we still have to learn about each other. You trust us, right?"

"I guess. There isn't anyone else to trust."

Her words were wise somehow and Jill twisted her body back and sat back in the passenger seat, pulled her arms to her sides. What had they done abducting a child? "Saving" her for the world. One step at a time, she thought. This universe. This whole dreamland was one step at a time.

"Millie. Do you want to go home?" Jill said because she had to say it.

"No. No. We're going to see my parents, right? They'll ground Joey," Millie said.

The confusion took Jill off guard. "No. I'm sorry."

Mary flung her arm across Jill's chest and whispered, "No."

"Yes. Oh my. We'll see your parents there and your brother, too." Jill said. A sharp tear left the corners of her dry eyes. It was likely from stress and no sadness. But the situation with Millie was tragically sad. Her life would never be the same. Neither would any of those children's lives be the same.

"Alright," Mary said, swiftly changing the topic. "We have one day's long drive to get to the Colony."

"The Colony. I've been there," Millie said. "It's really great. With a gigantic dome in the very center. You can look at stars. It really is something. Dad is so proud. He showed us pictures."

"Your dad is at the Colony?" Mary stared deep into the girls' eyes with tunneling seriousness.

"Yes. He works there. He comes home. Sometimes. But he hasn't come home in a long while," Millie said.

Mary leaned into Jill. "This really could be our godsend."

Mary cocked her head and gave a quizzical look, "You didn't, really. Jill, we're not parents. Never were, never will be."

"There is adoption." A scowl lit Jill's face.

"Look. We'll take her to her dad. There's only one Colony. That's what the broadcasts said." Mary scratched her forearm and started the car.

"Don't you want to go for a hike?" Jill said.

"No, not really. It's an apocalypse after all. I just wanted to see it one last time. Be in this place one last time." Jill sighed and closed her eyes. "Remember, we wanted to get married here. Real married on a rock top or something. In cool weather. Was that the sentiment?"

"When it was legal," Jill pouted a bit, frowning at her face. "You are right about that. This was our place, a safe place. We've done all these hikes."

"No need to do them again. I just wanted to find that moment we had, years ago when we committed verbally to being together, girlfriends, partners, lovers, whatever we were we didn't have a name for it, but we had a bond." Mary turned the key in the car, and it started. She let it idle a bit before and rested her hands in her lap.

"Well, did you find it?" Jill said.

"No. It's always been there," Mary said. "I just needed to hear it loud. Ring from the past, sort of. But confirmed. Yes, I still have it. That emotion. That departure from myself bringing you in. It was loud yesterday at the waterfall too. Confirmed here today. I felt the past and kindled the idea. It should last several more years. But this heat is horrible. This dry, dry heat will kill us if we hike."

And then they were moving again, cruising along at a clip.

CHAPTER 18

The sun peaked above the horizon. They shuffled along on the trip that should've taken about eighteen hours. It took three days. Derailed several times, they consistently found themselves behind schedule. They had to stage a wedding. They expected that first day to be easy. The stop in the small town in Colorado was a several hour detour. Intermixed were several stops where they explored the NeverSleep. The incident with the black truck and Uncle Mark really tested patience. Uncle Mark had delayed them twice. The trip was taking longer than expected.

They had made stops every two to four hours to not tax the Tacoma or the Jeep at the beginning. There they fell into conversation or NeverSleep, which seemed to stall things as much as if they had to actually sleep. It was testing their patience, minds, and schedule.

They had stopped for supplies, picked up road flares and food twice at gas stations. Road flares were Jill's weapon of choice. They still didn't have a gun, and they both believed it was best without one, especially because of Millie.

So many delays had led them to being behind schedule. They should've been at the Colony by now, and luck might not be on their side if the place was full up with residents. They had not planned for a situation in which a room wasn't available. Jill cursed their pace and selves for not caring. Not hurrying as fast as possible. The place was almost upon them, and they didn't even have their ducks in a row. A few photos on a camera seemed like a prayer to save them now.

They stopped again after three hours. They leaned back thirsty for the NeverSleep. It was a new and exciting place of reckoning. In this place, they could find and create the future. They were in California, the late great state. Coastal towns likely washed away. San Francisco was probably devastated.

Jill wondered if anyone would travel this far out. California has a new coast. She wasn't sure how far anyone could go out. The water was probably still creeping into the land. The climate hadn't fully turned yet, but they felt the heat. It might be a matter of days, revolutions, before the earth became what it would become. It had been simulated, but they hadn't really seen it. Jill stared out looking for the coastline. She had no news of what had happened.

At a far-off cliff on the rocky ground, Jill saw a figure. She wasn't sure if it was Uncle Mark covered in camo. The orange woven into the greens and grays stuck out, and she perked up. He was probably the only living person left in the world covered in camo. Mary's uncle stood before them. Jill didn't shout out. She didn't cough or inhale. She didn't want to upset Mary. She didn't want to change the mood. Jill genuinely believed he wanted to see them to safety. In a way, Jill relaxed. This man would watch out as the three of them drifted into the NeverSleep.

They each had a blanket they didn't need and a pillow on which to rest their heads.

Mary was out first, into her world. She must be so happy, Jill thought, to conceive something like this, as an Architectural Designer, to design the world and give hope to the planet. She used her design skills to think critically about what an entirely new world would be.

The billowing of smoke in the far distance seemed to drift over towards them.

Millie turned to Jill and said, "Uncle Mark?"

Jill smiled and breathed out through her lips. "Yup. A guardian angel, of sorts. Only Mary doesn't love him again yet. She will, though. She'll love him again."

"I think so too," the young girl chided. Then, she fell silent.

Still, Jill did not close her eyes. She couldn't find the place she wanted. She wanted more control, more remembrance. If anything was unbridled, it was NeverSleep. A person could get stuck in there. It contained. Jill wondered what it would be like to refuse to build, refuse to contribute. But then she remembered her motivation in the last NeverSleep. She built this young girl a home for the future, and it stood so beautiful. The reality was questionable. Maybe she never would understand. But she had to believe. She was doing good, and that motivated her.

Hands clasped over stomach, again flat on her back, Jill drifted. Her eyes shut. Her eyelids were hundred-pound weights in weak hands. They would never lift. Uncle Mark way up in the distance would watch out.

The billowing black smoke parted ever so gently onto a stage; a play started. She blew a deep breath at the red curtains, fringed in bound tassels. Similar to the steam of a train, it entranced, and like the engulfing power of Uncle Mark's truck, it warned. With Jill's gentle breath, she parted the powerful currents of smoke.

The heaviness of the world rested on Jill's gut. Her hands patted her center. With arms stretched wide, she flopped on the cement. Or was it soil for regrowth, the birth fluid of the world? As she dug her nails in, she lifted, weightless in this half world, one that she knew would be.

Jill crawled to her knees to prolong things, to linger on her thoughts before she got to work. Instinctively, compelled, she built.

Her eyebrows flinched, and she bucked them up and out in a direction and there a building surfaced. She saw the paned windows uniform along the sides. The school building grew upward, brick by brick, as she watched.

Hovering, crossing her arms, a roughly powerful being, Jill fell into this place. Her head darted to the left and the glass house centered in her view. The house was the one she thought about when she was out of NeverSleep. One that would drop straight down to the foundation if the glass broke if an earthquake hit. Had she made the right decision?

She followed the work with her eyes, almost laser glares that beaded and built, like a 3-D printer with an automated computer program. She saw the things that should go together, and she put them there at the same time. Her knowledge grew and her mind expanded to possibilities. This world was new and vacant, a dusty dirt beckoned growth, green, a sense of nurturing and softness against jagged edges, devastation wrought landscapes.

Floating in water so clear it wasn't there, Jill hovered like an airless being, only a spirit to navigate her, a will to build something she instinctively knew would eventually be there. This other world grew to be a playground, but she could only work. Her calling, the motivation that permeated the air, encouraged her, demanded she build this place.

Her head shook and stopped, even though her eyes still moved back and forth. When the lips popped open, forced with all her might, she found Mary and Millie awake and eating peanut butter crackers.

"You all are going to regret eating peanut butter all this time when there's nothing left except soon to be expired two-year-old peanut butter," Jill said.

"Is that all you have to say?" Mary positioned her head over her shoulder to look at Jill and then jerked it back as if she and Millie were playing a game or were deep in discussion.

She casually turned back to Jill, who rubbed her eyes trying to get her memories of NeverSleep back.

"Did you do good?" Mary said. "Did you do something good?"

"I think so. With my mind, I built a university. Millie will go there, so she'll have some place to go to school. It was right down the street from the glass house," Jill said. She arched her back, waking up like she had never done before.

"You?" Jill grabbed the wheat bread.

"Yes. I built it, glorious. A dream like I've never had. I acted as a leader and a designer. All the things happened at my will, all in an empowering, almost scary way," Mary said. She coughed into her hand to clear her throat.

"What was Millie's NeverSleep like?" Jill said.

"She wrote books," Mary said. "Can you believe it? Somehow, she had the gusto. Children's books from what I gathered. Someone, something, must've helped her. A prodigy?"

"This NeverSleep leaves us with so many questions. Things I'm afraid we'll never be able to answer," Jill said. She chucked dusty rocks at the tires of the truck.

"Tell me about your uncle, Mary," Jill said.

"Oh. He was great when we were kids, before we talked politics," Mary said. "I loved him. I really did. He was like … better to me than my dad. He would yell at my dad and tell him to treat me better. I was always cleaning up after Dad. The cans of beer lying around. You know how it is. To have a dad who's an alcoholic, but not really. He'd take days off and then binge. It was difficult, the yelling. But on the holidays and special weekends, Uncle Mark would come over for dinner or to hang out. He'd have one beer. Okay … okay … occasionally two. Anyway, he tried to be a good example, you know."

"I can't say I wish I knew what it was like …" Jill said. "You had it rough. You had parents, though. A loving uncle. I get it. Having my brother, that was all I really needed, someone, one person, to care."

"Really, I know, but Uncle Mark started talking politics. He eased into it at first, but then he talked about it all the time. He threw words around about the end of the world. Things to come. The overseers. Weird shit. It was all conservative based propaganda. The coming of the next Jesus, even. When we butted heads, it was about abortion or social justice or, or even the death penalty … climate change. We never agreed partially, let alone completely. We never ever talked about gay rights. It would've killed me to know what he really thought." Mary said.

Jill took a big swig of water. They weren't hungry as much anymore. Jill chalked it up to stress. This new world. But for a second, she thought the hunger had dissipated as it did on that morning several days ago, when she woke up. She was an entirely different person. She was without the tension of the real world, but now had a tension from the world she was in.

Hunger only came from habit, she thought, and there was no longer habit. It was all new. Every step she took, she was a new person, in a new life to live. For a second, Jill thought she might be all-knowing, unable to eat because she was a divine being. But weren't they all divine? Didn't they all build, even Millie? And because of that, they were all equally working toward a cause. There couldn't be one that was the One. And isn't that what religion is, defining the One?

She needed water in this place. This second coming for them all, wasn't one hundred percent real. Conservatives spun it a different way. The whole thing was a fabrication, something in between. A mid-way for each side who thought about this, what was next, the NeverSleep. Not what she expected, not what she preached, not something really anyone imagined. But the water she needed. Jill proved to be indeed alive, a mortal, because she needed water. Only time would tell when their lives would be finished. When some blood hungry Anti, some wild animal extremely angry with its own tension, or a child, Christ a child, would take them down, put them away, kill them, make them a builder unable to build.

CHAPTER 19

Jill dusted off the seat of her pants and watched a gecko scurry under a rock. It made its pit stop right where she had just been sitting. Did he NeverSleep? Did animals build for animals and humans for humans? That question was as futile as the rest.

At the car, she wrestled with her t-shirt, changing. She slipped off her pants and underwear switching them out. She stunk. A shower was in order whenever they got to where they were going. After another hour on the road, she tried to gather her thoughts. She fidgeted with the pockets of her new jeans, fumbled, and turned them inside out. She was irritable, she knew, and weary.

Mary came over to her and rubbed her back in comfort. "It'll be okay," she said. "They'll take us in. I know they will."

They kissed briefly and Jill's rosy cheeks glowed as Millie stared at them. She thought nothing of it. Not a peep or a question. She just watched and sat back, back with her magazine, now folding pages, amusing herself as the day grew hotter. It was almost 8:00 a.m., and the Jeep would have to climb for several hours into the mountains to get to their destination, where they were going or bust.

"The Antis though. What if they're all Antis? Or if their philosophy really carried into liberal minds like the broadcasts said at the end. That the liberal minds, the president even, were rethinking minor political stances, marriage equality, abortion, and interracial marriage included, so that everyone who took the NeverSleep pill could live together," Jill said.

"He was basically a moderate from the beginning. Aren't all presidents … a simple push over to moderate to get what they really want … besides a smidge of power," Mary said. "What if it's true?"

"We have our photos. That's what they said they needed to prove marriage. Photos of a marriage certificate or a photo.

That was on the last broadcast. We must prove our sanctity or something. Prove committed love. It was gibberish at that point," Jill said.

"It could've been the Antis themselves," Mary said. "But we don't even have the prints."

"We'll … We'll …" Jill said, thinking. "It's an old camera. They won't check the metadata. Honestly, there're snowboarding photos on this card from almost a decade ago."

The car chugged up the winding hill. The roadmap they peeled open held the exact spot marked days earlier after the second to last broadcast. They had said it like that. "This is the second to last broadcast. Everyone will be assigned their NeverSleep pill in three days. We have last instructions for you, so listen closely …"

Some people surely went straight there to talk to the scientists and have questions answered, a last-ditch effort to know, to do nothing and live. Jill stayed home. She could've curled up in a ball and died, but there she was in the mourning like they promised each other on the phone, starting life over again. Mary came. She had taken the pill like they said they would. She had fulfilled her promise and Jill, as stubborn about moving as she was, took to the road with Mary. They had come this far.

Jill watched Millie look out the back window, her teeth chattering on a narrow bit of metal against the window. She looked longingly for something. Jill imagined Millie's mother and father, Millie's similar experiences. Millie missed her parents. Jill knew that. But she had barely asked for them. Millie seemed, as she looked out the window, to hope her dad puttered around somewhere. In some ways, Jill hoped Millie's dad mulled around ready to leave. In other ways, she selfishly hoped he had died. Jill needed someone to take care of, someone to stand next to her for eternity, as long as she would ever live, alongside Mary or not. If the ferocious agreements or constant bickering came back, she hoped there would still be someone, a child.

"I know dad is here," Millie mumbled out past the window, talking to no one.

"I'm sure he is, honey," Mary said. "We'll find him." Mary

was upbeat and looking in various directions. Jill imagined that this was because both of them were excited to be at the end.

At the top of the hill, chaos ensued. Not the chaos Jill expected: people going to market from the outskirts like in a feudal kingdom, or professionals busy at work on robotics that would save the world. Neither of these things, these scenarios, were true.

The world proved devastated. A blank canvas to be rebuilt, by someone, by someone's NeverSleep.

Jill and Mary held hands as they walked toward the rubble, miles and miles of it. They asked Millie to wait in the car, rest while the adults checked things out. A slight murmur, "Dad." The words sounded hollow and full of despair.

Mary kneeled and picked up a rock that mimicked a moon rock in form and shape. The chunky, rounded block had no evenness. And it dimpled, like the face of the moon. The hard chunk wasn't a moon rock though, and this place, the most innovative place in the world, wouldn't be their last stop.

"This didn't fall from heaven," Mary said. "The most promising plan to get to safety is a pile of rubble. The Colony is gone."

They roamed for over a half hour looking for people, but they only found debris. Electronics were all trashed. Buttons were strewn here and there. Components, large processors, were mangled and smashed. Every bit of everything taken to with a baseball bat after a bomb went off. It might be irreversible. Not a shred could be saved. Nothing there proved useable, even if intact.

The abyss stretched for miles. They'd never cover all the ground. No one was left; No one was left alive. "They must've gotten out," Jill said. "But where did they go?"

A thick fog cascaded over the outskirts of what might've been a side door, an entry to an once dome-covered palace, hundreds of football fields big. A frame with shattered glass and the shards perfectly spaced were almost an ich apart, still in place. Translucent stained glass with opaque lead cames glistened. This wasn't a church. This place of safety wouldn't save them.

He spun in circles feet from where they stood. "Yahoo, he

heard them holler." All the Antis trucks were the same, but this one was certainly Uncle Mark's.

"Have some reverence," Mary shouted.

He held the car in neutral and as he crept backward down a slight slope; he gunned the engine for effect. "Look at the cars dancing."

"This is not a fortunate thing, Uncle Mark," Mary said.

"I'm just trying to lift spirits," he said.

"We have a girl in the car who is going to spiral into a cathartic shock once it registers her father is dead," Jill said.

"Not necessarily," Uncle Mark said. He held out three tickets. "For the NeverSleep Colony Red."

"What?" Mary said. "Uncle Mark, what do you mean?"

"Well. I've been there. You all are slow drivers. I went there and I'm back now … to get you," Uncle Mark said.

"Um. You only have three—" Jill said. She knew Mary couldn't say it.

"I'll take you there. But kids are more important. There's somewhere for me to go. I can be with the Antis or on my own. I hear the Rocky's will stay quite cool for a bit," Uncle Mark said.

They all three sat down when Millie came over to them, hopped out of the car. Jill wanted to be at eye level.

"We think your dad is safe. At another location," Jill said.

She was drying tears from her eyes that had streamed minutes ago. "Does he still love me?" Millie said.

"Oh hush. I know he does. You'll see him soon," Mary said.

Jill grabbed bottles of water from the truck and sat cross-legged with the group.

"What I wouldn't give for a camp chair," Mary said.

And Uncle Mark laughed. Mary held her head to his shoulder. "Why are you sometimes so good?"

"It took a lot for you to break away from me. It was that one last remark about your girlfriend that did it," Uncle Mark said.

"Yup. That was it," Mary laughed slightly. "You're so … You don't believe them, do you?"

"When you live a certain way for so long, at least for me, and your ideas change … What I'm trying to say is that you live the way you live, look the way you look, but you can change your mind. You don't have to be the same person all your life," Uncle Mark said.

"But you were with the Antis three years ago. At a protest. I saw you in D.C. It was you," Mary said.

"Think of me as a spy, if you will," Uncle Mark said. "I'm a follower, yes, but I'm also a leader with my mind. If I ever could've changed a mind, I would've."

Jill listened from what might as well have been a far-off corner. Both of them, Mary and Uncle Mark, looked at her, tipped their heads and returned to the conversation.

"But you walked the walk …" Mary said.

"I always loved you, and I never forgot your words, 'If you leave without saying you love the way I am, you'll never see the real me again,'" Uncle Mark said. "I guess I'm always looking for you. The real you. It's … it's from regret though that I accept people, everyone I meet."

Mary leaned in and hugged him. She wrapped lanky arms around his torso and sucked him in with a shrugging breath. "I love you," she spouted. Tears followed in light drops.

"I had friends on both sides, honey, but my ideals are in line with yours now. It's me trying to make up for what I wasn't. What I couldn't be," Uncle Mark said.

Jill penetrated Mark's eyes, even though he didn't look back. She tried to gauge his sincerity. The ability for a loved one to royally screw another over existed, she knew that. But was Mark as cold and cruel as an older brother trying to lure someone into an investment, or a son taking money from his grandmother to buy drugs, or a college kid spending way too much of her parent's money for that matter?

He didn't look back but flinched and his face shuttered over and then back to Mary on a lingering stare, a plea for acceptance. She was in the room. She was valid, and she saw a telltale lie, an obvious one at least.

"Do you intend to take us somewhere with paper tickets? Somewhere to live for the rest of our lives."

"Uh. Yeah. It's a wonderful place. I went in as a visitor. I hear they are still building. They learn about something and then they rebuild and make it better." Uncle Mark cast his eyes down and looked sullen. He really seemed to be convinced. But Jill was still skeptical. The things the Antis said were twisting, felt full of anger, but these sentiments he bore were even-tempered with no purpose. It was as if he had forgotten about the tickets altogether.

The three dimpled and creased pieces of paper rested on the dusty ground beside him.

"What are those made of, anyway?" Jill said.

"Parchment, I guess," Mark said. "It's the constitution actually," His voice raised, and his eyes lit up. "They chopped it up ... nothing more official."

"Well, I'll be ..." Mary said.

She reached for the tickets and flipped them over. Sure enough, Jill saw the unique but distinctive cursive writing and the weight of the paper. "Who would ever rip up the Constitution?" Mary said.

"The world is essentially over. The government ... well it's essentially—"

"Because of the Antis," Mary said.

Uncle Mark broke in, "What you're thinking ... Old Uncle Mark up to no good ..."

"Yes. That's exactly what I'm thinking," Mary said. "Jill you too?" She bucked her head up and at Jill. A tear drop formed with the reality of it all. The stress.

"Look, I'll prove it." He went back to his big black truck and ruffled some papers in the back, took out a SD card.

"Put this in your camera," he said, stomping back over to the group.

Mark's hair was unkempt, and he looked increasingly like an urban soldier in a post-apocalyptic world, a refugee from a failed government overthrow. The hairs thinned out on the top of his head near the forehead. Even below, the dirt of the burned world dusted him. His shirt had stains of greasy food and oil, maybe from his car or when he got gas in portable cans. The ones that rested on the side of his truck.

What strange cultish trucks they were. Individuals didn't ride in trucks like this. One of the Anti-trucks that popped up all over the country. Thousands of dollars of investment in a particular type of truck, spray painted with matte spray paint, marked you either in debt to the cultish mob or an outright member willing to help others. The thousands of dollars spent rigging up the bellows for the smoke marked you as holding a certain ideology … in case you weren't sure. You were basically on board the boats going to the arctic, even if it took another few years until they were ready. The one that would blow up the ice caps.

"Okay. Okay. I was at the attempted insurrection, and I stayed. It was really nothing. There weren't enough of them. They'd all gone to the sea or were too scared to lose their lives. Little did they realize their political faith would kill them months later. If they had only taken the pill. If they had only seen with clear, undistorted eyes." Uncle Mark dipped his head. "Somehow, I could see," he pointed toward Mary, but spoke to Jill. "Because she made me question my values against those of someone I loved. Someone I couldn't leave behind for my beliefs. I take everything with a grain of salt. I guess I guessed right on the NeverSleep," Uncle Mark said.

"Did you?"

"I stayed when they collapsed the capitol on purpose, sealed everything off. I helped."

"In that camo outfit?" Mary said.

"Yeah, in this same outfit. The administration was funneling people out to cars and convoys going west. This was two months before regular people reached to take the pills. Everyone staying and helping received compensation via tickets to the Colony. God called out their names for a few days of help to have a place to live, even though others would die," Uncle Mark said.

"A reward for loyalty," Jill said.

"We." The first word held emphasis. "Are very lucky."

Jill switched out the SD card with the wedding one and knocked on the camera a few times. "So, the other hope they gave over the broadcast was false hope."

"In a way." Uncle Mark's eyes cast down.

"Here we go. Something might be up with the battery."

"Here, let me see there might be dirt in there," Mary went to grab the camera, but Jill pulled away.

"Let me look." Jill scrolled through the photos with Mary

looking over her shoulder. They saw the president and congresspeople. An official at a podium with a gigantic set of long scissors.

"This is ridiculous."

"Everyone had to tunnel out something. Everyone got something to take on the road. Some took precious works of art. Someone got the president's dog. Can you believe it? Caring for the President's dog. He must've been worried sick." Uncle Mark shook his head. "I just asked for proof, robbed a photographer, begged for an SD card. Because you wouldn't believe me. There's no reason you should."

"Uncle Mark." Mary ran toward him and wrung her arms around his neck. "It's just—" She kissed him on the cheek, pet his head as if he were weary from a long trip or travels.

"I wouldn't have believed me either," he said.

"We … It's so different now. Who can you trust?"

They sat back down, and Jill chugged a bit of water, hoping they would continue to talk their issues out. She averted her eyes and looked off over a ridge top. The scene really was so beautiful. She thought the feud was resolved but wanted the two blood relatives to talk it out a bit more, in case one of them should die in this wilderness or get stabbed by a rabid child, get a flat tire, and run out of food. There were, of course, likely still Antis out here. An attack at any moment threatened them all. Someone willy nilly took a pill, hoping for death. Jill was sure.

"We're only eight hours away. Montana, here we come," Uncle Mark said.

Uncle Mark ditched the truck. They all agreed it labeled him an Anti and wouldn't do him or the group any good. Jill and Mary crawled into the cab and shot stares at each other.

Was this the happy family they thought they could have? Was this setting ridiculous, out of a dream, something never to be conceived or imagined? Jill was happy because they were all together, possibly the three most important people to her now and really since forever. Since her brother went to Europe and Jill headed for the hills. She wondered where he would be now. Possibly in the Alps or some other skiing territory, skiing away the days until the snow fully melted.

She knew her family now. Not like she ever imagined. Not like a sense of family cultivated in normal times. It would take years. Under stress, though, people morph, emotions run high, and Jill wasn't sure why bonds wouldn't run thicker.

Her job at the ski resorts was monotonous, person after person on the lifts and gondolas in her twenties. Each with their own anonymity. Some rode with total strangers, sharing a grasp of intimacy. As much as they wrenched out of her partner or as much small talk as she mustered. Either or. She didn't much care about herself, who she rode up with. Her whole life, she preferred it to be a stranger. Because what were two friends, two lovers, even to say to each other when engaging in a sport meant for solitary motion? There really was nothing much to say except that the sky was beautiful. The chill of the air is so crisp. The next day might not be as pretty. Jill took hold of every day as if it were the last of the season. Nothing else in the summer tempted her except the next year.

Looking out the window, she tried to feel that chill of the air, not even in the mountains of California. And now, they would go to Montana. Montanish, Mark had said. It was a place without a name. It was simply down a dirt road. Climbing might be involved.

Uncle Mark and Millie sat in the back, discussing the merits of the England's response to the devastation in the United States. For them, the new beginning was a new day for England to rise and take the lead as it had when America was born. Again, now, when America was dying, they would look to be a leader.

"The world is dying, though," Millie said. "The universe. The ice is melting."

"Unfortunately, yes. But we are going to find safety," Uncle Mark said.

"The two of them are quick friends," Jill whispered to Mary. "It'll all be new. It's all new still. She's still in shock from losing everyone."

"She's a kid and recovers. She is certainly keeping her sadness in," Mary said. "What was it like for you?"

"I was a little older, but it struck hard. It was like I had a cloud over me for months, then years. I'd look up and it would rain, but God damn it, it was never sunny. The world, to me, was constantly dark. It wasn't until I was older that I pushed the emotions away. When I was equal in independence with my peers. When they weren't grounded or on probation for staying out late, we were equals. Things I had gotten to do. Things that kept me alive, shaped me." Jill said, leaning onto Mary's shoulder. She rested her head on her thin brushed flannel shirt. "Did you pick this because it's a post-apocalyptic world? It seems to fit the fashion."

"Really? She jumped back into her seat. I mean. I am a flannel girl," Mary said.

"Not always so often," Jill chuckled.

"This is a new day. It's a day we need to confront with some extra padding and a little stretchable comfort. All while still being fashionable," Mary said.

CHAPTER 20

The world reeled, frame by frame going by, as Jill looked out the window. The scenery included a desolate rocky cliff followed by a barren flat of land, pebbles mounting in patterns that didn't quite resemble cairns. If they could see clearly on solid ground, they could make that cairn a marker for where they had been and likely would never return.

All three of the passengers played games with Millie. The alphabet game, where they found letters on billboards and road signs, mostly the names of places and things. They were stuck on Z. It tore the life out of Millie not to find it. So much so that when they saw a used car lot, Mary pulled off the road and looked for an Isuzu or a Suzuki. Wide eyed and bushy tailed, she sailed into the lot, almost as vacant as the earth seemed to be. Down a dirt road, the proprietors had stacked cars in piles. The four of them in the car stopped to gawk. By God, when Millie found that Z on the trooper, Jill cried. The earth was so desolate now. Millie might've asked what they were doing there or screamed the letter. Millie must've picked the latter because the smart and precocious child already knew the answer to the former. No one in the car had to even say I spy.

Mark wrapped his arms around Mary from the back seat. They were in a happy place again. They were family. It was her touch that made Jill realize this fact. A touch made without backing away. The way Mary eased into Mark's shoulder warmed Jill's heart. She thought Mary's might've warmed too. The uncle and niece would be together as long as possible.

Jill wondered if Mary would try to rehome Millie, so that Mark could have the ticket. It was her apprehension. To build new things, to build a place to live in NeverSleep, is one thing, but to choose between lives, to let one die or let them go into danger, is completely another. Jill put herself a little more down to earth when she recognized this. They would discuss it, talk it out. They would find a resolution.

Mark could survive for some time in the wild, Jill was sure. But that didn't justify switching Millie. But Millie might die like a million other children already had. Was Mark's maybe 60% chance of survival alone worth a 90% survival rate for Millie in the colony?

Jill watched and wondered. The ideas were something that escaped her. She couldn't vocalize her worry or concern.

They all bonded and played with Millie's marble. She told them it was her mother, and everyone should treat it as such. It glistened in the sun. The prism uncharacteristically placed made it the most beautiful thing on the earth. They each said so as they carefully passed it around and introduced themselves to Millie's mom.

When they stopped in Nevada, Jill was weary of Life. As the radio broadcast said, you would be in NeverSleep when you were ready, needed to recharge. The trio talked about how they best prepared themselves for NeverSleep. What conditions suited them? What could improve the experience?

Uncle Mark flaunted the fact that he had some secrets, and they all batted down the idea that he, a man among the Antis, could know more than them, have figured everything out already.

The cushions of the car were more comfortable than the ground. Yet, they all bedded down on the hard ground, lay flat on their backs, because that was what Jill had done and that had given her the best luck in the NeverSleep. The car seats molded their butts and thighs into sculptures that couldn't shake the shape.

"Where are we going this time?" Mary said.

"Wherever it takes you, I guess," Jill said nonchalantly.

"If we are rebuilding. How do we approach it?" Mary said.

"I'm not sure yet. I need more sessions. More NeverSleep experience," Jill said. "I found when I'm building, it goes much too slow. It's hard to move things one by one. It takes a while to build a building, right? If we are to rebuild the planet, if that's at least what we think we're doing, we should do it much faster … if we are to ever survive." Her voice cracked because it was true.

"I still wonder why you can move things more quickly than me." Mary muttered out the words and balled her fists.

"I could tell you why, but you wouldn't ever believe me," Uncle Mark said. He sat in the back seat. Arms relaxed from Mary's shoulders. He squeezed them and sat back. The edges of his mouth curved up. His choppy sentences became shorter, more mysterious because he either did not know or knew it would kill them all.

"Then don't tell us." Mary threw an empty soda bottle as her jovial uncle decided that they were no longer on temperamental terms.

"Alright, but you're going to ask when you wake up," Mark said. "Just grab something and hold on. See where it takes you. What triggers the brain lives. It's pure thought. Its emotion turned solid. You'll see."

***

Jill relaxed into NeverSleep. She even held onto her makeshift go-bag with some tools and food to see if it would follow her in. The bag did not appear when NeverSleep started. She could create all the things she needed, exact replicas in NeverSleep. She reflected on who she was here, a powerful woman able to build. Much like her Architectural Designer lover … spouse … wife, she created things.

She looked for her wife at the house she built. It was an easy fuzz of the eyes, wiggle of the body, head to toe, and she was there. She built the glass house just a few days ago for her love and her new focus, Millie. Millie's school was still down the block. She would need to learn to be a person in this new world. Stab-ready yard tools and blunt force objects wouldn't help her survive once real life started going, once Colony Red prospered.

As hard as she looked, she couldn't find Mary. She was sure that she would meet her there. They had discussed it beforehand … Find the glass house, find the school. Surely, she could navigate.

In a feverish moan she heard in Life, she recounted all the places she could be. She went to the school and searched the halls. She found a woman she barely recognized as a friend from her childhood, just before her parents died. She died too, just after Jill's parents, and it doubled over her pain.

"Katy," Jill said. "Is that you? My God, you must be the same age as me."

"I'm here, Jill, and I'm part of NeverSleep. I've aged just like you, but here on the other side. They call me a Think of sorts, part of the think tank, a panel of souls. I help solve problems. I want to save the earth from children, unbelievably." She laughed a bit and then produced a toothy grin. "You have a gift, Jill, to build this school. Most people can build to suit their needs, but this you build for others in complexity and precision. It's astounding," Katy said.

"I need more help," Jill said. "I can't do it on my own."

"You must build others to help," Katy said.

"Build others," Jill said. "What does that even mean? How can you build others?"

"Like you built me just now," Katy said. She turned to walk away. "Imagine it to be. You will find it. Find us. There are others looking for your NeverSleep to live on this other side. I'll live here now, Jill. I'll be here for you when you need me. When you want to catch up. But for now, you must build. See Mark. He'll help you build. He knows." And then she walked away, into a cloudy hallway just outside of her hazy vision, despite Jill's eyes staring, beading at her every move until all motion disappeared.

✳✳✳

Mary searched with her eyes fuzzed over, wiggling her body more than necessary to find, imagine, the glass house. It escaped her. What seemed like hours passed, and she was stuck by herself in NeverSleep, unsure how to get out. She didn't have the same acuity in this place, even with her architectural training and skills. Jill was a natural. She would help save the earth.

Mary was still searching for something when she partially came to. In the NeverSleep, she had traveled the world. She saw New York drown. Someone worked on a new dock, small and unassuming, about mid-way into Pennsylvania. She saw Kansas and a huge dome, a modern innovation, it appeared, that might stand the test of time. In a flash, she was in Minneapolis where the weather had turned deadly hot, muggy, and unbearable. To Mary, in NeverSleep, it was nothing. It didn't bother the random people she saw. Connection was not possible. She couldn't feel them or see the quiet in the bright light. No one saw her either. The wash of a dream made her entirely alone all at once.

Mary gasped for air and fell out of the NeverSleep, still searching, grabbing Jill's hand, and going directly back in. Jill didn't even stir.

When Mary reentered, Jill was there with her. They were together and smiled through a garbled bubble of water of a dream. They kissed.

"I found you," Mary said. The bliss grew, and it was more satiating than any other sense, to be surrounded by hope and building a new place, to be safe from the dark realties of the world, to be with the one she loved.

When they let go in NeverSleep, they let go in life and woke up turning to each other for another kiss.

"I missed you," Jill said.

"I was only gone a minute," Mary said. "We're here now, forever."

***

"I thought … I found a friend of mine, an old friend, not in age, but you know from childhood," Jill said. "She's dead now. She died incredibly young. It was exhilarating and sweet and she had so much to say to me in so little time. It all ran together a bit."

Mary cut in, "You mean Katy? You've talked so much about her over the years. That same Katy?"

"I always wondered what she would be like when she grew up, and, well, she was different that I expected," Jill said.

"Was she old? Did you dream about her?" Mary said.

"I think I might've." Jill suddenly fainted, lay back down. Weakness spilled throughout her body.

"You know when you do it. You waste your own energy. A person gives something, saves something … but also loses something. You must've done something really fantastic, from what I can tell." He smiled a glowing smile from his spot. Uncle Mark sat on the ground, legs crossed in front of him, picking the skin off an orange that might've been a day or two too ready for the trash.

"You can build things. You can become a builder. You can create, imagine people." Uncle Mark said. "Find a shred of something to do it. A shred of a soul or a person's prized possession. Some link."

"I don't think I created her, though. It was really her. All along she lived in the NeverSleep," Jill said. "It was really her, but I thought about her. She appeared."

"The last thing you can do in NeverSleep is fix problems. The last thing … I don't know quite how it works. If you can imagine a think tank, a political congregation of people created to fix problems. People that never go out into society, so they aren't influenced. Like a cabinet of confidants, an entire group of Thinks. Find them, that's all I know. They took the NeverSleep pill, and you'll find them. They are not builders, but you'll need them too."

"Your wise old owls are cut off from society?" Mary said. "Anyone removed from society can't really understand anything."

"First off, they're not my owls and second, they know things and you should seek them out."

"Look, I'm not here to play God or save the planet. This is getting too heavy. We have to find this place. This Colony Red. They'll direct us there. I'm not going rouge. If I'm going to play builder, or whatever it is, I want some direction," Mary said.

"Fair enough, Mary," Uncle Mark said. "But that one." He pointed at Jill. "She has a powerful NeverSleep and might be the one to save us all."

"God among Gods, Mary … eh. How do you like the sound?"

"Uncle Mark," Jill said. "How do you know all of this?"

"The Antis developed the pill. Now, you won't believe it,

but it's true. I was a monitor, a validator. I saw some pretty suitable test subjects before they shot them all."

"They did what?" Jill said.

"I'm not saying I was with good people. But Antis helped develop the NeverSleep pill in the beginning. They created it to cause the division in the population. That was all. To cause societal collapse." Mark flicked a chewed nail in the other direction. "All it really was, was to shake it up. Then, the ice caps melted. What they were doing was actually real then. Who knows now? Now, there is no basis for government. The main plot was to start an internal turmoil, looting, hatred of neighbors. The works. Chaos. Well, it didn't work as well as it should've, but here we are. No one took the government issued pill, and they died. The Anti's from distrust of the last steps of development, and the rest of society because of the confusion and mistrust of the government. But, because of gravitational pull and Life as it now is. Because of some reason, here we are and here is the NeverSleep. We have to promise to rebuild."

"I don't believe it," Mary said. Jill shook her head as well. "Word would've gotten out."

"Well, it's the truth. The Antis covered it up for their own self efficacy." Mark was plain-faced and sober. He hadn't had a drink in ages, but Mary could see him quivering.

"Why didn't they take it then?" Jill said. Jill's face said bull.

Jill and Mary got into the truck, shaking their heads. They were sure Uncle Mark was feeling some NeverSleep pill side effects or something. Surely, they weren't dreaming, Jill thought. This place they were in now, it wasn't magic, was it? The world really would crumble around them, wouldn't it?

CHAPTER 21

By late afternoon, Jill and her cohort arrived in Utah. The roads were still mostly barren. They didn't stop or rest in cities because Mark had warned them how people change. How when things change, people change. The cities were likely dangerous. They stopped alongside the highway to rest their legs and use the bathroom.

Jill didn't need to worry about pulling back into traffic or someone seeing her relieve herself. This place, this highway, had multiple smooth, recently paved lanes, extending far into the distance. The setting was pastoral, animals not yet keeled over, feasting on the fields where they remained. Sheep meandered outside of their cordoned space. Didn't matter to Jill, didn't matter to their owners, dead or not. The decision to work the lands, seek shelter in the Colony, or raid the grocery stores was theirs. This terrible Life had so many choices.

Jill ducked behind a low craggy bush where she saw cattle still grazing as if nothing had happened. She wondered when people would leave Colony Red and gather still growing vegetation, food, and water up? When they got closer to the Colony, scouts would be on the loose with weapons. The broadcast rules for the Colony said no one left without an ordeal. Not until the earth recurved into something habitable. Until they decided there wouldn't be further doom; That a lawful society might exist.

Stuck up in a safe place didn't seem bad for the short term, but in the long term, would her curiosity, her debased sense of home, get the better of her. She might seek out a person or a thing, an old type of chocolate she liked or a new lover, try to break restraints, find glory in another respect than what they would have her call work or rebel against the new system if her ideals didn't align.

When it was Mary's turn, Jill turned to chat with Mark. "Will we be stuck?"

"They won't let you out," he said. He chewed a weed from the fields in the corner of his mouth.

"It'll be a nightmare for a bit. But we'll get used to it," Jill said. She wasn't so confident in her words.

"The kid. They'll take her. And you don't have to worry about being married. They'll let you in, but you bet your bottom dollar they'll push you into the same bed if you even once hold hands." He laughed and kicked his heel up onto a rock, leaned into his knee for a stretch.

"Look. The last bit of snow. Oh, my god. How could we miss it?" Millie said. She cruised over to the puddle of whiteness and pulled her arms up like she was surfing. "Look just like Jilly."

"Ha." Jill bit her lip. "Yes, just like me." She wrapped her arms around Millie and held her. Rocked back and forth on stiff legs.

"You're so nice, Jilly."

Mark smiled, paused, and sighed before he spoke. "Let me tell you what's great about this life."

"What Uncle Mark?" Millie said.

"Finding the people you want to be with." He wiped at the corner of his mouth as he took a drag of his cigarette.

"You can come with us too," Millie said.

"I can't. It's too late for me. I have to wonder," Mark said with a pouty face.

Jill understood. It wasn't about the ticket or his cancer or his need to be a grownup cowboy. It was that he couldn't really get close again. Jill knew that or thought she had known it. She never wanted to settle down until her therapist made her realize it was exactly what she wanted all along. Mark was just where he was, and she didn't speak up. She didn't make a joke about tearing a ticket in half, offering herself to the wilds, or thinking of an alternative. His mind had been over it, Jill thought, and he knew himself. It was not her place.

"You know why they picked the mountains of northern California first?" Mark said.

"No. Why?" Jill said.

"Because that's where the new coast would be. Historically, port cities drew settlement, so the government assumed, especially with all that water, that they'd want to be in a new port city. Not the brightest idea in this day and age, in my opinion."

"No planes," Jill said. "There's no way to get to this remote location. Why did they pick it?"

"Because it's so unpopulated. So untouched all around it. It's pristine beauty. That's the only reason. They wanted to remind themselves about development, about growth. About the dedication to the spot so far left to linger in tranquility. No one who's been there can question the beauty, really."

"Aww. Mark. You're from the east coast. Southern east coast," Jill said. "It's all beautiful."

"Yeah, but the government officials have barely seen it. They don't know." He smiled and smoke cascaded out of his mouth.

"What would we do without you, Mark, as our guide?" Jill unfurled her arms for a hug.

"You would survive. But not everyone would. That's why I'm here. With my last shred of family. To make sure you get where you're going safely. It's my only penance for a sad, mediocre life, half of which was without the trueness of family."

Mark dusted his hands off and wiped a bit of muck on the road. "No need for hand sanitizer, right?"

"We can still get sick," Jill said.

"Well. I haven't so far. You haven't so far. What's keeping us from really knowing?" Mark said. "I will tell you this. When I woke up from the LongSleep, by God … It was the best sleep I ever had. The pain that I had in my lower back … was slept off. Like I found a perfect mattress and would never have back pain again." He gulped in. "You may not believe me, but it's true. One hundred percent better."

CHAPTER 22

The truck puttered to a halt on the side of the road. A stiff, hot dust kicked up and Mary paused as it settled. Then, Mary got out of the truck. Moments ago, she had said she needed to breathe. Someone had been chasing her, Uncle Mark, and she was glad for it to happen. Uncle Mark had been trying to find her. All this while she had chased Jill. Demanding to be a part of Jill's life and begging her to love her back. And Jill, love her as Mary must, didn't come running to her when she entered the room; Mary deepened in sadness every time she entered her presence. Jill's casual love was not the passion Mary needed. Mary looked broadly for sultry eyes and beckoning lust without fail.

Mary stood next to a small pile of gravel off a roadside pull off. "Jill, are we meant to be together?" Mary said. She crossed her arms, wondering if her downcast eyes would meet Jill's if Jill would look deeply into hers.

Jill came wandering over. The tension in her eyebrows glared. Once again it wasn't lust. But it was true concern. Something was wrong. Mary presented herself this way, full of discontent. She wanted Jill to look under the hood, to meet her halfway.

"Mary, what could you possibly think? I love you more than the world," Jill said.

"Yes. But are we meant to be together? Is this more than a lean on me, lean on you, casual friendship?"

"Mary, we will be together. I know we will be together forever, one way or another."

Jill pulled Mary by the hand. At first, she stood stiff, then stumbled in the direction that Jill pulled her. Up over the hill they found a soft spot of grass and Jill kneeled next to Mary who popped her knees in the air and leaned back, resting on her arms behind her.

"Mary there is not a better moment for me to profess my

passion to you. It's true my depression was worsening and then this. A moment of crisis like this is hardly a moment to think of anything other than staying alive. But I am here for you. There is nothing that is keeping me from ravaging you this very second. I married you in a moment of calmness. You made me feel confident in our actions. I had loved you for years, so it was easy to commit. I have known you for years, so it is easy to see the future with us together. But sex, I hardly … Remember that time in Estes Park. We were a little lightheaded from the elevation. We ran from a moose in town. Found the door bolted it and had the most magical sex, afraid to go outside. Afraid to open the door. Safe inside. I was safe with you." Her voice trailed off as she remembered.

Mary leaned in knowing this was the moment. These acts they were about to share would solidify or break their bonds. Jill tilted her head at Mary's neck and Mary gushed. Her face drew a bead of glistening sweat. She was humble and accepting. Jill's tender touch filtered into her mind.

Mary caved again as Jill pulled her in at the waist raising her up from her position leaning back. They faced each other on their knees softly kissing. Leaning in, they embraced each other with full force, kissing the backs of necks. Then, the simple kissing started again.

As Jill started to heave, not in tears but with overwhelming emotion, Mary grabbed her shoulders and leaned her softly down. When Mary pulled herself on top of Jill, it was what they both remembered. Mary's dominance was her will to please. She needed emotion. Her devotion begged to be returned with devotion.

Mary caressed breasts, scooched down shorts to ankles, kissed thighs in all their glory. She tumbled them left and right rocking love into their bodies together, as one. Then, thrusting up and back as Jill's head popped back uncontrollably. A moan prolonged a thrust. A breath was caught, and motions increased in rapidness. Moans became successive wanting deeper pressure or more articulate motions. Mary thought she knew which but wasn't sure until Jill's screech reached a peak. Mary reiterated she would be puddy to her, dote on her, everything she ever wanted for days on end, hoping to find love again. She gathered the memory of the experience she had years ago and made it come alive one more time. Their relationship should flourish. Surely, they would make magic every day. Surely, Mary would get her chance, but she didn't need it today. She just needed Jill's careful smile, one that did not want to upset the balance.

CHAPTER 23

Jill caught a glimpse of a multi-colored scarf on a tree. She had seen it days ago on the leader of the strange band of travelers. It was an unwelcome sight. Jill lifted it and gave a quizzical look as she buttoned the top button of her pants.

The man was just as absently cheery and dumbfoundedly innocent as before. A smile rose over his face so much that Jill saw his glee and his obsession on one fixed point, her. He would see right through them. While trying to sleep lightly, he stumbled a bit with his steps. He was plump and rosy-cheeked. His Mumu gathered at the knees, wafting in the slight breeze, presenting an obstacle as he tried to descend quickly, possibly worried he might miss something.

"Hi! it's Harrod," the man said, in a gallop down the path from across the hill on the other side of the street. "I'm so happy to see you."

"Aren't you supposed to be in Kansas … Harrod?" Mary said.

"Yes. We are. In NeverSleep. Duh," He smiled big. His demeanor was snarky and silly. "Have you joined us? There are some unexpected developments. A few new games and there are records set on our score boards for track and field events. You happen to know the culprit?" He grinned and pulled at his goatee.

They both shook their heads. "Where are your kids?"

"Oh. We didn't really need them." He cupped his hands and spoke to Jill and Mary aloud, but as if he were whispering. "They're so hard to train. I ran out of cookies, really. Oh, my, my." He held his clasped hands up to his mouth and blew air into them, muttering.

"You can't be serious," Mary said.

"You can't be serious," Harrod said. "Look. We got some fun stuff out of the way, but we need to concentrate on history management, the things that are forming NeverSleep. We're trying to capture them, make records, establish a foundation of what is. So, we could always come back to it. We want to be prepared if someone builds something wackadoodle, and it all goes under."

"Great," Mary said.

"You left those kids in the mountains?" Jill said, obsessing a little about the lack of empathy this man seemed to have.

"The kids. They'll be alright. We left them in the center of a town, down the highway a bit. One adult stayed with them. They can't travel. So, it's just as well. As I said before, we didn't have enough drivers."

"That one poor adult," Jill said.

The graveled slopes of the rocky land were lonely. It was lonely years ago when a few people traversed the land. It was lonely now, save the two distinctly different sets of people who looked at each other now.

Jill always wanted children. She thought Mary did too. That's why they failed each other. They both wanted something so badly that neither could give it to each other. Here was Millie, darling Millie, who bopped around as a child in a wonderland. And what Jill would give if that child disappeared, otherwise misplaced something, or found herself abducted. It would be a travesty, a travesty for everyone when she let loose. Her instinctual feelings and wants about stability and safety aside, she already loved this kid, and she couldn't think of anything positive about someone who could see it another way.

"It's not the same," Mary said.

"Oh, but it is." Harrod looked both ways as if the children heard his deep voice, as if they'd come for him if they heard him.

Jill turned about face and avoided looking this man in the eyes. Relaxation was not possible, and she thought about the horrid act he had committed.

"Where are they," Jill said.

"They're where they came from. All over. All over this world. They'll work things out. They grow and form community," the man said.

"It's not true. They need to learn and be nurtured. They're

so young," Jill said. Mary looked at Jill with weeping eyes.

"There's too many of them. We're ... shall I say, the government is ill-equipped. There's no space for children to have society in this world. Not until they release the details of the repair. The plan for mass NeverSleep building."

"Well. Let kids be kids," Mary announced. "At least they don't have to build."

A face popped out of the top of the ridge where Harrod had just come down. It was a rosy-cheeked devil of a look. He wanted something and would scream for it to go down kicking. The boy was nine and rearing to go. He licked his lips and squinted his eyes.

"He might be president someday," Mary said, pointing so Harrod would turn and see.

"Oh. That straggler," Harrod blushed. "Did we get them? Did we get their gas?"

"Com'on guys, get in." Uncle Mark picked up Millie in one fell swoop and tucked her into the back seat.

"Get them." And the children crashed over the hill toward the car. They wielded the same implements, rakes, hedge trimmers. It was the same bunch from that first morning after NeverSleep. At least Harrod was tempering their choice of weapons.

By the time Uncle Mark and Millie were upright and situated, Mary had the car out of park. Jill had edged herself around the car and hung with the door halfway open, her body halfway in, when the car from cold stop leaped into drive.

A buckshot sounded.

Three women in hunting vests popped bullets toward the car. They were rough and batted the long barrel of the gun down. Holding her arm around her shoulder, she said, "We need that car."

"Aww fuck. They're getting away," the other said.

The tires spun on the ground. Mark mumbled something about letting him drive.

"What the ..." Mary held onto the steering wheel with both hands tightly. Her knuckles flushed and turned white.

"That wasn't right."

"They won't allow them in the Colony. I can imagine with

their manners," Uncle Mark said.

Up the road were more children. They came to the road. Mary dodged one and another. It must've been one hundred children, all coming at them with poles and sharp objects. Everyone in the car was quiet, reserved. Millie looked out the window and pointed at someone coming right for her, no weapons or yard tools in hand. He galloped square into the side of the car and then popped off onto the ground in a ditch in the road. Mary mumbled, "I hope he's okay."

Soon, the children were behind them. Mary and Jill in the front seat looked at each other, then back at Millie. "He's right," Mary said. "You can't save them all."

They never planned for this overabundance of children. Children, kids, would die or go on neglected. No one anticipated an answer, even if the world stabilized. The household members, usually adults and one to five kids, floundered. It was like that for a reason. Jill imagined the chaos with only five. Overpopulation might easily be regarded as the biggest societal problem of NeverSleep. What if they filtered into the NeverSleep with their own agenda?

"Two more hours until the approach. Get your passports out, ladies," Uncle Mark said.

They really were close. It would be a matter of a few hours, and they would be to safety. Laughable, Jill thought, safety from children. She arched her back and stretched. The quick stop wasn't enough for her aging bones. Millie would be eighteen when Jill was fifty-seven. She would enter old age. By the time she settled with one of apparently millions of bachelors in her twenties, Jill would be well into her sixties. Old for the first time, she rubbed the skin on the backs of her hands. The veins stuck slightly out and a bit of green swam through them. The skin gathered and crackled in ways she hadn't noticed before.

"What are they even eating out there?" Clearly, Mary was thinking about the same things Jill was thinking about.

"I guess they stop at stores and food's still fresh," Jill said.

"They needed gas. And there are no towns out here. It's literally the middle of nowhere. Montanans like their privacy. I'm surprised no one has scared us off yet," Mary said.

"They're all Antis." Uncle Mark leaned back.

"Maybe. Maybe not. This Colony is here for a reason. That's all I know." Jill was solemn. For a second, she wasn't sure any other way was possible for the rest of her life.

"I just worry," Mary said. "About those children. It can't be easy."

"When we get to the Colony. We'll see. There must be a solution. The government. The shred of what's left will know what to do. If anyone does. They'll know what to do," Jill said.

Life in this world was dangerous. Jill just hadn't seen it because they hadn't heard how people got on and had not seen anyone else. But just as you'd expect, it was a person against the world, a person against nature, everyone for themselves. People, those who were left, were banding together and attacking people. Life was dangerous. They were creating a world of factions that might, much like the Antis, brainwash and convince, cajole, and consume people with their ideals, hidden very much in the open. The agenda was clear and concealed all at once.

The sun was cascading into the cliffs. Similar cliffs as the ones kids had maniacally popped out of and challenged the team of four. However, that man nurtured their hatred. He made them do evil bidding. It wasn't safe for kids, yes, Jill thought. In the middle of the world, all alone but with each other, they weren't safe. But it was the adults that were leading them into corruption, thoughts, and emotions they might never shake. For the sake of survival? Is this what this world was now … survival?

They went on their way, careening through the open air, looking for one more place to stop. One more NeverSleep to test powers, prowess, in a new land. If they weren't allowed to go to the NeverSleep once they entered Colony Red, they would be stuck with less knowledge and understanding. They looked for one more place, one more stop, to rest or think, or whatever it was that needed to be done to fall into NeverSleep.

CHAPTER 24

Jill snapped back into Life. Time became hazy, and a bit of vertigo set in as she lifted herself up. If enlightenment were possible, she might've experienced it just then. Even if she had made a mandala in the sand for hours upon hours, she wouldn't have found more peace. She experienced a moment of clarity, and the world might be better off for it.

Jill talked to someone close to divine, a deity. That spirit was Dillan. Jill conjured her up. The NeverSleep didn't forbid it, but Mary might have. Dillan knew about knowledge and power. Knowledge, she relayed, spun the earth. Knowledge solved so many problems. Then, she disappeared, never quite tangible, never quite more than a bit of haze and vertigo.

The NeverSleep was a place for all of them and Jill alone. It was a place where Jill, Mary, and Millie might live forever, and that was all she needed to know. The place would survive. And so would she. In this travesty, as the world unraveled, there would be another Life.

"I saw it. I saw the plan. What will happen? It seems so impossible, inconceivable." Jill said. Her fingers rubbed against her loose, stiff denim jean shorts. They were a dark wash. She'd worn the jeans to work. She cut them off the night before she took the pill in anticipation of the heat.

"I … I don't know if I can do this …" Jill continued. She cracked her knuckles and bit her nails in anxiety. "Here we are on a planet that is literally dissolving. Water is creeping into the coast. I'm sure, but I haven't seen it. I truly don't know. And this NeverSleep, this trance I'm going into is too much for me to handle."

Mary cut in. "What did you see? You were gone for what seemed like only a moment."

"The NeverSleep has builders. Ten thousand … People who are going in and coming out. They are recharging and building as they can," Jill said.

"What are they rebuilding?" Mary said.

"They're working at everything. They're building the earth. They're building life, society, culture, food, everything. It's a reimagining, and it's intense," Jill said. "Dillan said I'm a leader. I got one of the extra dose shots, and I'm to be a leader, if I can." She dropped her head because it was so hard to be this person she had to describe. She expected a headache to form, but it didn't.

She couldn't handle the pressure, the stress. A girl from rural Colorado messing with the world. Hadn't a cent to her neighbor's dollar, but she could make his house and hers if she wanted. Fairness, she thought. All unique. All the same. That's what she decided, at that moment, to strive for, fairness.

"Mary. I have to spin the world, somehow. I have to be alive, present in it. And oh, it's more. More than I ever have or ever could. But it's me. I'm this new person, dedicated to this cause. I can be this person. And this world … I think of it as just for the two of us. The thousands are there, but this place I'm building is also just for us. What I make if it's okay with you … is just for us. Our world. Our NeverSleep. Our new Life," Jill said.

Jill tried to relate the world that was being built, the world, NeverSleep. Mary partially knew what was happening. She did not understand everything. Jill had more power. Magic in a dream, in a NeverSleep that they all were creating, Mary too, as they both had guessed. But Jill's role was to create key components. Everyone had their part, but Jill must shift the earth, so that its gravitational pull didn't spin the NeverSleep back to Life. This required a prolonged stay in the NeverSleep.

"Who told you all of this?" Mary said.

"Mary, it was Dillan and a deity all at once. She told me this world was to be rebuilt," Jill said. "I think Dillan must turn the key eventually. She must shift the NeverSleep to Life."

"Great," Mary sighed. Jill watched Mary's body tense.

"It's just that she. It's too much, Mary. She has gone over. They overdosed her and she's gone over. Over in the Never-Sleep. She's at the core. She'll never be real." Jill's conciliation might not have been enough. She really adored Mary even more since they started their trip. They had a kid together now, for Christ's sake, but it wasn't because of the child. It was because of them. Because Jill finally saw the way Mary acted, her intent, her desire to be. It wasn't the acts of service or the presents, although there were many. It was her listening, her effort to be with her. Jill understood Mary would try when the going got tough to keep them together.

They had broken up years ago because of a slip in Mary's consciousness. She said, "I hate you," in so many ways. The words and actions stayed with Jill until she burst. Mary talked about the building anger and rage she was taking out on others because of it. Jill knew that the anger and dissatisfactions weren't good for them but also for others, their friends and relatives. The state of being, the way they were when the two of them were together and even when they were apart, hurt them both.

All Jill imagined was the destructive pent-up emotion. She fought with friends, as she told us, made enemies with co-workers, because she couldn't talk about what irked her with Jill.

When they ended the relationship, Mary calmed Jill's anger. They decided the breakup was the best thing for both of them. Knowing that Mary acted out because of her hurt Jill, but she moved on. The breakup was Mary's fault, Jill thought, but it was also hers. She beat herself up about it for months and years to come. And that guilt was enough to drive Jill away from Mary emotionally.

Now, in this hell of a place, Jill and Mary were sharing secrets and memories, hopes and dreams. Jill was finding out first-hand what she needed in NeverSleep. When they talked about their experiences there, Jill saw in a glance Mary's desires, her wishes and dreams. The interpretations were all she needed to try to make Mary happy, and that was so important to Jill.

Jill shut her eyes and went back into the NeverSleep. This time she would find more than Dillan. Dillan gave her a purpose, but she needed to find for herself her own limits.

CHAPTER 25

Jill held a pitchfork. It had not been there a minute ago. And then it was at her feet.

Mary had distanced herself a bit … stepped back in trepidation. She stumbled over loose, dusty rocks. A gecko moved to its purposeful place atop a makeshift cairn. Mary drew her breath for the words Jill would say.

"Did you …" Mary paused.

"It was the kids. They weren't there. I looked for them. But I found parents. Hundreds of parents in despair. If it weren't hell on earth, the hell of NeverSleep, I'm not sure what it was. They cannot build. They're stuck. Stuck in a temporal place. Mary, they want their children," Jill said. She motioned toward the ground and the pitchfork.

"Wha—I just don't see. It's all so unclear," Mary said.

Jill said, "I told them about the children we have seen. The wild lives of those left living. Children. The thousands or hundreds of thousands of them that there are." Jill held her fist to her mouth. "They want their children. They want the madness to stop. But they are separate, unable to come back."

"Jill, you brought this."

"They said I could. I said no. I guess I can." Jill kicked the implement over a small mound of dirt, the anger issuing the instant it rose. "This is the world. This is NeverSleep. It's not the end though, Jill. By far. We can transfer it when it's built. When we're happy."

Mary didn't understand, and yet she internalized that altogether it was true. Jill would never lie. She was too good, honest. Mary had seen her heart.

When they broke up some time ago, Mary held in her anger. Now she was prone to melt in front of Jill, let it all out good or bad, and she relished relaying it. In some sense of it, Mary understood that if it didn't work out, it wouldn't. So, in some sense, she threw her love to the wind. In another respect, she had done it all before and come back, so this time it must be for real. The relationship meant more and nothing all at the same time.

Bottled up emotions had no worth. It didn't work the first time around, it wouldn't the second. So, she let loose, and it felt so good in body, person, passion, and desire. Her inner being unleashed, she found out who she truly was … someone, a person, with an emotion that bled a personality. She was a new being, and she relished it.

Mary fooled the earth with her covering up. She pulled in the sense of being. She thought if they fought, they would look like a squabbling couple. She saved it for later and it backfired. Now she understood better, to focus on her needs … and also her wants and desires. This excluded the anger because, through asking, she got what she needed, what they in tandem needed to survive.

She would do it now … practice with the content of her speech not with the volume of her voice.

"Jill, I need you to calm down. I need you to be on earth, be in this place. With me. I'm losing you," Mary said.

"You're not losing me. It's so much more. I am making it for you. It's an act of creating, a catering toward. It's my foreplay and marriage all at once," Jill pleaded. She clasped her hands.

"You just sound outlandish." Mary caught herself stomping her foot ever so slightly, and she flinched. "We need some reason. You'll be with me, won't you? Are you disappearing into NeverSleep? Is that where you'd rather be?" A tear formed and did not trickle. It reminded her of the sadness that now grew. She developed an empty pang that pulsed, lacked feeling. Jill might depart for good, leave her to be. She numbed herself with a shot of anger. "You can't let us go."

"Mary. There is so much more. There is my desire to help. My need to help. I have to be this person I never was before. Caught in depression, unable to do a single thing. For once someone, the world, the NeverSleep, whatever is to be, needs me," Jill said.

"What about my desire? What about us?" Mary yowled in angst.

"It is a world for us to be in. It's safety and dream and everything anyone might want all at once. But this assignment, this charge, has given me life, given me the sustenance to be a better person, for you as well. This is our chance. We will run away together into the NeverSleep. The world is magical and unique, and it has your heart's desires. It is true. I've seen it. It's true."

"I'll never forget you," Mary cried her words like Jill was millions of miles away.

"I am here and there, and I can go back and forth. I can bring things. Maybe people into Life out of Life into Never-Sleep. It will be the capture of these powers that can do us all good. Please, Mary, won't you see?" Jill said.

"There is a place for together in this NeverSleep Life this place. And that is all I need, but I know who I am here and now. You, me, Millie. I don't know what else we can be— promise me."

"I promise. It will be our time and our place, and it will be a dream in disguise for everyone to see. It will be the magic of Christmas, a surreal Dali painting, and the hope of a generation. All that hinged in ecstasy for everyone left."

CHAPTER 26

After about an hour out from the last stop, NeverSleep, Uncle Mark turned very solemn. He lit up a cigarette and cracked the window next to him.

"Oh Christ, Uncle Mark. Quit stinking up the car," Mary said.

The touch of the now soiled and muddy Tacoma matched the air that Uncle Mark attempted, poorly, to keep at bay. Mary coughed. Jill's intuition expected him to speak the truth about something, changing the whole game. His serious demeanor showed through.

The fog of dust that kicked up around the car as they drove hid the truth. The earth was changing. Everyone understood it to be true. But unless you felt the heat that beat as the dust settled or felt the ground for the absence of water, you wouldn't really know. Only foresight or information, acknowledgment of truthful words, would let you really believe. Jill was silent.

"It's not like you will not get into the Colony and live happily ever after." Uncle Mark made a pouty face and took a drag of his smoke. Air gushed out of his lungs and out of the window. He tapped the edge of the stick's flickering light on the glass until the ash tumbled off.

Mary's and Jill's faces lit up in desperation, something they knew would not dissolve. This was it. This was the confession he hid so well behind a cacophony of crackling lungs, wheezes, and loud fist to mouth clears of the throat.

"I am dying. That's the end," Uncle Mark said. "There is no compassion in apocalypse. That's it. But there is hope. This girl is hoping. She brought us a light from a Think." Uncle Mark ashed his cigarette again. "Let's not dwell. You are. You needed to realize."

Jill didn't want to give away how she settled about it all. How strongly in one direction. Either way, she wasn't entirely sure. If Mark could read her expression as supporting Millie over him or even him over Millie, he would judge Jill in a certain way. She would have to double over and believe the other possibility. She must, for the silence woke the dead, pick a side, pick one to broach the topic.

"We never talked about this, Mark," Jill mumbled. She was solemn and plain faced. Any blood dripped from her face into core being, a self that needed to pick between two deserving people.

"There are plenty of children out in the wild, but I think we have a good one. We can't leave Millie behind," Jill said, finally her voice cracking. This time, she was as firm and clear as she could be. She gripped the underside of her thighs in the front passenger seat, knowing the statement would hurt Mary. The statement bellowed boldly, and she hadn't wanted it to be so.

Mary reached out and grabbed Jill's forearm. The strength was a caress. She held on to give faith for her to understand the passion. They must decide either way.

"They'll let us all in. You were the hero back at the Capitol, after all. They'll give you dispensation. Let you come in too," Mary said. Her face bent stiff in every crevasse it could. "They'll listen to reason. They must."

"They're very strict—" Uncle Mark said. He picked at his dirty cuticles and pulled his growing nails through a wily new beard.

"We owe you the world, Mark," Jill said. Her face glowed, sincere as when she told Mary she loved her. "How can we make this work?"

Mark ran his hand over Millie's hair and pressed his cheek to the top of her head. "This dear girl can have no other family. She lives with you all and she needs you all. She won't get along without you."

"Mark—" Mary said. Tears formed in her eyes.

"But we can build hospitals," Mary said. "In the Never-Sleep. We can build the treatment you need." Uncle Mark's face looked paler, more skeleton-like than it ever had.

"The cancer I have can't be cured. It's too far along. By the time NeverSleep develops, and the hospitals are ready for me, I'll be dead," Uncle Mark pulled his hands to his face and in a swift motion pulled them from the top of his head to his chin, waking himself up to the truth. "Besides, there's no hospital here. Isn't this really the only thing there is? Life? Isn't that the place we'll only ever truly be?"

Uncle Mark tucked his head into his chest and cleared, one more time, his throat, muffling it with his fist. Gasping after the act, only to do it again.

Jill recalled Mary telling her about her uncle's cancer. It was why they needed to connect. She would lament on Saturdays at the beginning of date night. More often in the past several months. She would say she needed to get in touch because of all that was going on. She needed to make amends. Or Jill would ask if she'd followed up. Ask if she tried to repair what family she had left. Family that was still living.

"So, you see. Roaming for me." Uncle Mark blew the smoke out hard, this time lips almost out the window. "What is out there, I'll tell you, is land to roam. Get a horse, find a magnificent tree. A bucolic spot. Nothing else. I'll tell you."

Jill imagined Mark out on the range, possibly stealing a horse from a nearby farm. She imagined him cutting up and cooking his own meat from cattle that still roamed, for now, freely in the Montana wilderness. What she couldn't imagine, hard as she tried, squinting her eyes closed to do it, was Mark lying flat on his back, exhausted, dying from a cancer he was unable to even treat. He would lay there awake several days until he finally passed from dehydration or wild animals picking at his distressed body.

"You'll be uncomfortable," Jill said. "At least have the sanity to want to die in peace."

"Other, living people, people who can change the world, need that bed," Uncle Mark said.

"Oh, don't be a hero," Mary said.

Uncle Mark had always been a hero to Mary. That's what she had relayed to Jill. He was the center of attention, always trying to solve a problem one of her siblings or cousins brought to him or assuage tensions and potential fights. He intervened when Mary couldn't get along with her dad. It was the most anyone had ever done; she recounted. She had to thank him for it before they all died … albeit at the hands of his sympathizers.

"There's one thing," Uncle Mark said. He packed his cigarettes on the back of his hand, ready to smoke another. "They will ask you. Someone will ask you in the Colony … if you want to take Sleep pills. These are to get you to NeverSleep, but they are extremely dangerous. They're … well, everything is untested or not tested as thoroughly enough … they'll put you to sleep permanently. This person when he gets to you as you first enter or a few days in, that he is evil, an Anti in disguise. He won't help you. He's there to kill you. This is my last piece of advice."

"Why don't they … arrest them … at gunpoint? Cuff them and take them. Citizen arrest or otherwise," Mary said.

"They're extremely hard to find. Like spies," Uncle Mark said. "They … They're sneaky and deceptive. And they're still out there. You'll have to navigate, and I wish I was there to help you." Uncle Mark mumbled under his breath and then spoke up a bit, "Besides, who is going to capture them?"

Jill couldn't believe the luck. The one good thing to come out of more than half the world dying was the fact that those deaths were all of a kindred spirit, something that never should've persisted, never should've lasted. But here they were, and now in disguise. The billowing smoke, the demoralizing speech, the radical acts of what Jill's kind called hatred now just done behind the scenes in a less populated world, one easier to hide in, easier to strike from.

"People like you?" Mary said.

"Look, I'm in it to change minds. You're sweet. I don't use force." Uncle Mark threw her a perturbed look.

"Aww. You're just one of them. Weren't you all along?" Mary said, stomping on the gas.

"Look at me. Do I look like I'm in disguise?" He patted his camo hat and then his vest with the orange woven expertly like no other.

The one thing Mark was always out in the open about was who he was. He turned into someone less couched in his beliefs. But he stood like the next one, aligned to a political side based on his physical appearance. Made one wonder why he didn't just change his clothes.

The car chugged up the mountain, everyone on their best solemn behavior.

"Ditch me here," Uncle Mark said. "I'll find someone coming out to pick me up."

"I haven't seen anyone come this way," Mary said. She denied the whole lot of what he was saying, every word. "You can't stay around here. It's uninhabitable. No grocery stores—"

"No other humans in sight. Look. The weather's fine. It's not flooded. Government officials just down the road. I saw a small town we passed. Seems fine to me," Uncle Mark said. "Besides, they set convoys for mornings," he said. "I can hop on the back or duck under it."

Begrudgingly, Mary veered off to the side of the road and slowed to a stop. They hugged but didn't get out. They didn't chance another attack from children in the wild world, what it had become.

"Take care, little one." Uncle Mark rubbed her hair, tussling it one last time. "Dears, you take care of yourself. If you let something go, it just might never come back to you." He winked at Mary and then smiled at Jill. "You have something special." Two hands grasped two shoulders in the seats in front of him and he shook them gently in unison. "See you in the NeverSleep."

Uncle Mark patted the tailgate of the Tacoma covered in splatters of mud, and Mary, tears streaming, pulled away. "I am no better than he is when he dismissed me from his life," Mary said.

"We'll come back for him," Jill said. Her heart burned truth, and she plotted a myriad of ways to get him back as they pulled away. "We'll find him."

CHAPTER 27

The Tacoma crept up the last little bit of highway, which stopped abruptly at two large doors they assumed were the front entrance. How silly that a place so secret could have a front. It looked like a complex of distributor warehouses. Each one slightly off kilter or otherwise extending out to the side. The front of the building, maybe a mile wide, made it hard to see beyond, but Jill could. As she lifted her butt off the passenger car seat, she could see the building spread a consuming mass, an entirely new world.

The façade was stiffly brutalist. The sheets of metal added support, but the seams extended the length of hundred foot or so panels. Welded with thick cames about two inches wide, the entrance was ominous and seemingly impenetrable. Two seams flanked a large ten-foot-high door noticeably thicker, unmarkable material. No human with no tool could alter it. A single sheet of metal transom ran between those two last seams. A fake archway was the only embellishment. This wasn't a traditional government building. It wasn't a place everyone could tap into a sense of history. This was, in a way, the restart, a start over if there ever was one, and this place alone might survive. They cut up the Constitution for Christ's sake.

Mary stopped the car and relaxed into the seat, holding herself steady. "What do we do, knock?"

"Well, I can't imagine why not," Jill said.

"I don't think we're meant to go in and out," Mary said. "I don't think this place allows freedom. If we go in there, if we want to go in, we'll likely never come back out … except maybe in our NeverSleep or whatever." She picked at her nails like this moment didn't matter, like it was a moment of reckoning.

"We can't follow your uncle, two clueless, middle-aged, out of shape women, and a child. We've been lucky so far, but we'll die out there," Jill said. "You love him."

"I realize. All signs point toward this place—"

"Isn't that what you've been saying since we woke up from LongSleep?" Jill said.

"Yeah. I miss him … Will miss him." Mary said. "He's a cowboy through and through."

"We can get him in," Jill said. "I'll beg and plead. It'll be our priority, and we'll make it a point at every turn."

"We'll do what we can … We'll both do what we can," Mary said.

"I'm getting out," Jill fussed with her seat belt and un-hooked it, staring at Mary. She pushed the car door over and rolled out of the seat into the street. "It's just … It's here. It's so big. Just in the middle of Montana."

They were about a hundred feet from the building, but the ominous front made it hard to tell how close she really was. A bit like an astronaut on the moon meeting an alien compound for the first time, she met the foreign. She took a deep breath and moved forward, one step in front of the other.

When Jill stepped into the red laser, she triggered some-thing and stuttered back, recovering her balance as she went. The line wavered on either side of her ankle and then cut off so she couldn't see it. It flickered and then came back on. She thought perhaps she was safe but grabbed her ankle. A warm sensation grew around the spot.

What sounded like a huge furnace turning on emitted a gentle roar only to cover the low buzz or an alarm or alert. It might've been part of the mechanics that engaged. She just wasn't sure. What she knew was that someone else knew she was there.

Mary grabbed the car window frame and jerked her head out the window. "What was it? What did you do?"

Jill stumbled slightly and then fell to the ground. She re-covered and got back up.

"Aww fuck. I'm coming to get you," Mary said, leaning back to tell Millie to stay put.

Once outside, she could see Jill pointing, arm extended, toward the flickering red line. She grabbed at her ankle with her other hand, stroking it.

"Is something wrong?"

Jill tripped as she tried to settle her foot and fell flat on her back. Her chin touched her chest and then slammed to the ground on impact. Darkness fell quickly, and she was glad to let it come.

When Jill came to, she found herself in a strange room filled with metal furniture. The place appeared not unlike a hospital. The walls were white. The hospital smelled and looked impeccably clean. Or it was a prison cell no one had lived in yet.

"Oh, that. Nope, you're not in a hospital," a woman in a white lab coat said. "This type of metal is light, strong, and cheap. You'll find it all over. Mining rock in Montana would have been so much easier, but before the NeverSleep … Montanans …"

Jill's face fell flush and emotionless, and she gave a great sigh. She resigned herself to wherever she found herself. Her pallor and strength would not permit a fight.

"Where? You … are." She fixed a syringe. "In the government Colony, Colony Red. Mostly government officials, but also recolonizers."

Jill swung her hand back and forth in front of her face, indicating, no, she would not like a shot.

"This? Oh, this just cuts the little bite you got outside. Would it, could it kill you, yes? Were you in NeverSleep? No?" she sped up the answers.

"No thank you," Jill squawked out. She remembered Mark's words, even if this wasn't the same thing.

She squirted the liquid back into the bottle. "Suit yourself …"

"Thank you."

"Where? What?" She tapped her fingers. "Who? I'm a doctor. I'm a colonizer, lucky enough to get in."

"Let's see anything else."

"When. You've only been out for five minutes … and why … Because the earth is collapsing, of course. Because the ice caps melted. Ecology will collapse first. The world is in ruins. You'll need to see a psychologist like the rest of us if you stay here. I assume you will because, voila," The woman held up three tickets. "You have tickets. Oh, my god. It's like you've won the lottery. People didn't kill you for these?"

"I think the man who gave them to us hid them well. He really deserves to be here, too." It was all Jill gave.

"Still a little groggy. Let's see. No shot. Lie down for a bit. You'll be better in no time."

"Mary … Millie …" Jill gasped some air.

"Okie dokie. They are in your room. It's a small one, but we assigned all three of you to the room," the doctor said.

When she fully woke up, Jill wiggled up onto her shoulders in a bed she had never seen before. In a room she had never been, a cubby of a room, she opened her eyes and saw Mary and Millie patiently waiting two bunks down. They looked up and over the edge of the bed to meet her gaze. Jill looked down and gasp, "Where are we?" Jill said.

"The doctor said he answered all the questions you'd ever have," Mary said. "I'm not sure what she meant. She was a bit, well, quirky."

"I think she thought I was confused, but I'm pretty sure we can gather exactly where we are," Jill said.

Mary hung her feet over the edge and sat up. "She said she'd be back to give us a tour. And she said congratulations on arriving. I guess that means we get to stay," Mary said.

"Yeah. She had the tickets. Good thing she didn't steal them.," Jill said, still a little achy.

Millie pulled out the cards and shuffled them. "Found them on the table," Millie said. She made quick work of a game of solitaire. It broke Jill's heart when she said she used to play with her grandmother.

Millie was the dearest child, such a good girl, such a compliant child. One that would have stood the journey with them and accepted them as role models going forward. She was a grace on this soon to be barren earth.

"Won," she laughed and went back to playing.

The trauma of losing her family would scar her or the change of the earth would turn her into something wild. Millie was neither scarred nor wild. She was a godsend and an asset to Jill and Mary. She tempered their anger around each other and gave them a focus, something that they shared responsibility for but agreed that it was of utmost importance. The child's loss of family had scared Jill, but this child, other children surely too, was resilient and could stand and outlast trials and tribulations.

"Polite guests," the doctor said.

This doctor was too much. Her thumb-twiddling sense of humor grated on Jill's nerves.

"I'm Dr. Abbot," she said. "I'd like to take you on a tour. I see that …" she looked down at her clipboard, "Mary and Millie have checked all three of you in. Glad that's over. Did you find it burdensome?" She looked at her clipboard again. "Mary?"

Dr. Abbot was a square woman with orthopedic shoes. Jill likened her to a nurse in the 1950s in that the style of her dress seemed dated, and the white faded from wash after wash. She had short hair curled on the top. One would hope she used a scalpel better than a comb.

"Oh, no, we just filed paperwork at the, I think, central station, and they assigned us our room." Mary leaned in almost to whisper to the doctor. "They cut up the Constitution?" Thoughts of learning from history dwelled on her mind.

"Ah, yes. Your tickets. Yes, the Bill of Rights and some other documents too. I don't know if we have an authenticator on the premises, but if something was in contention, we would figure it out … compare it at least to the other tickets. Anyhoo, yours shows the same texture and feel as the other puzzle pieces, probably fit, and there are … are …" she scanned her clipboard again more thoroughly. "There're some rooms left."

"We have—"

"Wait, not yet." Jill cut Mary off. "We have to see."

"What's that …" The doctor paused and teetered her pen between her index finger and middle finger. "Well … Shall we go?"

The doctor led them down various hallways and corridors. She pointed out government rooms where they were drafting a new constitution and holding judicial reviews.

"The gavels are repurposed. They came from the old government," Doctor Abbot said. "We didn't bring everything, so it's rare."

"Like it'll be an antique?" Millie spoke up.

"Not quite. Like an antiquity, but more like something that represents something opposite of what it had. It'll be in use until the wood splits. Then, it'll be an antique." She put her hand to her mouth and whispered to Jill, "It'll either be stolen or destroyed. It'll be the first thing destroyed if the Antis take over, or the first thing stolen if the government sticks. They'll slam it when they sign the documents, you see."

They walked around more hallways. The length of housing block 74T-5C Cheyenne extended over a mile long. The doctor whistled while she walked. To Jill, it was annoying. She felt the restlessness and thought back to their three-bunk room. Sex was out of the question. Maybe, maybe in the middle of the day, if Millie ever found a play date. Jill still wasn't sure if this was a place for playdates.

They walked past the cafeteria, which Doctor Abbott described as like a tech office. Just take what you want. All of it was free. She held her hand to her mouth again and spoke. "For now."

Jill wasn't sure what she was alluding to except the fact that it was a new government. It was a new way of life and inherently unstable. It was correct, Jill thought, that they shouldn't forget that.

"This is where they tend the gardens," Dr. Abbott said. "Really, only a select number of individuals can tend the plants. It's exceedingly high stakes, you see." She plucked up a cherry tomato that had fallen to the side and popped it in her mouth. "Ah, democracy at its finest."

The tomato plants whirled their vines all over the room. Unknown to Jill, and she wasn't exactly sure why she didn't ask, was how they got their oxygen. Pumped in? Open ceiling? Right now, at least it didn't look as if it were open. What when the ecosystem failed? All of this ominous power looked great, didn't blend into the environment like Jill thought it might have, but how was it going to last the centuries? She was sure time would tell.

Jill thought about what they had seen at the facilities and noticed one thing was missing. Children. "Um, where are the kids' facilities? Millie might want to—"

"Other wing. Restricted you see," Dr. Abbott said.

"Why is it restricted for God's sake?" Jill said.

"Look, the problem is, well, the kids ..." Mary said.

Dr. Abbott put her nose in the air and sniffed. "Yes. Yes. Quite a problem, the United States education system was." She sniffed and sniffed again. "I jest." After clicking her pen three times, she peered deep into Jill's and Mary's eyes. "You see. It's not as ... well you see ... We're keeping them in mass. There are so many. Anyone want to be a teacher? Eventually you'd get bumped up to professor, I would think."

"Let's just say, the kids have arrived. There are so many of them, they are well hard to manage. They've all had stress, unbelievable stress. They outnumber adults by far. There's literally five thousand of us in this country or soon to be, eventually, country. Which gives you perspective."

"Five thousand?" Jill said.

"Yup. Five thousand. That's the estimate. Only ones who took it were really government officials and some associated people who didn't give a fuck. Oh pardon, dear ..."

"I've been so deluded," Jill said.

"We both took it, Jill," Mary said.

"Right," Jill said.

"So anyway. These kids are in a, well, situation. They are sort of like in more or less jail like situation." Dr. Abbott bent at the waist and leaned in. "Look. You were going to find out, anyway. They were absurdly hard to manage. We had to bring them in. We're still going out and getting them. Convoys. Of course, it's only been a few days, but we have ten thousand so far." The doctor chomped down on her teeth three times, as if asking for a reaction from the others.

"Did anyone go to the NeverSleep? To fix it, I mean," Jill said.

"Oh, you can build in the NeverSleep, but you can't build people," the doctor said. "I mean really. The NeverSleep dream can't work. I mean, the Antis developed it." She blurted out a laugh. "You didn't know. That's why no one took it. The broadcast that last night said not to take it. There were so many mixed signals. They faked the president held at gunpoint for one last ditch effort. It's okay." The doctor patted Jill on the back. "But really, it worked. Half of the cabinet took it, and it worked. President? Well, a captain goes down with his ship."

"Uncle Mark. We need Uncle Mark," Jill said.

Mary shook her head furiously. "We really, really do."

"Is that who gave you tickets?" the doctor said. "We don't have room—"

"There are tons of rooms. Really. Literally thousands of rooms," Mary said.

"But once we get the kids to behave, we'll need the regular spaces. We are working wonders with sedatives. Besides, we have convoys of kids coming in every day. The trucks go and round them up from various locations throughout the country. We're still scouting. There really are thousands upon thousands more." Dr. Abbott said.

"There is so much room now," Jill said. "That's what matters."

"Sorry nope. And even if I said yes, which I can't, anyone not on an original document ticket is strictly not allowed,"

"It's not true. I can make or develop or re-form people. Whatever I do out there in the NeverSleep dream. I have to go there. I have to go now. I will form a doctor for your uncle, Mary. I can build him. It can be done. If it is all real, it will actualize. I have to find Mark," Jill said.

Mary hesitated. Mary must've wanted to see the kids in deplorable conditions. Jill explicitly did not. She wanted to get to that cramped tiny bunk and see if she could drift away into the satisfying NeverSleep a place for the gods. She could get to NeverSleep and create these people. Figure out how to create their parents.

But Mark held the secrets. He helped develop the pill. He surely could guide her on how to create people correctly if it could be done at all.

"I need Mark," Jill said.

"They already said nobody else. I need him too. Desperately … to get through this," Mary said.

"But they have so much room. I will work at Doctor Abbott. Uncle Mark is valuable to us and them. This is all so new. Look, he can help me with the NeverSleep, forming, creating people. He can. We have got to get him in," Jill said.

"I'll go," Mary nodded a deep nod and ran off down the corridor. Jill still held onto Millie's hand.

"Dr. Abbott, before you go," Jill held up her finger quizzically.

"Where is that woman going … taking off like that?" Dr. Abbott said.

"Restroom," Jill said. She paused until the scene settled in Dr. Abbott's mind. "Dr. Abbott, this girl here, Millie—"

"Oh yes, so tame. Good girl." Dr. Abbott patted Millie's head.

"She's looking for her dad. Can you tell us if Mr. Atchinson is on the roster? We think he might've been an engineer," Jill said.

"An adult?" Dr. Abbott looked quickly at what Jill assumed to be a register underneath other paperwork on her clipboard, skimming over the first, then second, page. "No. No. I'm sorry." Dr. Abbott patted Millie's head. "No. I'm sorry."

In an unreserved sidebar, Dr. Abbott told Jill that at Colony One mass devastation occurred. People died, and they didn't even recover the bodies. Not much was left. It must've been the bombs the Antis had left from the strikes on the polar ice caps, but they had firepower like the government no longer had. Now they were in a new location, Colony Red. They were taking precautions, but they could be attacked again. They waited for more building defenses. The Antis were still out there, albeit unorganized, waiting.

Jill bent down to Millie, "Millie, mommy and daddy might be in NeverSleep now. We'll have to find them."

"Most of the time, since the sleep, I've wanted them. I miss them," Millie said. "Can you help me find them? Are they still here?"

"I might help you find them. I hope I can," Jill said. And they were rushing down the hallway like they had never done before, taking a nap of sorts. To rest their eyes and find people in NeverSleep, they ran, hoping to find the pairing.

Jill thought about Dillan. How she found her in Never-Sleep. No one else who had passed away seemed to be there. Possibly only because Dillan had been vaccinated. Jill got the powerful shot. If Jill got half of what Dillan had to simply look around the testing facility, Dillan's shot would've done abnormal, unpredictable things as well.

She might find the dead in NeverSleep if they had taken the pill. Tensing every bone in her body, for Millie's sake, she hoped. To a little girl, she promised something; she didn't know if it would actually happen. But she promised, so she must make it so. She must at least believe. She brushed at a tear on the sleeve of her shirt. Scrunching her face, she put the unsavory thought away, ran from the guilt that it might be a lie. But the words she said to that girl would always be in the back of her mind.

"Doctor Abbott," Jill said, chasing her down the strip. "We told you about the engineer, Millie's dad. Surely, Colony Red owes his heirs a ticket. You must take this child. She's so well behaved. She is your responsibility as much as ours." Jill reached for Doctor Abbott's shoulder to connect with her and push her to accept a helpless child into Colony Red.

Dr. Abbot was not convinced at first, but Jill pushed, laid on the guilt of a nation leaving her behind. The government took care of its families, didn't it? It was responsible. It should act. Her argument proved at least a little convincing.

"Well, I suppose." She must've felt the guilt. Dr. Abbott tottered her pencil up and down against the clipboard again, as she had the habit of doing. "I suppose that's not typical. But I'm sure we can take on this one more; you've only been here a minute. Tick Tock. You'll have three days until you surface him, the other citizen. We have you on three registers right now, and until he gets here … then it will be a permanent record. You're in the new Colony Red of the world, after all. You're an original citizen. Be proud. People would strangle others for it." Dr. Abbott walked the other way. "Tours over. Find your way to your bunks until meal."

CHAPTER 28

In a moment of stress, Jill paused in her stride as Mary took off down the hall. Jill froze into NeverSleep, out of the world, Life, in an instant. It was in body and out of body, and she didn't collapse onto the floor. The world never spun for her as it did in this moment—perfectly still, perfectly rotational. That was the instant the mind cared and careened into what was possible.

She was in, but out, of Life, walking lucidly while she built a world, a society, the future. All of it rested, and she understood the weight of her decisions. She stressed. Her a woman, who barely gets out of bed in the morning, hurled into a position of powerful destiny. The catapult left her at a loss for words, actions. And NeverSleep pulled thoughts from the back of her mind and made them be. She must be good, she thought. For every doubt she had, she proved herself capable. She wandered her way through this trial, her time as a fish out of water. And she better succeed because so many depended on it.

She looked down at the core. The beginning, where she started. She saw the center and the movement of the planet in the ball. This would be the place to change things. This would be the world as it should be, and to make sure it would happen, she would have to reverse the direction of the world. Spin a ball twirling on someone's finger the other direction. It would be magic.

Jill thought about the planet, what it was and what it could be. She would create step by step what the world should be. It could not be a utopia and most certainly not a utopia in an instant because all that would amass would go awry. Each building block, each ideal from the new Trial of Socrates, loaded with all the concepts of the world that passed through Jill's mind, the minds of the nation, the world, and the unique experiences that only Jill came to have through her life.

They would create poetry and power, government in its infancy and distorted by what had already passed. The people of NeverSleep would find what harmony in nature meant by asking themselves to rethink what had been, one plant by one plant. She would shape happiness by placing a brick. Whatever she thought the house her lover desired was, it would be with her own soul. Whatever NeverSleep she created would be herself, for the populace, and for whoever was to be.

Stress mounted and subsided because she knew deep in the core a rotation spun. And here with her eyes she could stop it, turn it the other direction if she wanted, implode NeverSleep or set it on course. And with this power she had confidence to rebuild, from the first fire to the flag that capped the dome of the Capitol of the new state, if it were a dome, if a flag topped it.

Jill sucked in a deep breath, and without changing the rotation, blew upwards and onwards, perfecting a precision arc, adjusting ever so slightly up and down. The icicles grew on her lips. They grew far from Greenland. The cold amassed. And at the same time, she dropped a finger on the churning world. A pause on a spinning record, so she could catch up with the lyrics. And she lowered the rotation in one fell swoop. She brought the speed to what was. Her bones rattled.

The ice shattered and rebuilt in a reverse of the melt, swiftly and impractically. A miracle of intent made the place what it had never been full of life, full of the possibility of melting again 100 years later, carbon emissions aside. The cause of the ice's collapse could be much simpler than the lack of love in the world. The lack of companion for companion. A place void of loneliness kept the ice afloat, the icicles hanging.

It was her square, and it was everything, and she was not sure. The planet was round, or it was forever, engulfing stars to be what she was and what things could be all the same. This place with people was from her mind and might have their own. She might have a place for them, or they might want to have their own square, octagon, or cube of Life in NeverSleep as it would be in the world that would come about.

Dillan called from over an embankment just far away enough to define what was out of reach for Jill.

"This is everyone's place, Jill," Dillan said. "They picked you." She cupped her hands around her mouth to yell, even though Jill could hear her perfectly clearly. "You are the builder of worlds of entire beings. This is your plan. And if it is wrong, call who you may. This world is yours now because you've found the secret, found the right spin of the world."

"Dillan. Mary."

"When you received the shot, Jill. It became your obligation. They imposed a responsibility. And can you fulfill it? Yes. I think so. You just have," Dillan said.

She became glittery and bright, a firefly dancing in the void. A thing that included all things; Something so real and so missing everything else; Easily bothered and made a part of yourself all at once.

"But I'm lost," Jill said. "But I … we … what we had."

"But Jill, we can't be. Right now. We can't be together. You had Mary. You deserve Mary."

"Dillan. I tried to find you …"

"I am on my own. My deeds are otherwise bound to be erased, finding a time that counteracts what happened so we can write it down, so it never happens again. My deep research is just that, mine forever. They'll tweak your creations. All the NeverSleep's creations before it is again Life," Dillan said.

Jill didn't know how else she could come to terms with Dillan here, above her, in a chain of brilliance. Dillan was a lost love and someone she would always be with in spirit. Jill's passion, attraction, held her close to Dillan. Dillan's wisdom and imminence held Jill at bay.

Jill chose Mary at that second, without bonds of matrimony from God and without the strands of memory of the passionate newness of Dillan. Her purpose was to be with a woman who gave her love so open armed, absorbing rejection for years. It was so easy to love, now that her eyes were open to Mary's true intents, the love she cloaked in friendship.

Dillan would always be one of her lovers. What better a friend?

"What advice do you have for me? This is so complicated and the stress …"

"Find your soul." And Dillan disappeared. "And hold on to

Life and those in Life. Build what only you can build. Build
it for you and it will be for everyone. Rise to your occasion.
It will mean the world."

Jill became rabid for the first time in her life. She wouldn't
ever pine for Dillan's love again. Did NeverSleep create her
loss, create her madness of love? She resented Dillan and
thanked her profusely all at once. She disappeared and Jill
moved on.

CHAPTER 29

Mary had never seen NeverSleep quite like Jill. Jill had some special power over herself. She was compelled and determined, like she had never seen her before. Mary wished she had that power for a long time. She harnessed it, was learning about it, and her will to do good, to help, was even stronger.

Mary's own will had lapsed. She was less of a contributor despite the skill she had as an Architectural Drafter. But she knew it was much more than this. The world was much more important than a building. And she set her skills aside. It would be her time in time, once NeverSleep, the world to be as Jill proclaimed it, evolved into Life.

She shuffled her feet as she escaped down the hallway. Her growth was with Jill, not her career. At the moment, her home, the place she built for them both, with Millie, was of utmost concern. They would be together, and that was what she cared about. That was her NeverSleep, not actualized. That was more important than any other thing built.

Right now, Mary's mission was Uncle Mark. She stumbled a bit as she moved on her way, but not before thinking about Jill. Was this her way of proving she had compassion? She had an inkling. She wanted the best for the world, for them, for family, and bonds.

She changed Uncle Mark's mind in a way. Not by arguing at Christmas dinners, but by a lingering word on their last meeting. People change. The love of family overpowers. As much as Uncle Mark hated Mary's politics, her stubbornness won him over. Miles away, more distant than ice caps, and ages after they had last spoken, he changed his ideas to meet in the middle. His decision made their love, the love of their whole family, so much stronger. She felt the change she had issued to the ether. The ability to sway opinion from a distance in time and space.

"Those that love you will come back," Mary thought.

Jill was another that came back. A boomerang of a lover. A strong bond never, yet, broken. And in distanced passion, friendship became as powerful as love. Now that they were together, had seen both sides of it, they were attached for life.

"What do we need to be together? How can I help you?" Mary had said.

"This," Jill had said. "Your selflessness. When you lose focus on having me and think about having us, having the world be with us. That helps me. Makes me happy. Allows us to grow, create together." Jill played with and curled a lock of her hair.

Mary remembered when they first started flirting again. When Mary advanced on Jill. She attacked more or less, hoping that her desire might stay at bay longer, and their lives would come together for the long haul. Their passion was the growth that needed to happen between them for it to work.

"I love you, isn't it enough?" She had said months earlier in a declaration.

"I don't need you." It devastated her, and Mary left for weeks. Only she found Jill didn't call. Didn't need. Until she did.

Mary loved but nurtured the cause. She bolted. Now she needed to stay abreast of it, support and cultivate. Make herself be a need for Jill.

When they first started flirting again, it was a mission. The tempting glares took work. After the big letdown, after years of solid friendship, she assembled the kindling again. To say the least, everything shook. She came with intent, a goal, and that included suave flirting and pinning, She had to work all the harder to get back into a friendship that already had the basics: some sense of companionship forever, a tinge of mental intimacy, and a person to lean on when things got tough. They could already cry together, for Christ's sake. So, Mary had to work harder yet for Jill to see that there could be love, could be passion, could be more.

Mary poured her heart out one night about an ex and the hurt she brought her. Jill responded in kind words. They bonded, and it counted. To say Mary's tears were intentional flirting to be a lie, but to say she didn't lean into Jill harder would be tough to deny.

She brought her treats, did acts of service, listened with a caring ear. All these things pulled Jill closer. She did her part to make a relationship intimate, to make her loved. And it worked. Jill responded. Started to forget about Dillan. Dillan was just a fling. Mary hoped.

In the hours of the morning when no one wandered around otherwise awake for the sanity of it, Mary called Jill and then came over. She had something to say. Some sentences she must get out.

In fact, it was more than an "I love you." It was a message from her passion, and she knocked on the door before she entered this time. When Jill let her in, they both knew. The act, the middle of the night wakeful hours that tormented them both must resolve.

Mary's sexual energy was forward and meant to delight. But Jill wore her tension just behind closed doors. They fell into embrace upon embrace and licked parts of backs and thighs without restraint, without regard for what was appropriate on a post-relationship rekindling. Nothing about those moments kindled. No small fire grew bigger. It was an unleashing of the earth's core upon the world. It was their moment in the epic fires that would destroy the polar ice caps. They upturned the planet with their start anew. It was sin and hell; it was good.

And it was the rebirth, the realignment of the earth's core of a notion to do good. To help themselves help the world. They, in a single fuck, had realigned the planet. They saved the earth. They believed it.

They sat on the couch, fingers meeting fingers in on a middle cushion, deciding who would first obliterate what they had, make room for more love, or stop everything and default to friendship. The two of them didn't settle whose decision it would be, who would make the first move and take the responsibility. That person would have the weight of the world on them.

And so, they nudged along. Mary fingers to wrists. A, "Can I," from Jill. Mary petting fingers that stroked her back. A mutual, "Will we regret this?" A shoe flopped off, a pants button subtly undone, pleading, beckoning. Mary's arms splayed out so Jill could see, could help the zipper along. So, it would be Jill's decision and no others. Because Mary gave total consent.

Words became like shrapnel. If they spoke about the thing they were doing, something, the sex, would have happened. The words would be a record, something dredged back up when they thought about it. It was the actions that they only ever thought about on what could've been a one-night stand years into their friendship, years after the last time they made love. These actions they would, could think back on, pull out arousal and make worth of it again. So, they were silent, and it didn't happen. The words weren't there, so they didn't.

Jill's body had never been on top of Mary like this. She had always been first. Mary had always pushed Jill for her love. And yet, now she was Jill, giving everything back, giving her the world, and she might never get Mary in return. The world might collapse, or Mary would run screaming bloody murder. Their friendship could be doomed.

Jill's fingers laced Mary's bare nipples, tips to knuckles to the end of the gap in her index and middle finger. Fingers that would find their way to sex and satisfaction. Jill's satisfaction mirrored Mary's and Mary's hers.

The rhythm of the moment pulled them both in as Mary heaved and Jill panted, pulling their pulsing bodies over into the world of the living. Sprouting for both of them the exhalation of relief from almost a decade of misunderstanding. But if they hadn't saved it for now, what would it be?

And what Mary didn't need, lips on sex, Jill did. Jill moaned with the pleasure of the devil being fucked twice over. Her sin outlasted, courtesy of Mary's touch. Mary deepened her hands, wet and slipping in and out with more ease. As she tugged her other hand on her own clit, she pleaded for her own second taste, the rhythm of her breath only matching the thumbing of Jill's passion.

Satisfaction would never happen again. They would be left with this undying wish to be back in the thing. The world turned over for happiness, a moment of bliss. They would need to come back to it. There would be no regret because they wanted too much to be there again, without words to break the feeling, the actions that would pull them to sleep at night, alone, in their own beds.

That night they spent creating madness once, then twice. Sex only made Mary's want stronger. It would make her keel over at night in hot sweats if Jill slept somewhere else. It told her it must be. It was meant to be. The world would have it in no other way.

Jill responded in her typical defense. And Mary was back to flirting with kindness and giving, and it truly made her a better person. It truly saved both their souls. Mary called Jill a few days later to take the pill to try to keep living, or die trying to live, with her. The planet would kill everything, but the one thing that wouldn't die was Mary's desire. It just might save them both.

CHAPTER 30

When Mary took off down the hall intending to find Uncle Mark, everyone played their part. The doctors at Colony Red could help. Equipment or not, the doctors could do something. They had nursed Jill back to health in a matter of hours. Mary and the doctors could help him as much as he could help Colony Red. The deal could be reciprocal. If Colony Red even knew, if they even trusted anyone, they might all prosper. Uncle Mark had secrets, Anti secrets, and insights from before the fall of the government. Secrets that either the others were now trying to hide or secrets they didn't know about. Mary shouldn't have let her uncle die in the wilderness with cancer, for Christ's sake. Her family would be so embarrassed of her.

She had gathered up some belongings out of the bunk, put some food and water bottles in the tiny go-bag Jill had kept for months waiting for them to announce NeverSleep. She had stuffed a sweatshirt she had grabbed into the bottom of the bag. As she nosed around, she found a pack of cigarettes. She left them in along with the lighter.

As she approached the front door, she stopped to chat with the single person guarding what appeared to be the exclusive entrance to what some might consider a grand complex clad in sheets of metal. Those who considered it grand were certainly few, but well …

The desk monitor, who assumed other roles such as hallway guide, head of entrance security, and registrar, appeared non-plussed at Mary's approach. She lacked the gumption to carry her through this conversation, and Mary assumed she knew little about anything, including how to work the door.

In a frank way, she approached the idle sentry and said, without too much forethought, that her partner had collapsed in stairwell C off the H corridor.

"Mary," the desk monitor said, "isn't that it?" She was a

tad unphased by her presence.

"Actually, it's Molly." While trying to put on a face of immediacy, she spit out the words, "My husband Rick. He's down the hall in Stairwell C in the H corridor," she said again. "He might've had a heart attack." Mary's heart pulsed with the lie; blood pressure rose making her cough.

The desk monitor fluttered with the papers in front of her, looking down at a lengthy list. "I don't remember Rick but … I'll call a doctor," the monitor said.

"Please, it's an emergency."

The monitor dialed some numbers, but the phones were not working. "These technical blips in the systems are horrendous. We're still trying to work out the kinks. I'll go to Dr. Morris and get him to the scene. Will you watch the desk? Not that anyone ever comes."

As soon as the monitor had gone on her way, Mary took to the front door. Bar latch after bar latch, Mary struggled with the cold, stiff metal. The display must've surely been for show or to slow down and escape.

Looking to the left across the room, she saw a green panel box. When she got over to it, it appeared to be a breaker system. Mary guessed it was probably not for the whole building, just the immediate surroundings of the lobby. Fingers tensed on the switches; she paused. She flipped breaker switch after breaker switch, fifteen total, and an alarm rang with each one. Mary's ears lit up, and the world around her caught on fire. The lights blinked red. Turning something off can always turn something else on.

Swiftly, she moved back to the door and fumbled with the last of the door mechanisms before she slid the main door clear to the side. The air gushed in, and it felt heavenly, slightly sweet. The air in the compound was self-generated, fully sustainable in the lockdown. The easily movable suite of latches had been for show. Mary's strong confidence in the visibly enormous and strong complex wavered. She leaped forward, now free.

Out in the world, she quickly moved to step over where the red laser would have been if it were on. It must've been off, regardless, but despite her best intent, Mary stumbled on some rocks and fell flat on her face. She scrambled to gain footing and took off down the hill they had recently driven up to get to the stolid place.

Mary hid behind a rock about half a mile down the road. She had run to get there and now grasped for air to catch her breath. The luscious land of green filled in all around her, but under her exact spot, she could see a shed of pine needles. The tree above her had wilted, as well as the one next to it, and a few spotted throughout the distance that she could see.

Like the tree where Jill had left her wedding dress, this place was doomed. Hopefully, their marriage would not be. If she were lucky, Uncle Mark could survive and thrive with them in the flawed government complex, at least until they could get him the medical help he needed.

Jill had left the dress there with the best intents, the resolution that family couldn't be forgotten, memorialized. She could not bring triggering things with her as much as she wanted. But Mary went on a unique journey, one to find Uncle Mark, who found himself stuck in Life and needed help. She abandoned him for a young child who had a better chance of making it in this world. And she had immediate regret.

Family is family, dead in the grave or not. As Uncle Mark edged closer to the grave, these were the moments she needed most. The selfish cravings for what she missed in his life: what he had been, what he always wanted to be. Selfishly she wanted to prolong a doomed life. She needed him more than he realized, more than he thought he needed her. Still, she needed him. She needed him in health.

A small child came up to Mary as she exhaled. Immediately, Mary thought about those who didn't have a ticket to get into the Colony and where they would go. The government told everyone about the safety there and limited access, seemingly willy-nilly. Mary thought it another botched attempt at a government, democratic or not. If they couldn't build it, no one would ever follow. The best intents sometimes fall short. The brainchild of a new era might just not get off the ground with mere thousands behind it, all of which were sequestered into a building only to be characterized as a house of doom and despair, on the outside as well as the inside.

The child spoke, "Hi, I'm Matty." She seemed innocent, sweet, but Mary knew better. She guessed at the fate of children, their new plight controlled by adults on the outside of the Kingdom of doom and despair and controlled by their own will and whim.

"Hi Matty," Mary said. "Who are you with?" She reached out her palm and grasped her hand, hoping she wouldn't run.

"No one for now. I've broken away," Matty said. She eyed her goal, the big, boxy building.

"Is that what they told you to say?" Mary said. She knew better at this point.

"Yes." She cupped her hand to her mouth, miming a whisper, "They said to get into the building. Can you take me in?" She at once hushed herself.

"I'm afraid not," Mary said. "It's top security." She spoke to a child, "You need a ticket." Mary realized the outlandishness of what she had just said. This really was a makeshift, soon to be called sham, government. There were problems, yes, but the government's substantial redress was not incorporating the people, the democracy into its planning. It was the lack of transparency about what was happening now, during an environmental crisis, in a building so thick nothing was able to bring it down. The people wanted to understand. They wanted to survive day to day, but also to picture what the world would bring, how they would eventually survive.

A man popped around the corner, finger held up to nose. "Shh. We are helping. We're trying to round up these kids. But we need in ... Into that piece of junk of a building." He crept in a crouched position quietly over toward Mary. "We can't handle this many. There aren't enough adults. And the NeverSleep ... Will it ever really happen? Will it ever really be?" He cleared his throat. "We just want answers. We want to understand what this place will become, where we will be asked to go. Will the children in there get special treatment—"

"Oh, I doubt that." Mary said snarkly, digging to find out the truth. She didn't fully want to guess the answer.

"Well, that's why we wait," the man said. He combed his hair.

"How many of you are out here?" Mary said.

"Two hundred adults. Three thousand children or so," the man said. "We rounded them up just like the broadcast said. Brought them here. As many as we could."

"Sometimes … Well, sometimes the broadcast is wrong," Mary said.

He paused, about to speak, and shifted his weight on his leg. "They won't let us in. Said they will be full up once the convoys come back. Do you think that's fair? I mean, we were here first. I think they think we're all Antis."

"They're all out of sorts. There may be a way, but you must make them see the reason that your intents are good," Mary said. She wondered what the intents really were. The man didn't wear any identifying camo. He wore a stately navy-blue polo shirt with blue jeans. The man wasn't to be trusted. She had reservations about it all. If she were in the complex, would she even let them in, the hordes gathering in the woods just outside the last shred of government? It was a chance for them both, and Mary reasoned why the people in the complex might've said no.

"Were you friends with Mark?" Mary's pleading look must get across. The urgency resounded. "Has he left here? Did you see him come through?"

"He's up by the waterfalls."

"Waterfalls." She sighed thinking of the joy of her wedding and how this trip to a waterfall would be the other side.

"Nobody marked the place, but I can find it again. Do you want me to take you there?"

"Yes. More than anything. Do you think he's still there?" Mary said.

Mary found Uncle Mark napping by Waterfalls, just as the man, Hank, had said he would be. He rolled over on his side away from Mary, and Mary, as the matter was urgent, as his presence in the Colony Red was urgent, shook his shoulder.

"Aww. No. I can't do anything. I told you so," Uncle Mark said. "Oh Mary. Dear sweet … Have I gone?"

"No. Uncle Mark, are you okay? Can you get along?" Mary said.

"Less and less well, Mary. Less and less well. But since you're here. I'll help you as best as I can," Uncle Mark said.

"It's just. You're a Think, aren't you?" Mary understood the weight of her question. If he was, he must not die … should never die. She stepped in to give him her hand an extension of willingness to make things better between them, become family again.

"I am Mary. I am in NeverSleep. I helped develop the pill, so I understand what it does. But it's really better that you don't … You just need to rebuild."

"I have so many questions, Uncle Mark. Not about why, necessarily? Because I am who I am now, and this world is what it is. The pill has changed us all. All who are left. We are people. We are individuals. We are new and must accept it." Mary petted his side until he sat up.

The pallor of Uncle Mark's skin told something about the quality of his health or the NeverSleep rebuilding he just took part in. "I can't build much anymore. It takes too much out of me," Uncle Mark said. "You have questions. Those I can answer, but don't dig too deep or you'll be unhappy about what you hear."

"First. My first question and then Jill's. How can I find her if Jill goes into NeverSleep? I need to connect with her, help her," Mary said.

"They always go to someplace they sense is comfortable in NeverSleep. If they're trying to find someone, they'll go to someplace that existed. In NeverSleep, those places that they knew, that were important to individual people will be the historic places. They will be rebuilt because someone was close to them and loved them," Uncle Mark said. "If you understand Jill well. You will find her historic places. The places she will go."

"I … I understand. I'll find her on her terms." Mary said.

"Uncle Mark, you must come with me. I must get you back into the building, Colony Red." Mary said. "Jill needs you. She has questions."

"That place won't help me. It's cancer, NeverSleep cancer. I've put too much into it. The doctors can't even conceive of how to help me," Uncle Mark said.

Mary grabbed his hand like a child and pulled as hard as she could until he stumbled up and off the ground. "See you can." She remembered herself at twelve, asking her uncle for a superman ride a push through the air for a thrill. Now with the look of an ancient soul, scraggly Think beard to match, he could barely cough without a belabored heave and bend at the waist. Still, Mary was adamant, she needed him to fly.

"We must go." She pulled his arm around her shoulder, despite it he bucked.

"I can carry myself," he said.

Mary pulled the arm around again. "Hold me close."

Mary's goal at this moment included getting back into Colony Red through what might be an unprotected entrance without grabbing willy nilly, every orphan adult and child along the way.

The half mile trek back to the road and then the half mile trek up the road was laborious in effort and emotion. Mark stumbled and whined as any injured person could do, Think or not. He adamantly stood on his own for most of the trip, occasionally steadying himself by holding onto Mary's waist. Mary kicked rocks to make herself move more slowly, undo her pressure for immediacy, for resolution, or to at least get over the next hurdle. The pair moved rock to rock, tree to tree, just off the road until they got to the door.

A wail in the distance. "You leave us behind. You leave us behind for good." The bellow sounded loud and clear, a bull horn warning for everyone here and there to know. "We will rise when the subsistence ends."

Mary couldn't see, and Uncle Mark waved his hand diagonally across his body. Half a prayer, half a motion to signify they both should forget the sentiment. They had followed them there but would not strike. They would not go in. They were ready to rise and take over, not assimilate. But the time was not now.

With the laser off and the door shut, the place looked uninviting. She wondered what lurked behind an unguarded door. Several things could have happened. "Uncle Mark, I don't know how—"

"Mary, I have another ticket. I had four. My total allotment."

"But why? Because I am out here, and I am not inside."

Uncle Mark said. "I'm either a spy or not, but I want my niece to be safe. That holiday dinner, during that last one, your father swore off politics. He swore off a lot of things. You never came back. I heard him. The same boat, but I couldn't let you go. I never forgot." Uncle Mark pulled the paper and tore it in half. "One for you, my dear."

They knocked on the door and it opened, sucked Uncle Mark and Mary in and swiftly shut, the monitor latching each latch with fervor, swinging her whole body into it.

"What the. If they were all … let them all in …" the monitor said, not even checking the tickets.

"Why not?"

"Because they are gone. They are already against us. They will form and we will talk, but for now, our job. My job, as I understand it, is to not let them in." The monitor stomped back to her station. "If there was a police force. I'd have them arrest you." She pounded her fists. "Are you with us?"

"We … we are," Mary said. "I need to get Mark to my partner, Jill. It's our only recourse. They are going to save this place. You'll see." Grabbing Uncle Mark's hand, they took off down the hallway. They had wasted a significant part of the day, six hours in the sun. For them all to survive, they needed Mark. They brought him to save children, to save them all.

CHAPTER 31

When Uncle Mark sat in front of Jill, she had so many questions for him. She needed to have knowledge of how to build people, if she could, and what that entailed. She needed insight into where to find the problem solvers. And importantly, she needed understanding of how and why the NeverSleep wears you down. What causes it to zap your energy?

The last question he answered in curt words that meant that's all he knew and, it was serious. Health proved serious. Jill understood this to be true about Life but had awareness of how NeverSleep zapped her strength last time. "As much as you create, is as much as you lose." He swaggered the way he usually did when he felt needed, cherished for his knowledge or being. "You can share Life, though, too. You can reach out. Sense of touch is giving and bold. It recharges and melds with energy, power."

Tempering his ego and working to draw out as much as she was able from a tight-lipped man, Jill said, "Mark. I thought saving you from raging forests, wilderness, and an unstable ecosystem was worth a little more than that. What else can you tell me before I go in? My problem is these children. What do I do with them all?"

"Jill, there's the other place. The place in between here and there. You can't get stuck there trying to put kids with parents. It'll never work. The kids can't see their parents. Likely never again. The NeverSleep pill was about building the future," Mark said.

Jill stomped her foot. "But what about nurturing the past for the future? Listen, if I go in. If I can find those stuck in LongSleep like I found Katy, I just might find parents, one by one. Lead them to children. It will be a project, but it could happen. If they found their parents, they could still get what they needed in the NeverSleep and continue to live and work in this world until we are ready for NeverSleep to be."

Jill stammered. "Like when I brought the pitchfork back. I brought a pitchfork back from NeverSleep. Let's build this. Work here piece by piece. This will be the place to start over instead of there."

"How did you feel, darling? From that one item, the pitchfork. A thick wooden handle with metal spikes. How much did it zap you?" Mark said, leering.

"I can bring back more. It's a possibility." Jill was full of hope.

"It's your energy. You might. But I … It's a long shot in some respects. A person? Is that what you're asking? You'll need more gusto, I'd say."

Mark picked at his teeth, yellow from years of cigarette smoke. His dirty hands trying to help it all.

"Jill. You need to see a Think. You need to talk to them about solving problems. A Think, not a pseudo-Think like me; someone who simply knew how the NeverSleep pill worked. You can't just guess. You'll have to find them and it's tricky. It's hard to find them. Please be careful," Mark said.

"Millie." Jill kneeled down and held Millie by the shoulders. "I'm going to find your mom. You'll have to go with me into the NeverSleep, and we'll try to find her together, okay?" Jill sputtered out a breath wondering if she could maybe find her own mom.

"Okay, Jilly." Millie said. "I really would like to see her."

"Here. Hold my hand Millie, Mill. Don't let go as long as we're there in NeverSleep. Promise?" She was holding on to family, to someone she could never let go of for fear they would leave her like her parents.

"I promise."

The two leaned back on the scrap of floor that existed in the cell of an "apartment" the three were granted. Millie tucked her head into the crook of Jill's elbow. Jill ran her arm long around her head and held onto her hand, never letting go.

"In five, four, three, two." They drifted into NeverSleep, eyes focused starkly forward and staring into nothing, nothing incarnate.

In NeverSleep, Millie lived a new life. It's different for

everyone, Jill thought. She drifted into the NeverSleep holding another's hand. Simply touching someone brought that person into NeverSleep with Jill. She found this second time to be as true as the first and wanted to count it as fact. If she could scribe it on a tablet, she would.

"What was your mom's favorite thing, Millie?" Jill said.

"Oh, I guess her kitchen," Millie said, "Her chef's apron. When she put it on, she always pulled the ties around her body twice and tied it in the front."

"Tell me more," Jill said. Memories of her own mother's apron filtered in.

"It was a blue material, like gingham, like Dorothy for the wizard of Oz. It had a big apple on the front. She stitched it herself."

"How did the stitches look?" Jill said almost impatiently, holding onto something.

"They were loose, a bit of the patch curled over. Mom always wanted to restitch it. I sewed it on with her when I was young," Millie said.

Jill blinked holding onto Millie, and they were there in the kitchen with the apron. "Millie, concentrate on this. How much do you love, do you need, do you miss your mom?" Jill said.

"Oh, so much," Millie said.

Tears streamed from the emphasis Jill had put on her words. She heaved. She could've said her mom's life depended on it, for all Jill understood. She only translated her own words.

And Millie's mom, Rachel, was there. In an instant, just like that.

Rachel at once kneeled down and kissed her daughter three times. Her tenderness was heart melting. She took a square look, mumbled something about how much she had grown, and then looped her arms around Millie's whole body.

Jill collapsed in the warmth but only found her sadness. She only found that in this moment, she wanted nothing more than for Millie to be together with her mom, for now and always. She would switch places, her eyes drooled water she couldn't wipe away.

"Millie. How much do you love your mom?" Jill said.

"As much as anything, really, Jilly." Millie said. "As much as the earth."

Jill concentrated, as she had done in the past. She built up her sense of self, her awareness of it all, and collected pieces of a ladder. It was her building, but not really hers. It was a builder she controlled, but she didn't really know him. He was a vacant body, a builder, and that was his only job. An empty soul not yet filled.

The ladder twisted as if constructed immaturely, and it dissatisfied Jill. Jill pushed Millie's butt up the ladder. "Escape Millie. Escape fast," she said.

"But my mom," Millie said.

And she was already on her way up the ladder into the distance. Jill watched the pair and the climb rung by rung into a blue sky, one filled with temperate weather and delightful scents. Jill stayed on the ground, unable to climb, unable to muster the endeavor. She knew two in, two out.

When they came too, a flash of light streaked through the sky. The heavens opened up and as if a cloud was in the very room, lightning came, electrifying and shocking all that could be shocked. Uncle Mark was idle in the first bunk. Mary worried in the corner, knees to chest. The haze of smoke, a smoke that was not really there, beat down. The fuzz of the eyes transferred to the air, and it was mesmerizing and cloaking all at once. When it lifted, there were no people for a second until they all realized who they were.

As Jill was Rachel. And Jill fuzzed into no more, gone into NeverSleep, Uncle Mark tipped himself out of the bed, grabbed onto Jill, who was Rachel, and left into NeverSleep. In a split second, he was gone.

Mary threw her arms around her knees and pulled harder. He wouldn't return, she thought, and she for the life of her for her scared soul couldn't go in. This being her last chance at togetherness, she could not go. She lacked the strength to join the two she loved. For fear of the unknown … the unknown forever.

"Mommy," Millie cooed. "I'm so happy you're here. You're here." Her smile bubbled with glee.

Rachel must have instinctively known what happened because she turned to Mary and apologized. "This can happen. We can get her back."

"One life for one life is what it looks like to me," Mary said. She looked away, anxiously distraught.

"Try, Mary," Rachel said.

"How do you know my name?" Mary said. "I've never met you."

"But I met Jill, and she kept talking about you. You are her one true love," Rachel said. "Go find her."

Mary kneeled and collapsed flat backed like Jill always did. She ushered her arms by her sides. When Rachel came to her to pat her in comfort, she batted away her hand. "I have to do this on my own," Mary said. "Must … I will find her. The two of them."

With a hazy fuzz of the eye, Jill squinted and willed the person in front of her to be Mary, and it was.

"Oh my God, honey. I missed you. Why are you here? I need you in Life," Mary said.

"I switched, and I'm unable switch back. I've checked with Thinks and even if I could, I'm not sure if I would switch back," Jill said. "There is so much here that needs to be done."

"Can I follow you here?" Mary said.

"Don't even think about it," Jill said. "This is no permanent place for you; besides, I need you in Life to help me with things out there. I am helping kids find parents, and I need you to come in holding their hands so I can place them one by one. I need you, especially, because you can find me so quickly now." Jill winked.

Jill stammered the last words as she held Mary in an embrace. "We can always be together here."

"Jill, remember when you didn't want to go?" Mary said. "Remember when you didn't want to leave the house? Can't we go back there now? Can't we be afraid to leave together? Afraid the world will change? Afraid to change the world?"

"I am home, though Jill, it's a cloud of commitments here. I have free rein to build to be me. It's comfort and newness, but oldness. Really, all I ever dreamed I could be, and it's real. It's now." Jill morphed into someone entirely different. A beacon of purpose called her name, and she walked toward the light. As the world unsettled around her, she bobbed and weaved to stay on even ground. Now she was able to acclimate to anything, whatever threw her off-base. She was a new person, rising to what was asked of her.

"You've come such a long way. I don't believe your commitment to this all," Mary said.

"It's just. I have an effect. This is something I can do, albeit unrenowned—" Jill said. She picked at the air in front of her, at something Mary might not see.

Mary watched. "You are renowned. You will be. It is your place. It truly is."

Parting a haze before her, Jill swam into Mary and kissed her boldly, taking her energy, her full force, until she collapsed before her. "Oh, I'm so sorry. I forgot."

"You're still figuring out your strength, your meter of strength. We'll figure it out together," Mary said.

The wash of the NeverSleep sun overhead, the warmth of a perfect day, neither hot nor transferring a chill. Without wind. Without dampness, unless it was to cool sweaty limbs. The body of NeverSleep transcended weather. It was, but it wasn't. It projected, but a person filled it and asked for it. NeverSleep relieved. The fever of the day absent always.

"I need you," Jill said. "Every day? Every day you'll come to visit me?"

"Of course, I will," Mary said. "It's the least I can do."

"You'll build with me sometimes. Some places to be together, to have for us?" Mary was an Architectural Designer after all. Just not a builder.

Jill thought about Mary, the pencil and pen she always kept by her side. It was one of each, always. In the living room, at the work-from-home desk, at the bedside with a pad to scrawl notes on. It was a passion and a labor. Was she now free?

Perhaps, in NeverSleep, when the day of all days came, she would design again. Perhaps she would learn to build, get over perfectionism and ego, feel the calling once again.

Things had changed. Jill's life, living, had changed. She quelled Mary's passion. But they grew, would grow, and their eyes were on, at present, what was most important to each of them, each other.

"Absolutely," Mary said. She took back to her feet and hugged Jill.

Jill held the embrace as long as she could until she felt her knees weaken.

It was a miraculous kiss.

CHAPTER 32

Mary rummaged around the house looking for the tea kettle while she brewed her coffee. Finding the kettle tucked neatly above the microwave, she pulled it down and let the hot water drain in through its spout. The sweet taste called to her senses. As the coffee maker brewed, in an even stride with mug in hand, she tidied up, fixing the curtains and testing the ability of the door to open and shut either stiffly or of its own accord should she let go. Why was it always the impossible middle for a door in old houses? Each one took a different weighted tension to close or, perhaps, had a life of its own.

As she meandered around the house, she saw the photograph of the house Jill first built for Millie and herself in the NeverSleep what seemed like years ago before they even got to Colony Red or Colony One for that matter. It was mostly glass and stable, with steel or iron supporting beams. She witnessed the complexity of the rooms and the lighting. Set on an embankment, it overlooked a glorious farm field. A little school stood in the distance.

She didn't choose that house, though. They lived in the house in the photograph, rented years ago. She visited the house, and it had been the victim of a malicious attack. Shattered glass and spray paint across the entryway rendered it uninhabitable. Despite the attention, no one had broken in and stolen things from the owners.

Colony Red thrived. It bustled with government officials and the think tank recreating the government. When Jill was last there, it ended up being much too large for the number of adults left on the earth and much, much too small for the number of children they tried to collect and hold. Mary couldn't understand the lack of planning and cursed anything with an ounce of power in recent weeks.

Jill developed a program to train children to find their parents and respect them in NeverSleep. She handed off her technique to another while in the NeverSleep and she could go into retirement, tend to her wife, Mary, and honorary child, Millie. Bond with her uncle-in-law who was part of NeverSleep as well. Officials at Colony Red could take over the training regime to inculcate children into the new world folkways and way of living. So, as any great new civilization would do, they sent children back to their homes after they received training to find their parents in NeverSleep. If they misbehaved, there were repercussions. Parents, also after training, gained the ability to swiftly pop out and pop back in, taking their child into a mandatory time out. Most kids spent most days in the NeverSleep learning and socializing and then engaging in directed physical exercise during the night.

Mary returned to her home because of the government. All while the Antis were developing the NeverSleep pill, were developing an alternative to the polar ice cap problems. Using nuclear energy, they engineered cold. It was still a bit of a mystery to Mary, but the technology came out of NeverSleep. People were experimenting there, running tests. The group exported from NeverSleep, strategically and with purpose. Not only did they create things there, but technology, knowledge developed in different parameters, opened doors to possibilities in math and science that were never even conceived of before.

With this ability to put the earth back into its regular course, the compound in Montana was not entirely necessary, but it survived as a much more secure and suitable location for the government. The new Capitol amounted to a symbol. On vacations, government officials would stay with Mary because, of course, everyone needed a vacation, and the few people left in the world made friends. Of course, Mary actually liked to talk to real people and there were only three other adults in her town.

Despite this, Jill, Mary's true love and forever wife, would only be found in NeverSleep. She visited every day.

The ability to pull a living thing out of NeverSleep stumped all the researchers. They studied this without fail. The Atchinson Case they called it. The ability to transmute a person for a person. Reciprocity in cells and matter, but no more or less.

It boggled the most genius of NeverSleep minds. As much as they tried to recreate it, they were unable. People died trying.

Jill would tout that NeverSleep really became the best place to be because they were able to on a whim build or create anything, even if Mary said they fated it to happen. They'd get lost at the end of every NeverSleep and have to find each other the very next time. Part of the fun included traveling through the new world people had built. The mountains were higher for skiing, and the buildings were grander. No one called it the same world, but it also wasn't that different either. The one distinction became that every soul who entered NeverSleep built it. Each person made their mark.

CHAPTER 33

Mary was at the front door when she saw who she called the mom and child of the century make their way up the street. Millie skipped in utter joy, one of finding everyone even though some remarkably close, were lost. In a stutter step, she stopped, noticing her untied shoe. Immediately, attending to the violation often cited by people older than her, she over, under, through, pulled the laces tight. She popped up again stricken with the plague of childhood, a disregard of things too complex and things that might land sour. She worked her way down the street to home.

Mary stood at one of a handful of inhabited homes in the town. So many homes were vacant. One person struggled to clean a four-bedroom house. A single person struggled to fight the loneliness that filtered into something so open and empty. One person needn't tend a hearth fire if others weren't there to enjoy it. These thoughts rang in Mary's mind before she invited Millie and her mom into her home.

Millie and her mom, Rachael, lived with Mary in Life, the parallel place of NeverSleep. They rarely visited each other in NeverSleep. It wasn't a place for them to connect. Life provided that. Here on the other side of things.

Millie came bounding in first, with her mom Rachael tailing behind her, bending at the waist while trying to catch up and reaching for her to slow down to fix her shirt tail that had cropped up. Millie didn't wait and her mom choked up, breathing in and out with her forearms on her knees. A child just escaped her grasp. Both wrapped their arms around her in a hug and Mary took in the warmth of a child finding care.

"It's time for NeverSleep," Rachael said.

"Of course, mom," Millie said. "Can we see Uncle Mark today?"

"Sure dear. For a second," Rachel said.

Mary mockingly put the back of her hand up to her mouth

and said, "You don't really need to go into the NeverSleep because Millie has a parent here ..."

"Oh, but we do," Rachel said. "There is still so much more building to be done. Millie and I are building rules for the created environments to reduce effects on autistic children. We're working on sensory options for NeverSleep. It's really progressive research, actually."

"That's so great. I wish I made a difference. I hope the growing I do is powerful," Mary said. "But that's it. It's a hope."

"It is. The research is. The work is," Rachael said. She nodded and shifted her head, looking at something more on Mary's face. "You were an Architect," Rachel said.

"I was." Mary dwelled on thoughts of what she had loved and lost. Her life depended on people now. Living beings, to her, were so much more important, more fulfilling, than the work, things.

Rachael paused and put her hands on her hips. "Colony Red said the NeverSleep might actualize in a few years. They're on the cusp of bringing everyone into the NeverSleep. It would be the new world."

"We can all wish together and hope for the best either way," Mary said. She half consigned to Rachael and half hoped NeverSleep would come. What she rested on, what helped her move motion by motion, as each sun crossed the sky for another day, was her closeness to Jill. Everything she ever needed Jill provided. Or the frightening truth of what might be deterred her. One or the other.

"Do say hi to Uncle Mark for me, Millie," Mary said.

"Oh, course I will, Mary," Millie said. "Anything special?" After a brief thinking pause, she uttered the words, "Oh, he said he loved you."

"Mary, he really did ..." Rachael said.

"Well, I guess ... tell him Christmas will be mild, and I will visit his NeverSleep. But there better be a bit of snow. Tell him to work on that," Mary said.

Mary went back into her eyes and saw the man, Uncle Mark as she saw him for the last time when he laid his head down and gave Jill all the energy, he had to get the child into

NeverSleep to make that first leap, the first attempt. Jill was an old prop now and didn't need but a second of energy to funnel a child to their parents. She was a wily fox, unable to show her face for too long, but clever enough to get the job done.

Uncle Mark had died for her. He had fallen into a NeverSleep, one that could not be shaken off. He wasted his energy. Thought he had more than he really did. His ego impeding Life. He pushed his capabilities, while sick, to the max, and devastation resulted. He lived on for them now, in NeverSleep. Mary saw him infrequently but as much as she did in Life years ago. Holidays, birthdays, whenever days. They both held beliefs buried deep or pulled to the surface that might scratch or at least itch and start an argument. They held each other at bay for now, so they might regrow their relationship slowly.

Millie, however, announced herself best buddies with him. She loved to see his inventions, his works in the works. He checked in on him like a father, like a man who would eventually give her direction. He would. Mary set on it.

Destined to rebuild for a long time in the ether, damned to do virtuous deeds for people, for them all. They saw to it he didn't work on political systems, at least. But what was he building, what did he tinker with if not the weather?

Maybe Mary would see at Christmas.

CHAPTER 34

Mary found Jill in a playground where Jill had spent time as a child. Mary thought hard about the photos in their house, what was really Jill's house. She gazed into a photo on the fireplace mantel, and the image flashed, became a part of the back of her eyelids. And when she laid down to NeverSleep, the image surfaced again. The bright red see-saws were beckoning. And she went in, into madness again.

The NeverSleep obliterated Jill. She had been working too hard building, Mary had said. Jill had been sucking energy out of herself that didn't exist.

From the top corner of an elementary school's flat roof, the light shone down harsh and bright. The bleaching light cast no sense of mood. It had no discretion, either. The beam hit hard and direct. The concentration beamed on a square block and the light diffused as the sun at morning, onto the outreaches of the playground. If you looked hard enough, the light would spread further, encompass more. You could see deeper.

In the outreaches of the gravel lot, passed merry-go-rounds, swings, and a four-square court, were the see-saws. And Jill. Jill stood, rising from a lying position flat on the ground, stiff back, gravel pinching at the skin of her arms and calves. Short sleeves weather, Mary thought. It can be murder sometimes.

Jill brushed stones off her arms, picking at the last embedded pebbles on her skin. Craters in the skin remained when the rocks were gone. Jill waved to Mary, beckoned with flippant arms. Loosey goosey arms and hands, wiggling with anticipation and excitement. Mary's long journey, from light-years away, completed to be in Jill's arms. The same journey Sisyphus made every day.

"Come, lay with me on the see-saws, Mary," Jill said.

Jill and Mary locked hands and held them tight, resting

their feet on the handlebars of two adjacent pieces of playground equipment.

"They're both red," Jill said.

The thick, red paint looked coated as if year after year, for decades, someone slapped more paint on at the beginning of the school year. So authentic. Still, splinters ran through the color, shards with some weight peeled off, looking for a victim. The bare wood splaying beneath the chips of paint promised splinters to the most delicate of children's hands.

The wood splinters were a warning. The see-saw became a dangerous toy. Fulfilling to the brave, but feared by many, the see-saw earned its place among other equipment. This teeter-totter not yet utilized by children, would be in time. The thing wasn't a plastic model smooth in sheen and symbol. The teeter-totter, see-saw, was imperfect, a replica of what had once been charged with activity and emotion. It would serve its purpose again. It was recreated because it was once good and would create joy still.

"What?" Mary said.

"They're both red. That means we love each other. Right? We love each other," Jill said.

"You're worried about the divide," Mary said casually. "It'll be okay. They say we'll all be here soon," Mary shuddered apprehensive about falling into this world for good. She stiffened knowing that Jill was more than any fear.

"When? Did they say when?" Jill said.

Mary couldn't tell Jill what she wanted to know. Jill didn't swear by the government; she was only an asset, an assistant in the crime—the world. Mary's mouth hung open, and she hoped Jill would forgive her. They outright lied to Jill. This place. This resemblance of something they thought was the world needed to be built. The people, children even, needed to be controlled. And Jill acted as a builder and a tamer of children. She paired families back together, made sense of an upended world. The government, what it now called itself, abided that this was a good thing. This should continue. And so, it would, until the force of nature felled full swing.

"Tea?" Mary held it in her hands, a testament. Mary carried the tea from Jill's teakettle into NeverSleep, proud she could work a little magic herself. Mary brought a mug full of coffee too, into a world holding Jill in until its actualization. She smiled rather than drink the cooling coffee because her time, the intense feelings she felt in Jill's presence, were limited.

"I love this teacup," Jill said. "I love it all. The things you bring me, each day, something original from

"Life, something historic, something me."

"Something you don't need to build," Mary said.

"That's right. Something we don't need to build," Jill said.

"Jill, I'm a horrible builder. They took me off that," Mary said.

"But you make a mean cup of Life tea."

Jill nuzzled close. Her hands stroking the backs of Mary's, holding it in place, letting it go no further, preventing it from flittering away into some kind of life. Preventing it from raising a cup to drink.

"I just want you here. Be present. Be with me as you always are. Day after day. My recharge so I can build," Jill said.

Mary slumped in her posture, churning her energy into Jill, wanting to give her everything, anything she could. She, a lifeblood, gave Jill the energy to build. So were all the children she matched with parents. They gave her energy to do her work, so as not to fall into absolute darkness and never return. Then they would recharge in Life, return to charge into NeverSleep, and exit into Life, a duplicitous cycle of being.

"I don't want it all, but I can touch you. You're real." She rubbed the back of Mary's hand harder, knowing she would have to stop. And she stopped. "You stay out there as long as you can. I hate to imagine what it would be like if no one was awake or if Colony Red cleared out. Mayhem, mayhem for sure," Jill said. "I can feel your hands and your sweet touch give me more life than any place in the world."

Jill tried to justify the fairness, why this way of being called by some fair with stuttering words. To be together for mere hours a day, she said, left so much desire. She was imprisoned without her one life force.

Every day, Mary needed to find Jill at a new outpost, a new station in NeverSleep. Her burden became finding, creating a connection to appear, sometimes balancing a cup of tea and a cup of coffee. Jill never stopped building, never stopped joining families, and if it weren't for Mary, she would never stop.

"These moments are for us. I am here for you. The entire world is behind me to be here for you, our partnership even," Mary said.

"Mary," Jill said.

"This is life for us." Mary rolled off the see-saw board and kissed Jill passionately with such a feeling that it melted the air between them, and steam rose from the spot. "This is as real as we need it. And it is so much more,"

Exhausted, Mary reeled backward. The only energy she had left she saved for her chin in the air in agony. She would eventually have to leave and wouldn't be able to look back. Her touch spent, the bones inside her body sunk toward the ground and she wondered about Life and death. She pulled away from Jill and her temper raged. She yelled at the sky for acid rain that would boil her skin. This was no place for gods. Gods did not come here. This place emptied of godly will. The NeverSleep was subject to builders and their turmoil alone. Mary lay hard, flat back on the ground, the spot dry where Jill lay and damp beyond that bit. Mary screamed into the air again that she would never leave.

Mary would be back, and they would wait to touch.

She flickered into space; into something you might call space only because it was the absence of …

THE END

Acknowledgements

As I am prone to do, I would like to thank my wife. It's done. We can get pastries on Saturday mornings! Thank you to my mother-in-law for her patience and attention, and for always responding with whatever I need in seconds via text. Thank you to my brother who somehow, for some reason, will always support what I do. And thank you to my mom the reader, who I am always trying to impress. My friends, especially Emily, Erin, Laura, Sharmin, and Barb, are always standing close, ready to buy the first book or figure out reviewing websites.

I must acknowledge teachers, past and present, and literary adults I looked up to who simply encouraged me to write. There are so many who are probably too far away in memory to call. For every simple prompt I was given or intense critique I received, it was all I needed to start writing and continue writing. Thank you to the conferences who included me, the community at Provincetown, Massachusetts, and local LGBTQ+ Pride organizations, you build me up and you push my craft, directly or indirectly, to be the best it can be.

This book is a product of the GCLS academy. In one year, I applied myself to produce my best work yet with ongoing instruction from leaders in the sapphic fiction community. Without remiss, I especially thank Karelia, Finnian, Sheree, Tammy, Ann, Kim, Betsy, and all the instructors and students. Here I found an invaluable community dynamic. I would not have finished without my esteemed classmates who encouraged, applauded, critiqued, read, and supported than any group I've ever known.

Spectrum Books has been through it with me for a bit, and I'm so glad to have Andrew and Carl on my side. Their support and belief in the world of LGBTQ+ literature is inspiring. I hope to dazzle them even more this time, even more next time.

In advance, I thank the readers who are out there who might take a look, even if it's just one. It's because of you—we can fill the world with LGBTQ+ books and make it brighter, more part of the world and a world in itself. We can stay strong in little ways. Damn that election. We will pull through.

About the Author

S.E. Smyth is writing away as much as she can. She is inspired by history and stories that have not been told, pulling words from true events, her lived experience, and education in history.

S.E. has published has published two novels with NineStar Press, Hope for Spring (2023) and Criminal by Proxy (2022). Recent short work can be found in Scarlet (Jaded Ibis Press 2023). She writes the stories that are hard to tell. Her accounts are never exactly how they happened, and she firmly believes it is reparative to reimagine.